the Curiosities
a collection of stories

Carolrhoda Lab™
An imprint of Carolrhoda Books
A division of Lerner Publishing Group, Inc.
241 First Avenue North
Minneapolis, MN 55401 U.S.A.

Website address: www.lernerbooks.com

Main body text set in Century Old Style Std 11/17.
Typeface provided by Adobe Systems.

Library of Congress Cataloging-in-Publication Data

    The curiosities: a collection of stories / by Tessa Gratton, Maggie Stiefvater, and Brenna Yovanoff.
       p. cm.
    Summary: A collection of darkly paranormal stories, with comments by the authors on the writing process.
    ISBN: 978–0–7613–7527–2 (trade hard cover : alk. paper)
    1. Paranormal fiction. 2. Short stories, American. [1. Supernatural—Fiction. 2. Short stories.] I. Gratton, Tessa. II. Stiefvater, Maggie, 1981– III. Yovanoff, Brenna.
PZ5.S892536 2012
[Fic]—dc23   2011051335

Manufactured in the United States of America
1 – BP – 7/15/12

the Curiosities
a collection of stories

Maggie
STIEFVATER

Tessa
GRATTON

Brenna
YOVANOFF

carolrhoda LAB
MINNEAPOLIS

THE AUTHORS

Tessa Gratton is the author of the young adult novels *Blood Magic* and *The Blood Keeper*, and of the forthcoming Songs of New Asgard series. Visit her online at www.tessagratton.com.

Maggie Stiefvater is the author of several books for young adults, including the *New York Times* bestselling Wolves of Mercy Falls trilogy and the Printz Honor–winning *The Scorpio Races*. Visit her online at www.maggiestiefvater.com.

Brenna Yovanoff is the *New York Times* bestselling author of the young adult novels *The Replacement* and *The Space Between*. Visit her online at www.brennayovanoff.com.

THE WEBSITE

Tessa, Maggie, and Brenna also posted short fiction at www.merryfates.com. Many of the curiosities in this collection first appeared there.

THE HANDWRITING

Tessa: The fervent brown fox jumps over the recalcitrant dog.

Maggie: QUINCY, THE LAISSEZ-FAIRE GENIUS FOX, JUMPS OVER THE ESTABLISHMENTARIAN DOG.

Brenna: The ephemeral fox jumps over the bourgeois dog

BEGINNING

Sat, May 3, 2008   *2008! That's not even in this decade!*

From: Maggie Stiefvater

Time: 2:36 PM

To: Brenna Yovanoff, Tess Gratton

Hey guys, what do you guys think of doing a group blog where we each try and do a piece of flash fiction or a mini scene totally unrelated to anything we're doing? Each of us posting once a week, like a Mon/Wed/Fri?

Something to let us experiment with stuff totally outside our current range, and also a challenge, and a bit of promo if we keep it up.

Anyway, whatdya think?

From: Brenna Yovanoff

Time: 3:43 PM

To: Maggie Stiefvater

Cc: Tess Gratton

I think it sounds like a lot of fun, personally. This is the kind of thing that I feel helps me loosen up when I get stuck on my long projects, plus I think it's good practice, but I haven't been doing it lately for whatever reason. And, as always, when it comes to my own motivation, a deadline would be nice.

From: Tess Gratton

Time: 4:53 PM

To: Brenna Yovanoff

Cc: Maggie Stiefvater

I pretty much do that anyway, so I'm totally in!

How about the idea of some weeks being totally open and free, and other weeks all using the same prompt? I'd be interested in seeing the kinds of things we all do with the same seed, so to speak, but wouldn't want to be tied to that sort of thing all the time.

INTRODUCTION

by Andrew Karre
Editorial Director, Carolrhoda Lab

"I don't think we should edit them." I said something to this effect to Maggie way back when we were first discussing the merryfates.com stories and what became known first as the "not-anthology anthology project" and now as *The Curiosities*, the thing you hold in your hands.

— BUT NOT THE ODDEST THING HE'S SAID

"Let's not edit" is an odd thing for an editor to say when presented with a pile of short stories for potential publication—especially when those stories were created quickly and often as experiments. It is, after all, my job to conceal the massive effort authors put into effortless prose, to bury the drafts under a single, definitive version. And yet the effort and the process are fascinating and revealing—and not just for me. If you go to enough author readings—especially ones with teen readers—you can't help but notice the recurrence of questions like "How do you start a story?" or "What do you do when you get stuck?" or "In my stories, I always . . ." I have always wanted a book to address these excellent reader-writer questions. I never wanted a textbook or a manual, though. I wanted something more demonstrative than instructive—more performance than lecture.

With a title

← See Page 291

BURN THINGS DOWN

It is clear to me that, for many readers, the border between reader and writer is a thin, flexible one—thin and flexible in a way that, for example, the border between butcher and burger eater is generally not. Reading and writing are tightly linked pursuits. A story consumed today is a story created tomorrow. And so on. Witnessing this tight circle of creation and consumption is magical to me—a private highlight of my life as an editor. The circle is also, I think, magical to Tessa, Maggie, and Brenna. So magical that, like any good magicians, they couldn't bear to keep it private. And thus they built a stage on which to showcase their conjuring—and also to refine it. And that's what the Merry Sisters of Fate is, both as an online critique group and as this book you're about to begin. It is the public performance of the private act of story craft. It is writers reading so that writing might happen so that they'll have something to read tomorrow and so on for as long as there are stories to tell and readers to read them.

With that in mind, I hope you will enjoy this curious book of stories, and the stories behind the stories, for the magic they create and the magic that creates them.

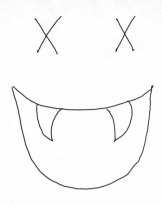

THE VAMPIRE BOX

by Tessa Gratton

To me, this is a coming-of-age story in the purest sense. It has all the hallmarks of the genre—there's the desire for autonomy, along with the impending separation from the familiar, not to mention the very pertinent theme of choosing the difficult thing. Only, Tess has given us the added bonus of the fantastical (vampirical!), placing the epic and the magical against a strangely domestic backdrop. —Brenna

I sat on this story for seven months, knowing the first line but waiting for the rest of the story to bubble up. I spent a lot of time thinking about it in the middle of other things. Like the line at the grocery store. Or in the shower. I knew there was a point but had to be patient. —Tessa

AND BY "SAT," SHE MEANS COMPLAIN TO ME MONTHLY: "I HAVE THIS STORY I WANT TO WRITE BUT CAN'T YET."

We have a vampire living in our basement.

It's my job to feed him while Dad is in Palo Alto at a convention. At 6 A.M. I pad into the kitchen in my bare feet and jersey nightgown with my robe hanging off my shoulders. I yawn, wishing I could crawl back in bed after the chore. It's the last week before finals, and I'm already in at Northwest State, so I don't really have to focus much. The motivation to show up at school is as low as it gets.

Half the freezer is piled with Tupperware blood-packs, and I dig out one from the bottom, grumbling to myself that Mom still isn't packing them with the oldest on top for easy access. I should just take over the butcher-store runs. Then she could just forget about it—which was all she wanted.

While the blood heats in the microwave, I heave myself onto the counter and stare at the basement door. It's painted soft yellow, but most of the color peeled away a while ago. I went through a phase when I was in junior high where I stripped a thin line of the paint off the door every time I passed it. The lines were like prison bars holding me back.

The microwave beeps and I hop down. I grab the lancet from its hook over the sink and pull the Tupperware out onto the counter. I yawn again just as I'm pulling off the plastic top and get a lungful of coppery pig's-blood smell. I gag like a cat and dance back, making a show of myself because there's no one around to see. When I calm down, I put my hand on the counter, palm up. I take the lancet, which is a thin triangle of steel about as long as my thumb, and put the tip to my pinky. This is my least favorite part. I grit my teeth and ready myself with a massive grimace, then jab the lancet into my finger.

Blood wells instantly, and I let a couple of drops fall into the Tupperware.

I'm supposed to be using Dad's blood. He drained a quarter pint of it before leaving, and it's hanging in the pantry with whatever his favorite anticoagulant is keeping it sort-of fresh. But it's bad enough our vampire is trapped in a cage in the basement. To not even give him the two drops of fresh blood he's promised seems unconstitutional.

With the Tupperware balanced carefully in my hands, I face the basement.

.   .   .

I was only five the first time I met Saxon.

For a week our water pipes had clanged in a staccato pattern that echoed throughout the house. Dad promised it was bad plumbing, but I woke up in the middle of the night and recognized that the pattern of clangs matched the rhythm of my favorite clapping song. I'd been playing it by myself against the kitchen floor just that afternoon. And now the house pipes wanted to play with me.

I crawled out of bed, snuck past Mom and Dad's room and all the way down into the kitchen. We kept the door locked in those days, but I knew how to climb up onto a chair and from there onto the kitchen counter to reach the key Dad kept hanging inside the spice cabinet. I managed it quietly and unlocked the basement door. It was where the pipes lived, because it was where Dad went every time he tried to get them to be quiet.

I couldn't reach the light switch, so it was very, very dark. Here is all I remember:

The floor being rough concrete.

The tiny red light bulb dangling in the center of the room, not making it any less scary.

Calling out, "Pipes?"

And he said my name. *Nicole.*

I clapped and ran forward. I tripped on something and fell against the bars of his cage. He caught me in both hands, and his eyes were right there in front of mine. Glinting red in the light. With his arms through the cage, he set me back on my feet and smiled.

He played a clapping game with me, longer than any grown-up had ever played before. We didn't stop until I was the one too tired to go on.

I curled up on the floor with my backbone pushed up against the bars and fell back to sleep. He tapped the rhythm of the song gently into the metal.

. . .

The wooden stairs are spongy under my bare feet from all the dank basement air. We need a new set, but Dad can't exactly hire a builder to come down here. Not unless he plans to feed the unlucky worker to Saxon.

I can reach the light switch, of course, but I don't flip it. I prefer the gentle red light. We have a carpet now, a long runner leading from the stairs to his cage. It's thin, and the chill of the concrete foundation still seeps up.

Dad uses a long pole to scoot the blood to the cage without getting near enough that Saxon could grab him. But I walk straight to the black bars.

Saxon is standing with his back to me. He's watching the square of light that fades in through the single window high up against the ceiling. The glass is shuttered over, but pink morning slips through the slats. It makes an aura around him, and I say, "Hey, angel. Breakfast."

He moves slowly, lethargically. But not because he has to. There's only about ten square feet inside the cage, and half of it is covered with stacks of books and magazines. "Morning, sunshine," he says back.

We smile.

I put my hands between the bars, offering him the blood. He could grab my wrists instead and tear fresh blood straight out of me, but he won't. Dad tried to make me fear Saxon after finding me asleep against the cage, but I knew at any time Saxon could have pulled me through and eaten me. I'd been small enough then to have fit between the bars. He'd have sucked the marrow from my bones before Dad woke up.

Saxon dips a finger into the blood and paints it across his bottom lip. He told me when I was eight that the blood tingles against his skin. I'd put a dot on my cheek and been disappointed when it only felt wet and sticky. That had been the first time he'd laughed at me, the first time I'd seen his rows of sharp teeth. When I scrambled away, he'd painted dots of blood onto his own cheeks and a long line down his nose, in solidarity.

I sit down cross-legged, with my knees against the bars. He sits too, cradling the blood in his lap. As I tell him about the TV show I watched last night where they had a mock battle between a samurai warrior and a Roman gladiator, he keeps dipping his finger into the blood and letting drops fall onto his tongue. He'll spend hours consuming every last bit.

When I move on to complaining about my trig teacher's bad habit of putting questions on the quizzes we never went over in class, Saxon holds up his hand. The musty gray sleeve of his shirt falls back. Dad brings him new clothes once a year, saying nothing more is necessary because Saxon doesn't sweat or pee or do anything but read all day. None of the normal stuff that makes a person dirty. But I wonder what he'd look like in a tailored suit or a really sexy pair of jeans.

"I've been thinking," he says when he has my attention, and dips his finger back into the blood. "When you leave for college, I won't have any reason not to rip your father to pieces."

I laugh.

But Saxon doesn't. He sets the Tupperware on the concrete floor of his cage and stands up. He wraps his hands around two of the bars.

My laughter turns into rocks that plummet down toward my feet. "You wouldn't."

"I might." He snaps the end of the word sharply.

I stand up and curl my hands over his. His skin is warmer than mine. "Saxon." To this day neither Dad nor Saxon will tell me how he came to be trapped here. All I know is that Dad feeds him, and somehow having a vampire locked in a box in your basement is massive good luck. Dad shot from junior partner to CEO in six months and now basically does whatever he wants. The only reason we haven't moved into a huge house in some gated community is because of Saxon. "It can't be that easy," I say, "or you'd have done it before now."

His fingers move under mine, and I swear I hear the metal creak. "The fool's been feeding me his blood for years."

I think of the drops of my blood in the Tupperware. And how often I've used the lancet. "What does that give you?"

"A taste for it." Saxon leans closer, and it's exactly the way it was when I was five years old. His eyes gleam in the red light. But this time he doesn't seem old or strange to me. He's young. He's my friend.

. . .

I used to sneak down when Dad left and help Saxon pick up the million pieces of rice Dad dropped on the cage floor to keep him occupied all day. We'd count them and drop them one by one into a tin mixing bowl.

Sometimes I got bored, but Saxon didn't seem capable of stopping before every grain was collected. He'd start making up little rhyming songs to keep me down there and telling me stories about people he'd known and lives he'd lived. My favorites were the ones where he had human companions who guarded him during the day, and whom he guarded at night. Probably because I could pretend he'd chosen to be here with my family, instead of imprisoned.

When I was in junior high I had a fantasy of breaking him free, bringing him to my school, and letting him go to town on all the teachers who made me talk in class, and possibly break the windows. Then we'd run off for New York or something, and I'd be a famous actress while he leaned back in the darkest balcony box and watched me. We'd spend the long hours of the night at private parties, the toast of the town. And all day we'd sleep in a quiet, dark room, waiting for the sun to go down again.

It was the only way I made it through Spanish class.

.   .   .

"What do you want?" I ask him.

He doesn't reply except to sigh very softly. I can smell the blood on his breath and see a small streak of it at the edge of his bottom lip. It's not as overwhelming as it was upstairs, when I first took the Tupperware out of the microwave, but I still don't like it.

I rephrase. "What do you want from me?"

"To go with you."

My very first instinct is to go to the workbench and get the key. To free him. I don't, of course, but I try not to ignore my instincts. Sophomore year, somebody told me to always go with my first guess on multiple-choice tests, and after that my grades improved noticeably.

I tighten my hands around his. "And then what?"

"Carefree nights and peaceful days?" he says with a smile.

I back away step by step. I'm off the carpet, and the concrete is rough under my toes. Like I'm five again.

"Let me tell you a secret, sunshine," he whispers, leaning against the bars. His cheek presses into one, and he wraps his arms casually around it and folds his hands together. "An imprisoned vampire is good luck."

"I know."

"But." He holds up one finger, the one he uses to feed himself. "A willing vampire—ah, sunshine, a willing vampire is what Washington had. What Charlemagne had. Elizabeth. Cleopatra—she got one from Caesar."

I don't know if I believe him. I want to. I imagine him again in new, clean clothes. Clothes he chose for himself. "I don't want to be those people."

"You wouldn't have to be. Hundreds of people you've never heard of made friends of us, too."

He could have killed me so easily, anytime over the last twelve years. He hadn't. Did that mean I could trust him? Or was he only biding his time for this very moment? Waiting, because to him twelve years was nothing.

My brain—my dad's voice—is screaming at me to go back upstairs. But the rest of me wants to know. Wants to know if he was my friend. Wants to know if I was his friend. Because if I am, wouldn't I free him?

If I run upstairs, I'm using him. Just like Dad.

If I let him out, he might kill me. Kill my family. Everyone on the block, everyone in the city for all I knew.

If I run, I am afraid.

If I stay, I risk everything just to prove to myself what I am.

"Nicole."

I blink. I'd been staring at him so long the light shoving through the slats of the window is strong and bright. Saxon stands unmoved, caught between the light from the window and the red light of the basement.

I walk into the sunlight and pick the key up off the worktable.

Contrary to popular belief, this is an ending.

A MURDER OF GODS

by Maggie Stiefvater

One of the things I'm most envious of is Maggie's ability to create these (sprawling ensemble casts,) filled with light and texture and noise, and all the players still fully differentiated. This is a story characterized by disillusionment and snarkiness, but it's also very tender. Despite the overarching presence of the gods, at the core this is a very human story. And I like that, too. (I like it most of all.) —Brenna

THIS IS SOMETHING I STILL BATTLE WITH AND LONG TO GET RIGHT. IT'S THE HOLY GRAIL OF FICTION— THE PERFECT ENSEMBLE.

I'll confess that I had only two things in mind when I began this story: writing a story with loads and loads of characters, and writing about fire. I'm ashamed to admit a lot of my stories begin with either one or the other of these. I can see hints of my current novel project whispered in this story, too, which was entirely unplanned. The seemingly ordinary narrator's position as the voice of reason, Grin's wanting to know where he fits in with this world—these are themes that I blew up and studied harder in my current novel. —Maggie

a common primary motivation

A LOT OF TIMES,
A FIRST LINE IS
THE ONLY THING
I HAVE WHEN I
START A SHORT
STORY.

NO PLOT.
NO CHARACTERS.
JUST...

"YOU WOULD THINK..."

You would think that in a world full of normal people, freaks would be kind to other freaks. But Finndabar, which at its core is a school for freaks, proves this wrong. Rather than being sensitive to one another's differences, the student body uses them for lunchroom entertainment. And believe me, when you have a student body like Finndabar's, there is plenty to be entertained by.

There's Stronghand Pol, whose left hand is twice the size of his right and can crush rocks. You can guess what else people talk about it crushing. The poor guy can't even go to the bathroom without people asking if he and his hand were getting a little alone time. And then Merilyn, who has the head of a donkey but the body of a vestal virgin. She also can make inanimate objects sing, but that's not what's brought up in the lunchroom. "Assface" is. Then there's Fergus, who can turn anything to gold with a single touch of his bare skin. While he's struggling to open his pudding with his gloved fingers, people ask him what he's "blinged" lately. We're a strange bunch, to be sure, with the power of untrained gods, the faces of angels, and the raging hormones of a herd of teenage Justin Timberlake fans.

I wonder what you call a group of children of the gods. "Herd" really is too innocuous. I know a group of jellyfish is called a smack. I think that's a lot closer.

The only one who doesn't talk smack to the freaks is me, which is ironic, because I am the only one who seems to be pretty normal. Unlike Rjork, I don't call

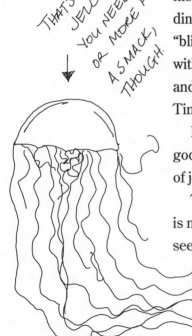

THAT'S A
JELLYFISH.
YOU NEED 2
OR MORE FOR
A SMACK,
THOUGH.

down thunderstorms in the boys' bathroom. Nor do I change forms when I get angry like Fionnuala. I don't have to eat my weight in eggs every day like Ben, either. I'm just me—probably the product of a pairing between a clueless mortal man and a nymph lacking in maternal instincts. No one here knows who their parents really were—only that at least one of them was of the supernatural variety.

It's not like it keeps me up nights.

It's a fun life, for the most part, here at Finndabar, though it's a bit dangerous. Every so often one of us accidentally kills one of the teachers or one of the other students. We never really forget that's why we're here.

But that doesn't really keep me up nights, either. Most nights.

. . .

Lunchroom. It's sort of the meeting place for all of the students, no matter what time of day it is. It's a modest name for a rather awe-inspiring room. All of Finndabar is made up of old churches—structures that were condemned because of disrepair or doomed because of their location right in the middle of a future superhighway. The churches were shipped in bits and pieces and then cobbled together into a massive, star-shaped piece of irony with the separate "houses" on each point of the star.

The lunchroom has the highest ceiling of the entire building; it's an old cathedral with a deep, brilliantly blue ceiling interrupted by vividly yellow ribs.

I TRY MY LEVEL BEST TO IMBUE MY STORIES WITH A SENSE OF PLACE AS QUICKLY AS POSSIBLE.

IF I DON'T THINK I'VE BEEN SOMEPLACE NEW, READERS SURE WON'T.

The slender, pointed windows that stretch over our heads always remind me of really tall women for some reason, hands folded on their chests.

In the morning, when the students were laughing and chattering sleepily over breakfast, the entire school seemed benign and beautiful. Maybe a flock. A flock of gods' children.

A few tables over, Grin Andersson was snapping his fingers, watching the flame that gathered on the tips of his thumb and forefinger in a rather bored way. He looked through the fire to where I sat and extinguished the flame. Abandoning his table of minions, he sat on the table next to my plate, making the old table surface creak and lean towards him.

I ADORE THE NAME "HELEN" AND USE IT WHENEVER HUMANLY POSSIBLE

"Good morning, Helen," he said with a grin. He always said my name with an emphasis on "hell."

I glanced up at his freckled face, his wide smirk of a grin underneath hard blue eyes and a riot of red hair. "Good morning, Grin."

"Care to join me at the fun table?" He scrubbed his thumb lightly across the table surface beside him, leaving behind a black singe mark, before jerking his chin in the direction from which he'd come.

"No, thanks. I'm busy being an island of sanity in a sea of utter madness," I said, shoveling a mouthful of tapioca pudding into my mouth. You had to give it to Finndabar's: they had really good tapioca pudding.

"Don't I know it," Grin replied. "But we could use some sanity over there. We were just talking about what a danger to society we all were."

I looked up at Grin, a bit longer this time. There was always something about him that put me ill at ease. Something about just how damn alive he was that made me feel like I was an underachiever. "I'm just trying to eat my pudding," I said.

"It's exceptional pudding," he agreed, still smiling. "I was just telling Professor Lansing the other day how exceptional the pudding is here. I wonder where they get it. I'd like to go shopping for it some time. I was thinking of asking Lansing about it."

"Now you're just being wrong in the head," I said. "Do you mean leave the school grounds?"

"Supervised," Grin said. "Just a few students at a time. Just to see what it's like."

I put my spoon down. "And the first time one of us accidentally maims another shopper because we lean over to pick up a cantaloupe and shoot lightning bolts out our ass, the government will come in and have us all killed."

Grin's smile was painted on top of a face that was something entirely different. "This is why we need you at the table, Helen. See, I knew you would be the voice of reason."

"Don't I know it," I said. "Now can I just finish my pudding?"

He made a little gesture like he was tipping a hat to me and retreated back to his own table. Later during breakfast, one of the juniors turned into a goat and ran through the breakfast bar, splattering pudding everywhere, and pretty much proved my point, I thought.

. . .

As the student resident advisor of my house, I get a room of my own, which is a rarity. It's not big—just a tiny, wood-paneled room that used to be a confessional—but it's quiet and it's my own, which is important. I keep my door open until 10 P.M. in case any of the students in the house need my help for anything, and in reality, my room is usually occupied by at least two others until almost 11.

Tonight it was Minerva, a beautiful girl who looked nearly normal but for her four arms and long, long fingernails. She sat on the end of my bed, looking at the pictures on my walls and hugging her arms around herself.

"What happens to us after Finndabar?" she asked. "Do we graduate? Do we leave?"

"I don't know," I said. I handed her a cup of tea and sat down on the chair by the desk opposite the bed. The room was so small that my knees were nearly touching Minerva's. "Do you want to leave?"

Minerva stared into the cup of tea. It was black, but not as black as her eyes were. They were wells of darkness, her eyes. It was unnerving, the pupil that covered the entire surface of her eye, until you got used to it. Her long nails tapped, tapped, tapped on the edge of the cup, and she didn't drink it. "I'm getting so hungry, Helen," she said, finally.

I didn't say anything, because I sensed she wasn't done. I just drank my tea and waited.

"I'm so hungry," she said again. "I think I am hungry for the souls of men."

THIS IS A TRICK OF DIANA WYNNE JONES (ONE OF MY FAVORITE AUTHORS) THAT I WANTED TO TRY OUT. SLIP IN THE EXTRAORDINARY UNDER THE RADAR AFTER YOU'VE LURED THE READER INTO THE FAIRLY ORDINARY

"Oh, Min," I said, and put down my teacup. I took hers, because she clearly wasn't going to drink it, and I rubbed her cold hands in mine. I couldn't offer her what she wanted, and I couldn't tell her that she'd be free to go when she hit eighteen. "Let's go watch *Sleepless in Seattle.*"

"Thank you," Minerva said. I gathered other students on the way down to the media room, students who were listless or fighting or bored, and together we watched *Sleepless in Seattle,* and I didn't get back to my quiet room until eleven.

. . .

"How does this work?"

I jerked awake, my eyes seeing nothing but darkness and the glowing green numbers of my alarm clock: 1:30 A.M.

"Do I just tell you what the problem is, and you make me feel better?"

I sat up slowly, disoriented in the darkness. I knew who the voice belonged to: not a member of my house, but familiar nonetheless.

"Turn on the light," I said. "I can't think with the light off."

Grin lightly clapped his hands together, and a moment later light flickered into the room. I saw him on the end of my bed, his hands spread like a book in his lap, flames flickering in his palms.

"I mean the real light. Put that out before you burn off your dick," I said.

"I didn't know you cared what happened to it," he replied.

I didn't bother to dignify his comment with a response. I reached over and clicked on my dim bedside light as he closed his hands together, extinguishing the light. He looked pale underneath his freckles.

"I don't suppose I have to tell you how much trouble you'd be in if you were found out of your house," I said. "And in my room, to boot."

"No, you don't."

"Okay then, talk. What made you come over here instead of talking to your own resident?"

Like all of the students who came into my room, he looked at the pictures on my walls. Photographs and magazine images: the turquoise sea and a tangerine sun above it. White beaches and white cliffs. Twisty trees ripe with fruit and olives.

"Because you're clever, Helen," he said, head tilted back to look at the wall better. He stood up, my bed rocking precariously, so that he stood face-to-face with an image of a sailboat bent low over a sapphire ocean. "Because we're too busy being monsters to use our brains."

He traced the line of the sail and I winced, remembering the singe mark on the breakfast table. But the paper remained unmarked beneath his careful touch. "What are these things, Helen? Do you wish you could go to these places?"

"I thought you came to talk about you," I said.

"I didn't say that," Grin said, putting his hands in

EVERY TIME I READ THIS LINE, I THINK... MAYBE I'LL MAKE THIS A NOVEL the pockets of his cargo pants and still carefully studying the photos instead of me.

"Yes, you did," I replied. "You said you had a problem."

Grin didn't say anything, and it struck me that the line of his shoulders looked somehow vulnerable, in comparison to his usual cocky stance. I let my voice soften, just a touch. "Grin, you risked a lot to come over here. Just tell me what I can do."

He turned to look at me, still standing, the light from below throwing strange shadows across his face. "I'd like to know who my parents are."

I didn't say anything. Not because he had more to say, but because I didn't know what to say to that.

"I think we should have at least that," he said. "If we have to stay here and we can't leave, even for a few hours, and this is our whole life, then we should at least have that. We should at least know where we came from, even if we're never going anywhere."

"What do you want me to say?" I asked.

"I want you to say what you always say. That it's stupid and that I should forget about it because it would cause more problems than it would solve. I want you to be the voice of reason, Helen, like you always are."

I was surprised that he thought of me that way. Not as a wet blanket. "I don't know," I said, shrugging. "I really don't see how that could cause us harm. I think that's a fair question."

He sat down in front of me again, blue eyes staring into mine so intensely that I was afraid he would see just how badly I, too, wanted to know who my parents were. Why I was here when I didn't light fires with my hands or turn things to gold or turn into a goat.

"Okay then," he said. "Okay, I'll ask."

He seemed about to say something else, but he just said, "Okay then," again.

"Good luck," I told him.

. . .

Because of our class schedule, I didn't see Grin until dinnertime the next day. He sat at a table by himself, no food in front of him, elbows on the table, just staring down. One fist clenched and unclenched, over and over again. I didn't have to know what had happened. He'd asked.

What did I think would happen? I felt bad for not advising against it.

I would've gone to him, but my table was swamped with juniors having hissy fits over the new sofa placement in our house common room. And by the time I had settled them and gotten up, Grin was gone. For some reason, all I could think about was the longing way he had drawn a finger across the sail in my favorite photograph.

. . .

I awoke to the sound of screaming and the ground surging beneath me. It turned out to be just my housemates leaping on my bed—but the screaming was real.

"Helen!" shouted Hera, one of the younger nymph

daughters who always smelled of fish. "Locke House is burning!"

My gut dropped out from under me, and I scrambled around in my bed to look out the tiny window across the courtyard.

In the night sky, orange and red burned the darkness away, smoke scudding across the courtyard between the houses. I saw teachers knotted in the smoke, getting hoses organized, and Illia, who had a talent with vomiting water, making his long-legged way across the lawn. Evacuated students from Locke drifted back and forth like a school of fish, following each other's lead. Leaping out of bed, I told the girls to pay attention to the teachers if they told us to evacuate, and then I bolted down the halls, intent on making my way to Locke House.

"Where are you going, Helen?" Professor Lansing asked me, standing in the middle of the hall that led to Locke.

"The fire," I said. I didn't know why I didn't say anything more coherent.

"It's under control," he said. His voice was hard. "Go back to your house, please."

I wanted really badly to say his name, but I bit it back with effort and just said, "Is anyone hurt?"

"It's under control," Professor Lansing said. Then he said, more kindly, "This business has nothing to do with you, Helen. You would do best to stay well out of it."

But I knew better.

. . .

The next morning I went to Locke House. As I walked down the twisting, crooked hallways made of church lobbies and cloakrooms, I saw where the fire-making had begun. A black handprint on the right wall became two black handprints on the left became a long, dragged, seared stretch of plaster. The motivational posters in the common room had been burnt to a crisp, and the sofas were overturned, burned-out shells, like landlocked, ruined ships.

My heart thudded in my hollow chest as I ran my fingers along the burnt claw marks in the doors, the smell of smoke burning my nostrils. Windows were broken and paintings smashed over radiators; it wasn't just a fire. In my head, I pictured the rage that had accompanied the flames.

I turned around and left.

Professor Lansing's office had been rendered useless, and so he was doing his work from the empty guest room in Hallow House. He looked up, surprised, when I walked in.

"I'd like to see him," I said. "Can I see him?"

"I'm not sure that's a good idea," Lansing said.

I folded my hands in front of me, trying to convey my usual sea-of-sanity image. "Surely it can only help, me talking to him."

Lansing considered for a moment and finally sighed. "I don't think you'll like it."

But he took me to him, in the isolation room. I'd never been to the isolation rooms before, and I don't know what I had expected. A tiny closet, I guess. But it was a huge, auditorium-like room, lined with tile like a bathtub or an ugly mosaic, with small windows situated high in the walls. In the middle of the room, Grin sat in the middle of the floor, back to me.

Lansing shrugged when he saw me looking and then shut the door behind me, leaving me alone with Grin. Grin didn't move, though he must've heard the door and my footsteps as I walked across the floor and finally sat in front of him.

He looked up at me, and I jerked when I saw the brilliance of his eyes. There was fire in them, somehow, behind the blue, and he was so very fearfully alive that I crossed my arms over my chest in retreat.

"I knew you'd come," he said.

"There are better ways to deal with your anger," I said.

He smiled fiercely.

"Why do you think we're here?" Grin asked me.

"To keep from slaughtering pedestrians with arcs of flame?" I suggested. "To keep us from killing normal people?"

"I don't think it's normal people they're afraid we'll kill," Grin said. "I think Zeus and Odin and Venus and the rest are afraid of what we'd do to them. That is why we can't know them. That's why we can't get out."

SHOCKING, REALLY, HOW MANY OF MY STORIES COME DOWN TO EITHER FIRE OR REVOLUTION.

I looked at him, because I knew he wasn't done.

"Let's break out," he said. "Let's go find that sailboat."

I didn't say anything.

"Tell me it's a bad idea, Helen."

I uncrossed my arms and let him take my hands. His fingers were tough, like they had been scarred again and again by the fire inside him.

"It's a bad idea," I said, because I knew it was true.

"Tell me not to do it," Grin said.

"Did you find out who you were?" I asked him.

He leaned forward. "No. My file wasn't in Lansing's office. But yours was. I know who your mother was."

"It's a bad idea," I said again. Outside, a flock of crows flew past the tiny windows, black wings sailing in an azure sky. No, not a flock. A murder. That's what a bunch of crows were called.

Grin's mouth was right on my ear, and his hands squeezed mine. "Athena. Makes sense, doesn't it?"

"It's a very bad idea," I said, louder, but I stood up, his hand still in mine. And together, as we walked toward the door, I felt as alive as he was.

THE POWER OF INTENT

by Brenna Yovanoff

Brenna doesn't write about magic very often, and I remember this story so clearly because it IS about magic, but Brenna magic. The spells happen subtly and without exploration of any magical philosophy, and is less about amazing magic *than* metaphor. *I often think of my magic as a sprawling, visceral, messy creature that slinks through my stories—but like most things, in Brenna's imagination magic is a cold, sharp weapon. —Tessa*

> THIS IS THE KIND OF MAGIC I PREFER, BUT I THINK IT'S MORE DIFFICULT TO DO WELL *

I've always been fascinated by the idea of wishes, and more than that, the idea of wishes gone bad. When I was really young, I had an audio version of "The Monkey's Paw" [by W. W. Jacobs] and I think it scarred me for life. This story isn't as gruesome as that one, but then it still has an element of danger—the complication of a rogue wish. —Brenna

Anything I could add seems off-topic now.

* No offense to your magic, Tessa **

** AWWW! SARCASM SUITS YOU SO WELL!

25

I am two and occasionally four times more invisible than anyone else at school.

I don't mean that I'm ugly. If I were, I think that people would see me. And maybe their stares would feel cruel and impertinent, but at least I'd know that I was real.

I'm not ugly, though—just transparent. Forgettable. I blend in. I can disappear in a heartbeat.

My best friend, Embry Gleason, says that this is the principle of how objects that are Harper Prescott tend to remain unnoticed. Embry is better at physics than anyone else in the junior class. She can build a model glider out of balsa wood or cardboard or mashed potatoes. She could probably engineer a pretty sizable bridge. I can't even put up shelves.

But there is one trick that I can do. All I need is a pen and a piece of paper.

All my life, my mom has been telling me not to—not to be careless, not to be tempted. That just because you can do something doesn't mean you should. But what she doesn't know won't hurt me. Mostly, I use the trick for little things—to make sure the science test is only on the material I know, or that Mr. Lester doesn't assign us extra homework on weekends.

It goes like this—write it down, then tear it up:

The lesson ends, the bell rings. Class is over and people start to file out. Lester has forgotten to announce the reading.

Later, the wish takes on a life of its own. It comes true. Simple, right?

. . .

But here is where the trick went wrong.

"My mom says I have to go to the homecoming dance," I told Embry in the library at lunch. "Apparently it's what 'normal' people do. It's completely going to suck. You should come with me."

But I knew she wouldn't. Even if Embry had wanted to attend a school function, her mom never lets her do anything.

"Don't even go," she said. "Just do your pen trick and make your mom take it back."

"I can't. I'm not supposed to do that stuff at all, but especially not on people. What if she found out?"

Embry gave me a bored look. "I think you want to go. You want Colin Cray to see you in Rosie's old prom dress and fall madly in love with you and ask you to dance to 'Lady in Red' or 'Unchained Melody' or something else equally wrist-slitting."

"I don't," I said, but I was thinking about the possibility despite myself, thinking of his hands on my waist. His eyes gazing raptly down into mine.

The thing about Colin Cray is, you don't get to be that handsome and that popular without having some pretty predictable tastes. He wears DC skate shoes and dark, worn-out jeans. He worships girls like the Solomon sisters, who have long, tan legs and fabulous hair. He does not even exist on the same astral plane as girls like me.

You shouldn't use magic on people—even hedge magic. I know that. It's too imperfect, too unpredictable. But what about for something small and harmless? What about just once?

The trick is to be specific, but not cluttered. The trick is to know exactly what you want.

After the bell rang and Embry left for trig, I sat alone in the library and wrote the spell to counteract Colin's adoration of Valerie Solomon, undo the way he looked at her.

Colin thought he was so in love, so in love that it hurt his heart, but he was wrong. That was before he noticed Harper Prescott. He saw her at the homecoming dance, and even though she was still and quiet, and even though she was wearing a borrowed dress, he saw her for who she was. And then he was in real love, the kind that doesn't change.

Write it down, tear it up. The wish comes true.

Simple. Right?

. . .

The homecoming dance was about what you'd expect. The gym was dark and full of paper streamers. People were wearing fancy shoes, looking cleaner and more serious than usual. Everything else was pretty much the same.

I stood alone in my beat-up sneakers and my cousin Rosie's old prom dress. It was purple taffeta, with a short, poofy skirt and a bow on the back, too fancy for a semiformal and too big in the chest.

Colin was there with Valerie. They kissed under a huge archway built out of pink and gold balloons, holding hands and looking perfect together. I kept waiting for him to glance in my direction, but he didn't.

After nine songs I decided that maybe I was just too far out of the way; maybe I needed to be closer. I crept over to the crowd by the DJ table and slipped in with a bunch of the kids I only knew from PE, wondering why they would even bother to show up to a dance at all since, based on their conversations, they usually spent their Saturdays getting wrecked somewhere.

Marcus and Sharif laughed way too loud and made out with some of the girls from general track, while Gopher Fitch just leaned against the wall, staring at the crowd. He was watching Bethany Stephens dance to "Wild Horses" with Austin Quaid, looking gloomy and drunk.

Colin and Valerie were out there too, turning in circles to every slow song. They kissed extravagantly to "Unchained Melody." I bit the inside of my cheek and looked at my shoes.

On either side of me, Marcus and Sharif were wrestling with their dates, flopping around like fish. Between them I was completely, perfectly invisible.

Gopher was there with one of the girls from our PE class, but he didn't look at her. Sometimes he slipped behind the bleachers for a few minutes and came back out looking more wasted than ever. He watched Bethany and Austin as colored lights washed over them in slow rainbow waves. Bethany's hair was long and dark and glossy. I knew that she would never look over, the same way Colin Cray was never going to.

Beside me, Marcus kissed his girlfriend like he was trying to do CPR. When he nearly elbowed me in the head, I gave up wishing on Colin and went outside.

Just outside the gym was a cluster of cottonwoods. They'd cut the lower branches so there weren't any handholds, but if you're nimble, you can climb onto the lid of the Dumpster, and from there it's not that far to the roof and then just one quick step into the nearest tree. When you are invisible, you can do anything you want without getting in trouble.

I sat in the cottonwood, watching people leave the gym in twos and fours, stopping under my branch to paw each other awkwardly in the dark. I shivered against the bark, ruining my cousin's prom dress, wondering why my magic didn't work.

Gopher Fitch came out of the gym alone and didn't head for the parking lot. I pressed myself closer to the tree and sat very still while he put his head down and puked in the shadow of the Dumpster. He did it quietly, like he was trying to disappear.

I wanted to call down to him, ask how he was. But that would mean drawing attention to the fact that I was sitting in a tree in a giant prom dress, while one of the most aimless boys in school got puking-drunk over a girl who was never going to look twice at him. I didn't do anything.

After a few minutes, Sharif opened the door and leaned out. "Hey, Gopher, are you okay?"

"I'm fine," Gopher said thickly, pressing his cheek against the wall. "It's fine. Go away."

Sharif started to close the door, but he wasn't quick enough. Marcus shoved past him to stand over Gopher, laughing like it was the funniest thing he'd ever seen.

"Give it up," he said, while Gopher leaned his forehead against the building, his face in shadow. "She's never going to get with you."

Gopher didn't answer. When Marcus jabbed him in the ribs, he twisted away, turning toward the dark chilly sky and the cottonwoods. Toward the girl sitting huddled in the bare branches. His eyes were wide and glazed, staring into mine. He opened his mouth, started to say something, but no sound came out.

"What are you looking at?" said Marcus, glancing over his shoulder.

"The girl," muttered Gopher. "The one in the tree."

I shrank closer against the trunk, pulling my legs up and tucking them under my purple dress.

"There's no one up there."

"There was," said Gopher. "I saw her."

Then he put his head down and heaved some more, and Marcus shoved him in the back and told him what a loser he was for getting all sloppy over Bethany, for not just asking her out, and Sharif stood with his hands in his pockets, looking awkward.

I sat in the cottonwood, shivering. Trying to forget the naked feeling of Gopher Fitch's eyes on mine, like I was the only thing worth seeing. Like he was never going to look anywhere else.

See page 113

The expression on his face had been stricken, and I'd done it to both of us. Because I was needy, because I was lonely. Because I was too stupid to remember that Gopher Fitch's real name is actually Colin. This was the consequence, because I'd asked for it. I wrote it down, called it into being, and now it was mine because that was how the magic worked.

Simple. Right.

Gopher Fitch slumped against the wall, staring up at me while Marcus flicked the side of his face with his index finger and tried to make him flinch.

I sat in the cottonwood tree, hugging my knees and trying not to sob.

5 Signs of A Tessa Story

1. SOMEONE DIES AT THE END

2. THERE'S MAGIC. PROPER MAGIC.

3. 3x LONGER THAN A BRENNA STORY

4. KISSING

5. RATED R FOR BRUTAL MEDIEVAL VIOLENCE

5 Signs of A Maggie Story

1. ANGST

2. CARS

3. SARCASM

4. KISSING

5. GENIUSES

5 Signs of A Brenna Story

1. TAKES PLACE IN A HIGH SCHOOL

2. EVERYONE NEEDS THERAPY

3. 1/3 THE LENGTH OF A TESSA STORY

4. KISSING

5. GIRLS IN PERIL.

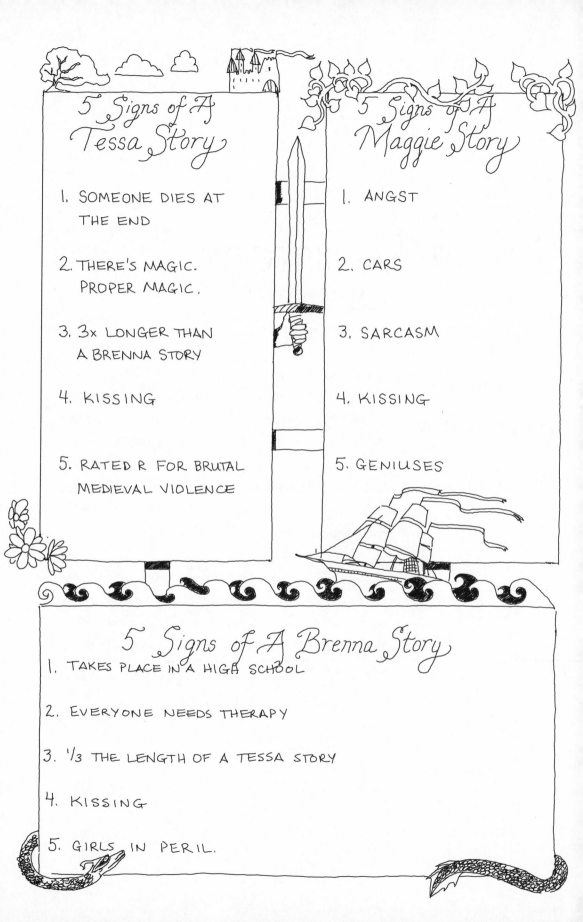

A HISTORY OF LOVE

by Maggie Stiefvater

like piano wire—{ *This is a story about secret love. (Yay, secret love!) As you may have guessed, I have a special place in my heart for all things uncomfortable and covert. The thing that makes this particular story both hilarious and poignant is the juxtaposition between the couples. The drama of Daphne and Apollo provides a nice backdrop for the genuine love story, which is slow and understated and real. And also proves that sometimes hand-holding is just as good as kissing. —Brenna*

Although I adore reading funny stories, they are a devil to write. I very rarely attempt to be intentionally funny through a story, but this was one of those times. I sincerely hope you laugh at least once, and if you don't, please don't tell me. Also, please note: I was a history major. —Maggie

I am lady-in-waiting to the goddess of Carlton University's history department.

Today, Daphne, the goddess herself, was invited to go to the new mall with Brendan. Because she hates being alone with him, I have to go with. I don't mind because Brendan, being the Apollo of CU's history department, has his own manservant and fool, Andy. Andy and I get along because we both understand what it is like to be attendants to campus royalty.

So it is a beautiful spring day. I have cut Psych 102 to be a part of this trip, and Andy has skipped a required meeting with his advisor. I sit in the backseat of Apollo's BMW with Daphne, because Daphne cannot bear to be in the front seat with him. What if he looked at her! Gasp! Her reputation would be mud.

Andy sits in the front seat with his window rolled down. It blows his sandy hair straight back from his forehead and whips Daphne's hair around like a shih tzu in a tornado. She looks pissed as she and Apollo argue about the best way to get to the new mall.

"The new cut-through would be faster," she says. She makes a big show of patting down her windblown hair; the gesture is lost on Andy, who can't see her in his mirror.

"It might be, but I'm driving, so we're going to try using my brain instead," Apollo replies.

"I would drive if you ever climbed off your chauvinistic marble pedestal. Instead we must take your

I ENJOYED PSYCH 102, MYSELF, AND WOULD NEVER HAVE CUT FOR A MERE SHOPPING TRIP.

MAYBE IF THERE HAD BEEN ICE CREAM INVOLVED, THOUGH

35

chariot, and it's going to take us fifteen minutes longer to get there."

Apollo adjusts the rearview mirror so that it reflects Daphne's face. "Fifteen minutes longer to look at you, then."

Andy and I text each other. I see his head duck as he looks at his phone, and my phone rumbles silently in my hand.

Me: wow i love our kids. we should have more of them.

Him: we will. i forgot to mention im pregnant

I see his head turn ever so slightly as he listens for my reaction. I cannot laugh, or Daphne will emote on me, so I tap out another text.

Me: i just peed myself

Him: me too. i think it gets better after the 1st trimester

Apollo swears as he gets cut off by a blue minivan. Daphne gives the minivan driver the finger.

"We should get married, Becca," Apollo said (I should have mentioned that that is Daphne's real name). He sails into the left lane and gets into the turn lane for the mall.

"Could I drive your car if we did?" Daphne asks this already knowing the answer. Apollo's lips press together in a sad line. He loves Daphne, but he loves his BMW more.

Furious texting from Andy.

Him: emma emma emma we should joyride in this tonite

This is my favorite kind of Maggie moment. It's hilarious and makes me want to hang out with their characters

I FEEL FOR APOLLO, NO ONE UNDERSTANDS MY LOVE FOR MY CAMARO EITHER

Me: dont make promises u don't intend to keep

Daphne makes a noise of awe as we pull into the mall parking lot. It's packed. This is the second mall to be erected near the campus, but this one is The Largest Mall in Maryland with Open-Air Public Areas! It also has a Pottery Barn. So of course everyone has come to see it. Brendan finds a parking spot at the far end of the lot, which is where he normally parks anyway, to protect his car's delicate paint. Andy's head ducks again as Brendan displays his superior reversing skills. Brendan's neck cranes and he sets his jaw like a turtle as he verifies that the BMW is equidistant from the two vehicles on either side.

Him: i know where he puts his keys

Me: i have an evening class

Him: dairy queen is open late   ← ICE CREAM

Me: you're on

"I'm wearing heels," Daphne tells Apollo.

"I'll carry you," he says.

"If you touch me, I'll . . ." Daphne is not witty, so she leaves the threat open-ended.

Andy gets in one last text to finish it off:

Him: . . . make emma slap you.

We climb out into the hot spring day and adjust ourselves for the trip according to our personalities. Daphne smooths her tiny khaki skirt and fluffs the hair at her nape to better volumize her curls. She hands me her purse. I drop my cell phone into her purse and stomp my feet to get the feeling back into them—they've fallen asleep since I was sitting on them in the car. Apollo inhales deeply, making his nostrils flare, as if the scent of new asphalt inspires him, and then caresses his BMW key as he remotely locks the doors. Andy slides his cell phone into the back pocket of beat-up jeans and picks some lint off Apollo's collar.

"Let's roll," Apollo says. We are already walking. He tries to put his hand on Daphne's back, and she shies away like a spooked deer, putting me in between her and him. He frowns prettily. She pouts sadly. He knows this is against the rules.

"What shall we see first?" I ask, because they are so busy not talking to each other I fear that we will end up in Sports Authority.

"Borders," Andy suggests. It's a safe suggestion. Though he and I have cut class to be here and Apollo and Daphne spend much of their time as denizens of the history department, we cannot change what we are: book geeks. But I know what will happen when we get there. Apollo will try to follow Daphne, so she will pull me into the modern history section and use me as a human shield until Apollo loses interest and goes back to the Russian history section on the other side of the shelf, taking Andy with him. I am not a modern history person. It smacks of political science, which is not a real major.

"I want to go to Hallmark," I say. "And Things Remembered. And other boring old-lady stores."

"Why?" Apollo's perennial look of confusion

is replaced with true bewilderment. He holds the door open for all of us.

"I need to get something to mark the occasion." I pat Andy's stomach as I pass by him. I remember that the others are not in on the pregnancy joke just as I realize that Andy's stomach is flat and hard under my hand. I was about to smile, and I saw that he was too, but instead we exchange a look that feels like it lasts a minute.

"What occasion? Lunch?" Daphne looks pissed at me. I am not supposed to have conversations that she is not a part of. Then she looks pissed at Apollo, who let his shoulder touch her shoulder. "I don't get it. Emma, you should leave the funny to Apollo."

Andy and I bust out laughing, as Apollo hasn't been funny since the day his BMW got a scratch and he made his voice three octaves higher than usual. Apollo, however, looks flattered and grants Daphne one of his most shining, godlike smiles. Daphne looks startled, as if she hadn't realized how awesome he could be when he smiled.

She lets him walk beside her all the way to Hallmark, and he keeps glancing over at her without trying to touch her. That leaves Andy and me to walk behind them, just us instead of lady-in-waiting and manservant for once. In the store, Daphne and Apollo head down the wrapping-paper aisle while Andy and I walk to the stuffed animals.

I hold up an elephant to Andy; its eyes are slightly crossed. "Hi, I'm anatomically incorrect," I say, moving the elephant's head in time with my words.

CHEMISTRY IS SOMETHING ELSE THAT CAN BE COMPLICATED TO ACCOMPLISH IN A SHORT STORY. YOU REALLY HAVE TO DISCOVER A LOVERS' SHORTHAND

39

Andy pushes some animals aside until he finds one that he likes. It's a horse with a green mane and tail. "And I'm more practical for most third century B.C. land wars."

"Are you going on about the Alps again?" I ask him with my elephant.

"I can't stop thinking about it," Andy's horse replies. "It was a significant FUBAR."

"I still get more views at the zoo."

Just then, Andy's head jerks up to look over the display, and I follow suit. Apollo has an arm braced on either side of Daphne, carefully inserted between gift bags hanging on the wall, and amazingly, it looks like he might kiss her.

Suddenly, Daphne bursts out, "I changed major."

Apollo leans back. "What?"

"This morning," she says. "I put in the paperwork. I got assigned a new advisor."

"So?"

"Poli-sci," Daphne gasps out, her voice desperate. She crosses her arms tightly over her chest. "I'm becoming a political science major."

Apollo lowers his hands from either side of her and steps back. He is looking at her with an expression of utter loss and betrayal. I am reeling a bit myself. A poli-sci major? It seems so drastic. But Apollo really had left her no other choice.

"I will stop saying bad things about political science," Apollo says, formally. "I may even take some modern Russian classes."

But things have changed, and we all know it. She's not even the same species anymore.

We leave the store, Apollo and Daphne several feet away from each other.

I reach down and take Andy's hand.

IN RETROSPECT, IT SEEMS SO OBVIOUS THAT I STOLE MUCH OF THE ATMOSPHERE OF MY OWN COLLEGE EXPERIENCE FOR THIS STORY, BUT THAT'S THE THING ABOUT CREATIVE THIEVERY... ~~OBVIOUS~~ OFTEN IT'S NOT ONLY APPARENT UNTIL MUCH LATER.

Odd, considering I went to an all-girls college prep. There should have been plenty of girl-on-girl action.

GIRLS RAISED BY WOLVES

by Brenna Yovanoff

Brenna writes about[high school in a way I never experienced] it: as if high school were a million different worlds, all coexisting, and they're not only each legitimate and meaningful, but important. Without magic or monsters she makes these characters matter. I both wish my high school had been like that and am vehemently glad it wasn't. —Tessa

The most obvious conclusion one could draw from this story is that girls are mean. Which may or may not be true. The underlying conclusion one could draw though, is that sometimes being who you are—whoever you are—is hard. Sometimes, you can have it all together and still drive yourself crazy. —Brenna

Hadley:

Valerie Solomon is perfect.

Her makeup is flawless and over-the-top, and her hair is always completely amazing. It never looks like someone styled it with an eggbeater unless she means it to.

We're in the west-hall bathroom during the five-minute passing period between first and second, and she's alone, which is weird because Valerie is insanely popular, and she is never, ever alone.

She stands at the mirror, painting on lip gloss, pursing her lips for her reflection. I don't want to look, but I have to anyway.

Valerie is the girl all the other girls have a crush on. Not like a kissing crush—I mean, I guess some of them could have that too—but the kind of crush where everything a person does is irreproachable. The kind where you just want to be them.

So when she turns around and looks at me and says, "Hey are you going to that party at Clara Finn's this weekend?" it's like being acknowledged by the pope or something. You don't know if you should kneel, or bow, or avert your eyes before some vengeful god strikes you down with lightning.

"It's not really my scene," I say, which is a massive understatement and also implies that I have a scene.

She nods like she's thinking hard about something. Then she holds out her hand. "Here, let me see you," she says.

It's in the narrow window before the late call, but

after the second bell. If we don't leave now, we're going to miss roll, but I step closer and hold very still while she stares at me.

Valerie:

I don't know much about her. Just that she's on lacrosse, which is the toughest sport Saint Paul's has for girls, and her arms are thick and kind of built. She's always covered in bruises. Usually that would be sort of gross, but on her they look almost decorative, like some kind of exotic body paint. Like someone has been dotting on purple splotches with a paintbrush. Her joints look hard and sturdy. She could take a punch, no problem.

I'm nearly done to death. I know I'm not supposed to say that, because this is the prime of my life and I am blithe and youthful and privileged and blah, blah, blah, but no. I am overly done to death, and yeah, I really mean that.

The texture of my life is so dense, so all-consuming, that I stop being able to think about trig or symbolism or who won the war. It's like this time in eighth grade when Logan Baines told me he was going to kiss me and didn't do it, and then it was just like this thing hanging over me for weeks and I couldn't relax or concentrate. I never knew when that kiss was going to come out of nowhere.

Now it's exactly like that, except for ski trips and parties, and I get kissed every weekend, but the feeling of waiting never goes away, like I am scrambled to pieces in my own skin.

The waiting is always hanging over me, and all I want is for the other shoe to drop.

Hadley:
Valerie sticks out her chin and rakes her hair back from her face, turning away from me. "You should come anyway," she says to her reflection. "Or at least not worry about people or scenes or whatever, because that's just stupid."

"Why?" I say. And I mean, why come to Clara's party, but also, why does she care one way or the other?

"Because it's better to just do what you want. Whatever you want. You should do what it takes to be tough," she says, and her voice sounds tired and annoyed.

"How do you mean?" I ask, not knowing quite how to take this. "What do you mean by tough? I mean, are you tough?"

"I used to be, sort of. But that was back when I was young and dumb or however you are in eighth grade, and that's stupid. I mean, it's all Black Labels and Marlboro Reds and rebelling just to fit in."

The shape of her mouth is bored. Over it, and I nod. A Marlboro Red is a cigarette. I have no idea what a Black Label is.

"Can I give you a makeover?" she says suddenly, talking fast, like I might say no. "Just a tiny one. A two-minute makeover."

And I nod because I want her to, even though this is not how I would have pictured it. Makeovers are the

True fact: when I was 17 a guy said exactly this to me (or else, something very close). I never really knew what it meant because like Hadley I had no idea what a Black Label was, but I liked how it sounded.

45

kind of thing friends do, not complete strangers standing in the bathroom after the late bell.

She opens her makeup case and gets out a pale, iridescent liner. She draws a shimmery line around my eyes, then follows it up with a smear of glitter and candy-pink shadow. She does my eyelashes and my cheeks, rubbing in cream blush until I am very, very pink.

"There," she says, stepping back. "Now you look like me."

I don't, but I do look different and kind of harmless. Even though I wear makeup sometimes, it never looks this soft when I put it on myself.

Valerie takes a deep breath, zipping her makeup case. "Here, stand right here and don't move. I want to try something."

So I stand with my arms at my sides, watching as she walks circles around me.

"Perfect," she says under her breath, and her voice is shaking a little. "You really do look just like me."

Her voice is so dark and ferocious that I flinch. I start to tell her no, that I'll never be as pretty as her. I'll never be Valerie, who is indeed perfect, even though her eyes are strangely red. Her mouth is working like she's trying not to bite her lip.

"Are you okay?" I ask.

She shakes her head and swallows hard. I half expect her to start crying.

Instead, she hauls back and punches me in the face.

*I believe I immediately went back and reread this from the beginning.

DATE WITH A DRAGON SLAYER

by Tessa Gratton

This is a pretty Maggie story. I mean, it's a story I think I would've written if I'd been Tessa instead of Maggie. Something about the banter and the teen voice and the angst seems very . . . I might just pretend I wrote it. Sometimes that happens when I'm remembering Merry Fates stories: I remember a Brenna story as a Tessa story or a Tessa story as one of mine. Sometimes I find stories of mine that I don't remember writing. I always thought they were Tessa's or Brenna's. Basically what I'm saying is this is a very Maggie story, and if you ever ask me about it in person, I might lie and tell you I wrote it. —Maggie

One Monday I sat down at seven in the morning to write my story, and five hundred words later I deleted everything. I started over, and after nine hundred words realized everything was wrong. By noon I'd scrapped three stories, and by three I was lying on my living room floor in utter despair that I'd have to post a piece of crap because nothing was working. I stared at my ceiling and decided I wanted to write about lying on the carpet in despair. Only, for a better reason than writer-fail. Somehow, I pulled this story about courage and assumptions and dragons out of my butt. And it's my favorite ever, basically. —Tessa, who could fill a book w/ deleted beginnings.

As soon as I wrote this line, I knew my narrator's voice.

Sean Hardy is a dragon slayer.

It was a small dragon, only about the size of a barn, but still. He killed it. They mounted its head on a flatbed truck and drove it around the country. Annie and I paid five bucks each to slip into a dark tent smelling of mold and musty seashells—it had been a saltwater dragon—for three minutes. They flashed the lights on and off and shot trails of fog at your ankles like they needed to make it scarier. The head just sat there, maw half open and greenish teeth filed down so nobody accidentally cut themselves and sued the carnival. Annie cowered back, hands clutching at her purse strap, but I reached out and touched its nose, just over the left nostril. The scales were rubbery there, and surprisingly soft. It reminded me of my dog's belly.

. . .

Turned out, Sean Hardy came from a long line of dragon slayers, but he hadn't known it. They weren't Sigurd's line or from any of the well-known Giant Killer clans. It was only this branch of a long-forgotten family that, back in Eastern Eurland in the fifteenth century, made a name for themselves going up into the mountains and returning with a horse-load of dragon eggs and hearts. One of their youngest daughters married a skald who moved to Eirelann and went native. They immigrated to the United States about three generations back and lost all the stories from back in Eurland. But Sean Hardy's father did have a dragon tooth with one serrated edge a bunch of archaeologists said had to be from one of the Baltic saw-mouths that died out four hundred years ago. I guess that was proof.

He was hailed as the heir to Sigurd despite his somewhat questionable pedigree. Three war colleges gave him honorary degrees despite the fact that he was only eighteen, and he got a half-ten commercial deals. Everybody knew his face. I have to admit, it was one you'd want to know, too. Eyes as gray as smoke, that ruddy look of the Eirish, but with shockingly bright yellow hair.

We never heard him talk, except to say carefully scripted things like "Frosted Puffs: better than dragon tears" and "Only you can prevent troll attacks." At school the prevailing theory was that he hadn't actually killed a dragon, and if he was interviewed live he'd be dumb enough to say so. Annie, of course, defended him as if her own life depended on it. She said he was brave and had the heart of Thor. I said Thor was brave, for sure, but not very smart, and who'd want a guy with a great heart but lacking in the brain department?

But whatever the case, when reports of a dragon rumbling the rocks in the Adirondacks came in, not only did they send in Sean Hardy, but the Vice-Jarl of State also declared a countrywide competition for a morale-boosting public date. Because apparently Sean's only request before risking his life for the country was a simple dinner with a pretty girl.

Confirmed my opinion of him right then and there.

THIS SORT OF SLY SKEWERING-OF-MODERN-SOCIETY HUMOR IS A TRICK I LIKE TO PULL IN MY STORIES

But it didn't stop me from putting my name in.

Come on. Don't judge. There was a scholarship attached.

. . .

My family's been dedicated Children of Loki since as long as we can remember. I'd say that gave me an edge in the luck department, except that there were probably thirty thousand other girls whose families were Lokiskin with their names in the pot too.

My mom said it was destiny. The hand of Wyrd reaching out to pluck me from the teeming masses and set me on my true path, blah blah blah. I didn't argue, because what was the point? I'd get a gorgeous new dress, a free trip to New York, a fine meal with a guy who was at least easy to look at, and then get to attend any college I wanted, no matter what the price. And I could get into pretty much any of them.

No sweat. I wasn't nervous at all throughout the week of television interviews, through the very public shopping spree along Fifth Avenue with Mom, Annie, and a half-ten fashionistas who'd plaster me and my dubious fashion sense across the blogosphere. I wasn't even nervous after they convinced me to pick a teal dress with thin straps I wasn't sure I could wear with a bra.

I didn't get nervous until I knocked on the door of Sean Hardy's penthouse suite, two cameras with their white-hot lights making sweat tingle on the back of my neck.

. . .

Despite the very sparse description of the dress, I wasted 10 minutes looking at dresses on the Internet.

And there he was. They'd put a tie on him that comple-
mented my dress. Little salmon-silver-and-teal swirls
were the only color on him, though. Gray jacket and
pants. Gray eyes. I did notice a small trefoil tattoo on
his earlobe. I stared at it. Through all the interviews
and photos I'd seen, I'd never noticed it. They must
Photoshop it out. Or use some great cover-all makeup.

He cleared his throat, offered his arm, and we
were off.

. . .

Sweet Sigyn's teeth, was dinner awful. They put us in
the middle of a huge dining room where all the rest of
the tables had been cleared away. Instead, there were
cameras and reporters and a couple of priests, even. I
guess they couldn't stop laying magic to protect Sean
in the morning when he went out to face the dragon.

I barely tasted the whatever-it-was some celebrity
chef had spent hours or days fixing up. Sean ate basically nothing too, and he kept trying to talk to me
about TV shows he liked, books he'd read. Polite
stuff, when all I wanted to ask him about was how he'd
killed the dragon, and if he'd touched that soft spot on
its nose.

. . .

We walked back up to his suite, which was only a
floor above mine, holding hands. His fingers weren't
smooth, and I changed my mind about him being
a fighter. It was possible he knew his way around a

AH! DO I SENSE A LITTLE CHEMISTRY?

THIS IS WHERE, IF THIS WAS A MAGGIE STORY, YOU'D KNOW THEY WERE GOING TO KISS AT SOME POINT.

But because it's a Tess story, there's still a chance she might stab him.

I imagine it exactly like the skin on a horse's nose.

spear. His family was healthy middle-class these days, so it was unlikely he'd roughed up his hands with manual labor.

I was so busy thinking maybe he wasn't so full of shit that I didn't notice at first when he leaned in and kissed my cheek. "Can I come inside?" I asked.

THIS WAS NOT → THE KIND OF KISSING I WAS TALKING ABOUT.

Sean Hardy blinked and made a real expression for the first time all evening. He frowned.

I just waited, slowly raising my eyebrows and putting on a tiny, polite smile.

He pushed open his door, pulled me quickly in by the wrist, and slammed it shut in the faces of all those reporters.

While Sean stripped off his coat, snaked free his tie, and went for the minibar, I leaned back against the door and thought about what in Hel I was doing.

"Soda?" he asked.

"Yes, god yes." I didn't move, though. The suite was shockingly sterile, given that I was pretty sure he'd been living in it for a few weeks. Vacuum tracks pressed into the carpet, the TV remote lay next to hotel brochures, the bed I could see through an arch was perfectly made. No suitcases, no half-full cups. Nothing but his discarded tie, curled on the carpet, suggested life. And that hadn't been there half a minute before.

Through the door I could hear frantic conversation, and I turned the bolt. Sure they could find a manager, but would they? If this was Sean Hardy's final request?

Sean poured a can of Coke into two glasses. Then he just stood there with one in each hand. The carbonation popped and fizzed. I walked to him, took one, and then sunk down onto the floor. The carpet was dark blue and thick, so I kicked off my heels and sat cross-legged. The skirt of my teal dress was full enough to fall into my lap and protect my modesty.

I tilted my head up at Sean. He stared at me for a moment, then joined me on the floor. Whereas I sat with my back against the back of the plush sofa, Sean stretched out completely. He set his Coke next to my knee, then lifted his legs so he could untie the shiny dress shoes. His socks were striped green and red.

SEE! CLEARLY A MAGGIE STORY. I LOVE STRIPES! RIGHT NOW MY SOCKS ARE RED AND WHITE.

I laughed.

Then Sean Hardy slid me a grin so unlike anything I'd seen from him before I felt like not only had we known each other for years, but we'd planned this whole thing start to finish. Every step of the dance had gone exactly as we'd wished, every moment was a triumph.

It was a nice fantasy, so I said, "Couldn't have gone better if we'd planned it."

"Right," he drawled, half his face scrunched, the other half skeptical. "I've wanted an awkward date with a girl clearly using me for my money at a closed restaurant the night before I'm basically guaranteed to die for so long."

That killed my smile.

Sean winced. "Sorry. I'll try to be less melancholy."

"Naw, no worries." I shrugged and had to adjust the extremely thin shoulder strap so it didn't fall off. "Melancholy is in. Totally sexy."

"Good. Be sure to tell ... somebody. My mother. The newspapers." Sean spread his hands out over him, as if displaying a front page headline. "SEAN HARDY: WENT OUT SEXY."

"You really don't think you can do it again?" I leaned down so my elbows were on my knees, then took a drink so I didn't have to look at his face. It suddenly mattered.

I heard him shift against the carpet. After a pause he said, "Well. Maybe. I don't know. Last time ..." He trailed off, and I glanced up. He was watching me. When I caught him his eyes flickered to the ceiling. "Last time, Vera, I didn't have weeks to think about it. I just saw the dragon, ran at it, killed it. There wasn't all this brooding and stuff. When you don't have time to be afraid, I guess it's easy to be brave."

This is why I like Sean Hardy.

Pushing aside his untouched glass of soda, I stretched out next to him. From my side I studied his profile. He had nice lips, but probably by the time he was forty his nose would be too big. If he lived that long. My stomach tightened. I was hugely glad I'd barely eaten anything. "You didn't actually make this your final request, did you?"

He sighed. "Don't tell."

"What did you really want?"

"Tickets to Australia?" He turned his head.

I smiled a little. It wasn't really funny, hearing the

edge of fear in his voice. I reached for his hand and took it again. This time I asked, "You know how to use the weapons you need?"

"I can use a sword. And spear. And pistol." He used both of his hands to flatten mine, to splay it between his fingers. "But I think what I need is a bazooka. Or a tank. They won't give me one of those."

"Not so epic," I whispered, "if you kill a dragon with a tank."

"And that's what's important."

Not me, was clear behind his words. *Not my life.*

HERE IS THE ANGST. AND THAT, REALLY, IS WHAT MAKES IT A MAGGIE STORY

The moment I'd hit send, entering this stupid contest, I'd been thinking of taking some pork out of the freezer to make for dinner. By the time I got home from school and Dad was back from work, it would be thawed. It was just a little, inconsequential thought to pair with pushing a button. I hadn't cared about Sean Hardy, or the dragon, or the contest. I hadn't expected anything from it, but I had expected to be alive to eat a pork loin dinner my dad and I grilled on the front patio.

(IT HARDLY MATTERS THAT TESSA WROTE IT)

I rolled against him then, and kissed his earlobe where the trefoil tattoo darkened his skin. He didn't move. I pulled it between my teeth and bit down, hard enough he grabbed my wrist. Hard enough that, when I leaned back, a small white line cut the tattoo in half. I watched it flood with color. Pink and then red. Like his tattoo was bleeding.

THIS IS THE SORT OF KISSING I WAS TALKING ABOUT

Sean raised his hand and touched it. His mouth pulled into a frown. "That hurt."

"Good," I said. I sat up. "Don't die, Sean Hardy."

He sat too. I was close enough to him I could see the flecks of blue sprinkled into the gray.

"If you die," I continued, "I won't be able to use this damn scholarship. And I really want to go to Cornell."

"I'm pretty sure they won't retract the funds," he said. His eyebrows pinched in just slightly, though he was trying to school his expression. I could tell because it was exactly like it had been at dinner.

I didn't respond. Just crossed my arms under my breasts. One of my shoulder straps fell, but I ignored it.

Sean Hardy slipped it back into place, his finger skimming my skin ever-so-gently. "All right, Vera Joansdottir. I won't die." He smiled. "Just for you."

. . .

I don't know what people said that night as I sat on the balcony with Sean Hardy, waiting for the sun to rise. Waiting until they came for him.

At the knock, we both stood up. Sean gripped the railing, and I touched his ear. I pinched it softly, and he whispered, "Ow."

"Want me to tell them you're passed out? That I was too much for you?" I stared out at the indigo lighting the eastern sky between the silhouettes of black skyscrapers.

He kissed my jaw, just beside my ear. "No."

I stood there alone as the sun crept up. As traffic and grease and daylight reached ugly fingers toward the balcony. I thought of the soft left nostril of the dragon and of my mark cutting in half the trefoil tattoo. At the last possible moment, I went into the suite, turned on the television, and watched Sean Hardy walk up the mountain. *

* I have not yet decided if he survives the day. †
† HE TOTALLY MAKES IT.

SCHEHERAZADE

by Brenna Yovanoff

Like I said in my introduction for "Ash-Tree Spell to Break Your Heart," the authorial voice sometimes becomes invisible, and that is a very particular sort of skill. This story, however, is the opposite of that. This story is so very peculiarly Brenna that by the time I get to "It's nice, living alone," I can hear Brenna's voice narrating it. I always envied her precision, her way of neatly establishing both the deadly and the whimsical. —Maggie

I adore stories that explore what brings two bad people together, as opposed to heroes falling in love. The evil soul mates and how they find each other. Brenna is especially good at this. I pretend she wrote this story specifically for me. —Tessa

How do you know I didn't?

The house seems wrong as soon I step into the front hall. I take off my boots and hang up my coat, smelling rain. And that's fine, because it's raining. Except the furnace is on, and the warm, dusty smell should cancel out everything else, and I closed the window before I left. I know this. I know I closed it. The breeze blowing down the hall from the kitchen is cold and brackish, straight off the river.

In the kitchen, the window above the sink is flung wide, screen in tatters, rain trickling down the wall and pooling on the counter. With electric clarity, my gaze leaps to the magnetic utensil strip on the wall. The nine-inch chef's knife is missing, and suddenly my heart is going a million beats a minute.

"Turn around," says a voice behind me. The tone is low, predatory, and makes panic race down the back of my neck.

When I turn, a guy in a damp canvas coat is standing in the doorway.

He's my age, maybe a little younger. Tall, but with stooped shoulders. His hair is shaggy, wet from the rain. The missing knife is in his hand. The way he holds it is casual, easy. There's nothing skittish about him, and that's what makes my heart lurch in my chest—the easy way he holds a knife. I look at him and don't say anything.

When he smiles, it's almost sweet. "Don't you want to know who I am and what I'm doing here?"

I shake my head, willing myself to look composed, but for a second my mouth won't shut.

"That's okay," he says, hefting the knife. "It doesn't really matter."

"My boyfriend will be home any minute."

"No, he won't." And this time when he smiles, it's hard and chilly and gets nowhere near his eyes. "His car's been gone for two weeks. I don't think he's coming back."

"He was on—on a business trip, but he's home now, he'll be coming home tonight, any second. If he finds you here . . ." But the threat trails off, empty in the bright glow of the kitchen.

He just nods, giving me a hard, scornful look. "Right. Where's all his stuff then?"

And I'm steamrollered by the knowledge that this is no accident, that he's been watching me. That Dalton has been a done deal for quite a while and this guy knows it. His gaze is flat, without texture or depth, and I already know that something's wrong inside him—a flipped switch that makes him walk into a girl's kitchen and take a knife off her wall.

He moves closer, unhurried, staring into my face, and I know for sure that he's the textbook definition of dangerous. Not troubled or misguided. He is a stone-cold psychopath. ✗

"Why?" I whisper, but I already know that the explanation, the reason will mean nothing and all I really care about is if it will hurt. How much it will hurt. How long this is going to hurt.

"I want to know what it's like," he says, easing his thumb over the blade, testing it. "To kill someone."

✗ Yes, this is a recurring Brenna theme.
Or fixation. Depending on how you look at it.

"They'll catch you," I say, backing away from him. Two shuffling steps before the countertop presses into my spine and I go rigid and still. "Don't you care about being caught?"

For a second he doesn't seem to hear. Then he grins, shaking his head. "How will they catch me? It's a break-in, a burglary gone wrong. Happens all the time. Everyone will be so sad for you." He smiles like the idea pleases him.

"But there are so many things that could give you away. What about DNA? It's almost impossible to kill someone at close proximity without leaving something behind. What if I scratch you? What if you leave a fingerprint somewhere, or clothing fibers under my nails? And you need a plan to dispose of the body. Unless you want to go down for first degree, you can't stab me in my own home and then just leave me here—too much evidence. Do you have a car?"

He throws his head back, incredulous, still smiling. "And you're telling me all this . . . why?"

"Because—" and my voice sounds shrill and much too loud. I take a deep breath, smile like I'm selling real estate or dishwashers and start over. "Well, because you're doing this all wrong. If you really want to kill someone, it has to look so much like an accident that no one will even investigate."

For the first time, his smile wavers. His jaw is tight with something like rage. "And how do you know so much?" In his hand the blade looks very sharp, reflecting the glare from the overhead light.

His expression is watchful, and I'm certain that he's imaging my blood.

I take a deep, shuddering breath and blurt out, "When I was twelve years old, I drowned my sister."

For a second he doesn't respond. Then he moves closer, looking almost troubled. "Why?"

The story rushes together in my head and I claw through the pieces, trying out answers and discarding them: because I was jealous of her beauty and her popularity, jealous of our parents' affection for her, angry because she broke a toy that mattered to me or always teased me or never loved me?

"Because I wanted to know what it was like," I whisper, trying to look how he might think a child-murderer should look. Honest, but unrepentant. "Because I'm like you."

He covers the space between us in two steps, and suddenly I'm frozen, balanced on the point of my most expensive kitchen knife, chin up, head tipped back at an awkward angle. "Are you lying to me?" he snarls.

The steel is cold against my throat. I shiver and breathe out but never look away from his face. "No," I say softly. "No, I wouldn't lie to you."

"Good. Because if you're lying, I will gut you here and now."

"Look—I'm just trying to help you. If you want to kill someone, you should do it where no one will find the body. Or where people die anyway. Where it will look like a freak accident or a crime of necessity. I can help you," I whisper, biting down on every word,

I LOVE HOW AMBIGUOUS THIS ALL IS!!!

horribly aware of how my pulse beats in my throat, thrumming against the knifepoint. "We could find someone really good—disposable, a lowlife who deserves it. Some people just aren't meant to live. I can show you how to get away with it."

"Right." He sounds disgusted. "Why would you do that? Why would you help me?" His face is close to mine, cheeks red, teeth bared, but anger is better than flat, affectless nothing. Flat means no remorse, no reasoning. It means one centimeter away from being stabbed to death in my kitchen.

"Please, I told you about my sister. I told you a secret!" I gasp it, almost wail it, trying to sell the promise of camaraderie—that it will be me and him, two sick customers, partners in homicide. The promise that I am not lying.

He nods, stepping back, looking dazed, and lets the knife drop from my throat. I go limp inside but don't sigh aloud.

"And if I walk out of here," he says, sounding almost sad, "what'll stop you from calling the police?"

"You know about me. I could never turn you in— you'd tell them what I did!"

He sets the knife on the counter, looking lost and pitiful, like maybe all he's ever wanted is for someone to know about him.

"We should make a plan," I say, giving him a quick, sideways look. Almost flirtatious? "Meet downtown somewhere, do some recon. If we dress right, we can pass for vagrants or barflies. No one will remember seeing us. We need someplace with loiterers and lots of foot traffic—maybe the bus station? In two hours? Let's meet behind the bus station."

My voice sounds wrong, a little forced, but his eyes are hopeful and he wants so badly to believe me.

"You better not stand me up," he says, shaking a finger at me. "I know where you live." But he says it with a smile. On someone less homicidal, it would sound almost like he was making a joke.

I let him out through the back door and watch him go, waving from the porch steps.

After he's over the fence and out of sight, I go down into the basement and stand at the workbench, sorting through my supplies. It's nice, living alone. I can leave things lying out now. Taser-plus-piano-wire is very efficient, but I like cyanide for strangers.

The story of my sister was a risky move, hard to sound convincing. The memory is clear but featureless, gone over so many times I've worn the details off. I don't even remember what it felt like.

I didn't want to do this so soon after Dalton, but the neighborhood seems content to take that for the heartrending tragedy it was—her longtime boyfriend, poor girl—and I don't see any other way. Some people just aren't meant to live.

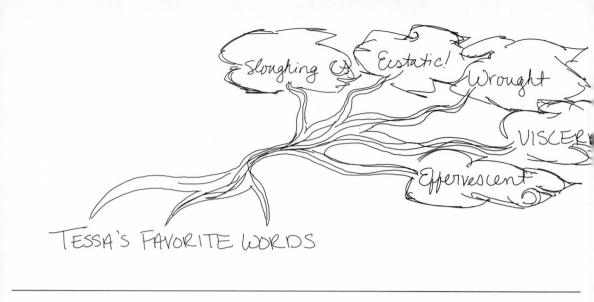

TESSA'S FAVORITE WORDS

BRENNA'S FAVORITE WORDS

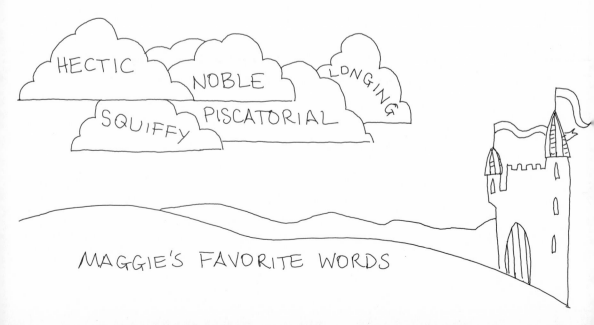

MAGGIE'S FAVORITE WORDS

PROMPTS

One of the reasons we named ourselves the Merry Sisters of Fate was to play up the idea of mutual creation—the three women who spin the same "story" but each have different roles. The spinner, the weaver, the cutter. (We may have spent several hours near the beginning discussing who is who . . .) But each fate has a different specialty, different preferences, different weaknesses. To me, the common prompts exemplify this. We pick an image, a fairy tale, or some piece of folklore to use as inspiration, and each of us writes a story. They can be any kind of story, so long as it comes from the prompt. I'm always amazed at how different the stories turn out—the ways that Brenna and Maggie will find aspects that never occurred to me. The prompt weeks have been my favorite since the beginning because it feels like a real chance to play—there's characters and world and story already, so I don't have to worry about them. I can twist and experiment and have fun. —Tessa

♡ RULES

The prompts are one of my absolute favorite aspects of Merry Fates. The idea of a common starting place is really exciting to me, because as a staunch supporter of the arcane, I'm always looking for the most obscure, mysterious, esoteric parts of a thing—the underlying theme or unspoken implications—and the prompts are the perfect venue to really dive into the core of a story. Not just the characters and the action of it, but what it means. Also, I am unapologetically obsessed with what things mean. —Brenna

I always think prompts are going to be easy. After all, part of the work has been done for you! But a story is really a reverse telescope of narrowing opportunities. With every sentence you write, you reduce the number of paths open to you as a writer. And it's hard enough when you're the one doing a narrowing, choosing how you box yourself in. But a prompt! It immediately slams several doors before you've even said "boo." All of the paths seem to point unerringly toward a very literal interpretation of the image or fairy tale. For me, then, the challenge is to figure out how to open those doors back up again, to be clever with my handling of the subject matter. In the end, it's like all the other stories I write. I have to ask myself, what am I really trying to say? What question am I trying to ask? What is the magic really going to stand for? And then I have to put the prompt back on top of that. When I look at it that way, it becomes a puzzle with the edge pieces already done. The weird part is always looking at what other people have done with this puzzle, though. I mean, we all had the same edge pieces, didn't we? How in the world did they get a city scene when I made a moose? —Maggie

I'd like to read your moose story.

OUR NEXT PROMPT!

THE SPIRAL TABLE

by Tessa Gratton

I have a long history of (despising Arthurian legend.) Yes, I once wrote a trilogy that relied heavily upon it, but that doesn't mean I had to enjoy it. So while I was thrilled at a common prompt, the idea of using King Arthur for it gave me hives. But I'm rarely one to shy away from a challenge, so I agreed. All I had to do was find a way to write this story without my hatred being visible. The answer was obvious after some thought: delete Lancelot and Guinevere. Have Arthur stand on a table. Add knives and murder. Ta-da! —Tessa

where "obvious" means totally not.

AS SOMEONE WHO WAS ACTUALLY PHYSICALLY HATCHED FROM ARTHURIAN LEGEND, I REGARD THIS AS A PERSONAL ATTACK.

Call me Mordred.

I ALREADY DO.

The wizard asked her to help him build a table.

For all her seventeen years she had lived between nine crumbling columns at the pinnacle of a low hill. Spreading around her like a living moat was a ring of apple trees.

She crouches now over the earth beside the column she calls "Between All Things," mixing a potion for the Queen of Faerie's son, who is plagued by nightmares. There is no sun here; it is always morning or evening and only the color of the sky suggests which. Now the wide sky is purple-tinged, and she knows that soon it will be dusk-time and her herbs will have to wait.

This was my first real attempt at 3rd person present.

Through the false gate between the "Never-going" column and the one named "Forever-falling," the wizard appears. He wears the leather armor of men, an iron sword hanging at his hip. "Morgen," he says, and the apple trees whisper her name back to him.

Without glancing the wizard's way, she tips over the clay pot with mixed crushed lavender and valerian and skullcap. Like tea leaves, they whirl against the cracked stone floor as though swept by eddies of water, then fall into a pattern. She stares for a moment and then as she stands says, "Yes," and sweeps her bare feet through the divination. "Whatever you have come for, the answer is yes."

They face each other across the grove of stone: one lithe and young, her fingers stained blue and her braids as tangled as lake weeds, the other like a piece of driftwood too heavy to be swayed by the current.

I love this line more than it probably deserves.

"Your loyalty does you honor, child," the wizard says, holding out a hand.

Thinking of her divination, she goes to him. Better for the wizard to think she makes her decision for love.

. . .

The first words from the boy-king's mouth when she enters his hall spit with anger. "I will not, Cai, I will not stay here." His hand slams onto the long table, rattling cups down the line.

"Sir." A warrior pushes back his seat, a great bulk of a man with thick braids the color of tallow. "Here is the best place to keep the wolves from our door." The gathered warriors bang their thick clay cups in agreement, drowning out the boy's protests. By their bracelets and sword hilts and rings, Morgen knows them for lords.

The king says, voice strained with calm, "The fields here are over-eaten, and if we continue to force ourselves upon this valley, they will welcome the Saxons, Bedwyr."

The wizard strides over the straw-strewn floor and bows. "Arthur."

"Myrddin! Tell them we cannot stay here. They will not listen to me, because my words are meaningless to such warmongers and idiots." The boy throws up his arms.

From the doorway, caught between the warmth of the hall and the early spring chill at her back, Morgen hides a smile behind her fingers. She has heard stories in the wind and chatter from the pixies about this new king. That on the battlefield he is unrecognizable in his wrath, but his mercy gathers men and loyalty at an uncommon rate. Mostly, though, she has heard that the land loves him, too.

"We have wintered here," the wizard says, "and should move on so that the fields may be replanted."

Clamor rises from the gathered lords, and as they argue, Morgen watches the king. He is younger than she expected, and he observes the cacophony with his mouth turned down in a furious pout. A twisted iron and copper ring sits heavily about his neck. Tilting his head, he stares up at the low roof beams, at a pair of mourning doves huddled in the shadows beside the smoke hole. Just as Morgen thinks, perhaps, the stories have exaggerated his command, he stomps up onto his chair and from there onto the table itself, planting his boots so hard chunks of dirt fall off the heels and skitter across the wood.

This was the inspirational image for this story.

Silence cuts through the hall. The boy-king says quietly, so they have to listen, "I am leaving and taking my court with me. I will not ruin this valley. We will find a better place to camp until the summer warring."

Without waiting for an answer, he hops off the table, landing with his knees bent and balanced. Flicking his hand at the wizard, he strides toward Morgen. She steps aside, but the wizard says, "Arthur."

The king stops and notices her. "Who is this?"

"Morgen, Arthur. She's come to help with the table."

"The faerie?" Arthur walks the final space between

them and peers at her, hair to toes. "You don't have shoes."

"You don't have a beard," she says.

His scowl opens up and he laughs. "Welcome to my court, Morgen the Faerie."

. . .

Traveling with Arthur is slower than traveling with the wind, but soon they arrive at the fort where the table will be forged.

A great wooden hall rises from behind an ancient ring of earth, and Morgen can smell the sea. It was a fort belonging to a lost tribe, Myrddin tells her, used by the Romans to corral cattle, and rebuilt by Arthur's father's father. From the cliffs they can see in all directions, but the ground is fertile and the place will do well for their magics. Earth and sea and sky, coming together.

She closes her eyes and digs her toes into the grass. It is as the wizard says. Here she can build a hearth for the deepest magic.

. . .

They begin with a slab of stone cut from the cliffside and worn smooth by a thousand crashing salt waves. All the lords and Arthur himself hold the ropes that drag it over rolling logs, up and up and up from the beach. "This will be a symbol of our rule, of the wholeness and greatness of our island," he declares over a feast, with torches licking the shadows away and fat popping in a dozen bonfires.

. . .

Morgen is given a gown of smooth red wool and a girdle of linked mother-of-pearl, but even as she walks the halls of the king she refuses shoes. In the great hall, where the round slab is raised up by squat oaken pillars, she crawls over and beneath it, etching tiny words around and around and around again, while the wizard cuts the thick spiral where the iron will be laid.

I prefer magic to require hard work.

She kneels beneath the slab in the morning when the young sun spills in through the doors at just an angle to light the underside so she can work. A shadow flashes over her runes, and she glances at the boots pacing slowly around the table, scuffed leather and chunks of mud trailing in their wake.

A whisper of skin on stone tells her Arthur runs his fingers along the edge of the table as he walks around it. She holds herself still, uncertain if he came here to be alone, until the king releases a sigh full of sorrow.

"Why does my table make you sad?" she says.

"Morgen?" Arthur crouches, resting his forearms on his knees, with his head tilted so he can peer under. "What are you doing down there?"

"Working."

Before she can crawl out, the king crawls in. He fits perfectly beneath it when sitting with his legs crossed, and when he lifts his face his nose is a breath away from the smooth stone. "It smells like old things."

"It is old."

"Not like us."

"We feel old," she says, imagining her finger

tracing the arc of his nose the way he's traced her table. "Is that what makes you sad? All the weight of kinghood?"

He meets her eyes, and in this shadowed privacy whispers, "I am sad I must resort to this."

She knows he means her table.

"I want to inspire and unite on my own merits."

"Why am I creating it, then?"

Another long sigh blows his breath against her cheek. "Because when the Romans retreated they left a void here, and everyone has raced to take it apart and destroy any good they had done. We had roads and trading and communication, and now the roads crumble; we have pirates instead of merchants, and without their force, no one listens. This island needs an emperor again."

"You have done so much in just a little time. Why are you impatient?"

"I had stories on my side, wild tales of a boy and his faerie sword. I had cavalry when no one else did. But stories are good for conquering, not for finding peace, and at every battle my enemies learn from me. I need something to hold my rule together, here, at home. To bind the others to me."

"There are better ways. Ways you know well."

"How can I risk them, with what is at stake?"

"How can you not, with what is at stake?"

He remains quiet, and she moves closer. The king kisses her.

. . .

In the forge, where sparks and ruby coals tumble over the ground, she picks her careful way, hair braided back, sleeves and skirts tied up, to hammer magic into the metal. The smoke reeks of stringent herbs, and none but she can breathe.

It is a marvelous, terrifying production when the metal is ready. They build the largest forge fire ever seen, on logs of yew and mistletoe bundles, to heat the spiral in one piece, and it is carried hot and glowing by nine men to the table and set in at once for the magic to quicken properly. Yelling and curses crack through cool dawn as they scramble from the forge to the hole knocked into the wall so the door is large enough.

The spiral scrapes harshly over the stone, and Morgen and the wizard together shove it into place with oak wands. It locks down, sending up a ring that reverberates in the ears of all.

Morgen raises her eyes, wiping sweaty hair from her face, and finds the boy-king watching her. He smiles, sorrow melting away.

. . .

The wizard leads her into the empty hall in the hours before dawn, when everyone sleeps. She is weary, but the spiral table invigorates her, calling to her skin so that she immediately presses her palms down. Where stone should be cool, this is as warm as a man.

"It is beautifully done," the wizard says, standing behind her. "As I would expect from the Faerie Queen's ironsmith."

Bending at the waist, she leans her entire body against it, ear to the iron, and closes her eyes. The song it sings is of roots and rivers and currents of wind, living ropes tying the men who touch it together. It is earth and fire, air and water, and she has drawn them together.

The iron screams, and she jerks away.

The wizard's dagger grinds into stone, sparks blinking and gone.

She stands back, staring at him, only able to wonder at his purpose.

"You'd made that so easy." He slides the edge of the blade against his finger, drawing blood.

"Why?" She is so unbelieving, she finds it impossible to be afraid.

The wizard points the dagger at her. "It is the final magic. Your sacrifice, to the table."

"But it is complete. It needs no such thing."

"I have seen him watching you. You with your bare feet and ocean eyes, you have become the spirit of the island to him, Morgen. He would sacrifice himself to you, apple-keeper, healer, wind-whisperer."

She draws back her shoulders, but the wizard gives her no chance to speak. He lunges, and Morgen falls back with a yell, kicking out her feet. They crash down, and she swings her arm at his face. The iron ring around her wrist hits his cheek, and in his moment of surprise she claws at his hand, takes the dagger, and runs.

· · ·

The king sleeps in a heavy tent, out among his warriors. Morgen tears back the flap and darts inside. A banked fire casts no light, but the moon is bright enough to glow through the cloth. Arthur sleeps as he walks: sprawling and loud.

Her breath bursts in an uneven rhythm as she flings about in her mind for something to tell him. Some truth that he will understand, before the wizard comes.

That she is bound to him, not by magic, but by love.

That he is bound to the earth, not by magic, but by spilled blood.

That the wizard is bound only to himself, and the trees themselves will one day devour him.

She kneels at his head, leans to kiss him, and pauses, lips hovering over his.

"The witch is trying to murder the king!"

The wizard's yell is just outside, and as the tent is again torn open, Arthur opens his eyes to see her crouched over him with dagger in hand.

"No," she whispers.

His eyes look past her to the wizard's towering figure, blocking the firelight outside.

Love at his bedside, and power at the door.

The boy-king grips her wrist, tightening until she cries out and released the dagger. "You will never trust love," she says, wrenching free of him. She means it mournfully, but the words twist and churn into a curse before they reach his ears.

Standing back, she claps her hands together, and the sound is echoed by thunder and the crashing of waves. Wind gusts into the tent, yanking it up from the ground in great flapping chaos. The king ducks and covers his head as stakes are flung in the air. The wizard cries out, and all the waking warriors cower.

When the maelstrom lays itself down again, the girl, too, has gone.

I almost convinced myself I could give this story a less unhappy ending, but that wouldn't really be in keeping with the prompt.

This story is in
my top 5 favorite
Brenna stories
of all time. It might
even be # 1.

THE MADNESS OF LANCELOT

by Brenna Yovanoff

I am a fan of structure, I must admit. I love the hell out of it. A lot of structure in a short story or novel breaks down the fourth wall, and often that's a bad thing for fiction. A story is a lie, and generally you don't want to remind the readers any more than you need to that you're lying to them. But when it's done well, when you make the reader want to know it's a lie, that it's not true, it becomes like a song or a poem. The refrain reminds us that this is not real life, because real life some-times doesn't have a purpose. This story of Brenna's is one of those structured pieces, and it reminds me of an old ballad: girl, boy, country road, and the sad, sad refrain of a cigarette-smoky voice. —Maggie

One thing I look forward to most about common prompts is finding out what Brenna is going to do, because she takes these prompts and manages to find some core truth or hidden sentiment under all the folds that I've never seen. Her prompt stories often make me feel like a very literal writer. Even when I'm writing about magic. —Tessa

All the Avett girls are strong swimmers. In a county of cattle ropers and turkey shooters, this is what we're known for. There's nothing more peaceful than diving below the surface. The lake is my secret, my refuge.

But this is not a love story.

. . .

Asher Phipps is four years younger than me, but a good deal taller. When he was hardly more than a baby, his daddy, Otha, died in a threshing accident. Afterward, Asher's momma was no good for anything anymore, so he started tagging after me. He had a sweet country lisp and a toy duck on a string. He used to follow me everywhere.

I watched him on yellow afternoons, showed him how to make pets out of beetles and dolls from corn husks, took him swimming in the creek.

Now he's mostly grown, and we haven't spoken in years, though I still see him nearly every day in the summers. Sometimes his mouth is open like he's about to say something, but the sound never makes it all the way out. Sometimes I catch him looking at me, this raw, ragged look that I don't know how to answer.

Before this business of misfortune and grief, he was the golden one, hero-strong and best-loved. As for me . . . well, I'm the girl from the lake. It's been a long time since they didn't find me strange.

Asher's change was sudden, whereas mine happened so slowly that no one could make note of it for sure. I might have always been this way.

It wasn't his momma dying, although that happened. And it wasn't the recession or not getting that scholarship. All those things were bad enough, but when he lost his sweetheart, his store of strength, of perseverance, seemed to end.

When she died, the whole town turned out for the funeral. I did what I always do—went out to the lake and swam deep, looking for answers. In the murky glow of a stifled sun, I saw blackness and shadows, indistinct. I saw nothing.

This is not a story about revelations.

. . .

Before there was the lake, the town was situated at the lowest point in the country, snuggled in tight between two hills. When the steel plant came in, they needed water for cooling. They tore down the houses, carted out the planks and shingles. They left the foundations like a monstrous ruin, a long-forgotten world down in the weedy tangles and the mud.

On most days, I visit. I swim out to the middle and dive right down to the bottom. There in the gloom I am closer to our past, running my fingers through silt and slime, reaching for a world that used to be ours, all lawns and carports, leaning garden sheds. Avett girls can hold their breath forever. I wind my way between rotting stumps where trees supported tire swings. We used to live here. I would live here again if I could.

This is not a story about coming home.

. . .

Asher runs what used to be his daddy's bait shop, only now I guess it's his. The shop was there when people used to go fishing in the creek, and now that the lake has taken over, the shop stands farther up the slope, just off a pair of barbecue pits and a rickety picnic area.

During the slow hours, Asher sits out on one of the broken-down picnic tables, waiting for sunset, for closing time. The girls from town come twitching around to see him, smiling cherry-red smiles and flirting with their eyelashes. They all want him to take and marry them, if only to have that triumph, to prove they each are fine enough that he'll love them. If they can make him love them, then anyone will love them. His eyes are always somewhere off in the middle distance, and tragedy has a glamour to it, if you only wear it right.

This is not a story about sorrow.

. . .

It's a slow, hot evening in August, and when I come trudging up from the lake, I'm not startled to see a herd of girls gathered around Asher.

He looks up, looks past Annalee Marquart and Callie McCloud, to where I stand with my dripping hair and sopping canvas shoes.

"Viv," he says, and his voice sounds cracked and rusty. Just my name. Nothing else.

Callie glances over her shoulder. She's younger than me, but aggressively put together, with curled hair and heavy lipstick. When Asher stands up and pushes past her, she looks stricken, then furious.

He comes across to me, eyes fixed on my face. In the trees, seven-year cicadas are crying clear to Colvern County. "Viv," he says, "can you tell me something? Just tell me what it's like when you dive?"

And I don't say anything, because it's not the kind of thing you can say. I know what he's asking, but that's not the same as knowing how to answer.

I would comfort him, console him for his loss, if I were still his friend. But was I ever?

This is not a story about loneliness.

. . .

How can a person ever know the true, honest heart of another?

This is what I'm thinking as we stomp and thrash our way through the canebrake with blackflies and no-see-ums whining around our heads. This is what makes the goose pimples come out on my arms and the shudders run through me. Not the chill of my wet clothes, not anticipation of the crisp, authoritative splash when I break the surface. But this, this certainty that Asher is too far from me now to ever know me again, and yet he wants an antidote, expects me to cure him of his pain. At the bottom of the lake there are the gloomy shipwrecks of memory, but no answers.

Fools like to talk about the little town church. They say it wasn't dismantled, but only left behind. They claim the steeple stands even to this day, dark and ghostly, just visible when the water gets low. That's

The house I grew up in was by a reservoir that used to be a town. Lots of talk about a church steeple, totally not true.

83

nothing but a tale. I've been down a hundred times and never seen it.

This is not a story about God.

. . .

Asher wades out first. Just stumbles forward and plunges in. If it were me, I'd have walked farther down the shore, to where the bank slopes off and the ground is all bare gravel and fine sand.

He goes deeper, water churning up around him, and I'm struck by how badly I want to comfort him, fix it all if I could. I raised him half his life, but that was years ago, and it's taken me this long just to uncover the mysteries of the place I grew up. I don't know him any more than he knows himself.

From the bank, I watch him flail away from me, toward a world he can't survive and can never understand. The world on the bottom is mine alone, not because I conspire to keep it, but because no one else in the history of our incurious little town has taken the time to explore it.

"Asher," I call and then start after him. "Asher, wait. Why are you doing this?"

"Because you're the only other person who knows what it's like," he says, looking back over his shoulder. "Because you know how it is to wish and wish for something you can't ever have back."

"It was never like that." And now I'm splashing after him, shaking my head. I say it unashamedly and right out loud. "I never loved our town until they sunk it."

He stops.

He nods but won't look at me, standing hip-deep in the artificial lake, run through on the realization that I'm not broken. That he is wholly alone in his sadness, when all this time he's been so desperately sure it was the two of us.

His eyes are a pure, moody ice-grey, like swimming out to the center. Like going under.

This is not a love story.

SHEER GENIUS.

It also makes me want to tell everyone what things are by saying what they're not.

M & A
4EVAH

THE WIND TAKES OUR CRIES

by Maggie Stiefvater

There are two things going on with this story. No, three. First of all, it is about Arthur, and I love Arthur. I just do. I like him in pretty much all of his forms, although I think Lancelot is a douche and I don't know why Arthur hangs out with him. I think I prefer the older Arthurs, before they came up with the concept of courtly love and sketchy Sir Lancelot. So, there's that. And then the second thing is that I am trying to be Tessa in this story. She does historical voice so well that I of course had to try my hand at it (I won't tell you how much longer it took for me to be Tessa than if Tessa had been Tessa). And then, the final thing that's going on here is I was trying to write a sort of narrator that I'd never attempted before: a sort of person I have often met but never been. —Maggie

The real secret to writing like me is killing someone violently in the end.
MISSION ACCOMPLISHED!

I love the smell of intestines in the morning. Why have I never ended a story with a dinnertime evisceration?—Tessa

My Eoin was sixteen years when they rode through. Eoin, I loved him; he was my seventh, and the others nearly killed me coming out, but not him. He slid out like a fish through a fisherman's hands, and like a fish, he never did cry, just twisted in the goodwife's arms. Later, when he was older, my husband and master did his part to beat a tear from Eoin's blue eyes, but he wouldn't cry for him either. I did the weeping for him, while I listened from the other room, and the wind took my cries away. My husband beat the others as well, but when he beat them it was a steady, methodical, rhythmic sound, like weaving, or intercourse, or raking up hay. When he beat Eoin, it was the unpredictable scrabbling of a foal standing for the first time, or the chaotic crashing of the ocean on cliffs. The beating would stop whenever Eoin stopped getting up, but Eoin never seemed to learn to stay down, any more than he learned to cry.

Eoin was like a stubborn green willow wand: he would bend but never break. I was proud of all my sons, but I was proudest of Eoin, partly because I was the only one who was. And love means more if it is hard to do.

The day they came in on their horses was summer at its end, ripe and crisp as an apple, the sort of day that makes lords long to be chasing foxes to ground and maidens to bed. There was no mistaking them. Who else had chargers like they, their coats every color of oak leaves? Who else, in this season, had brilliant caparisons draped round their horses' shoulders

OFTEN, I WILL SET UP MY STORIES AS A CHALLENGE TO MYSELF, AND THIS, THIS WAS MY CHALLENGE — TO TELL A STORY IN THE VOICE OF THIS WOMAN WHO THOUGHT NOTHING AT ALL LIKE I DID.

and cloaks pinned on their own? Who else rode with the faerie-woman on her chestnut palfrey, her face proud as a man's?

My sons all watched the knights process along the edge of our fields, their horses pressing up against each other and then dancing away, restless with their own strength. My daughters watched them too, but like me, they were not fair of face, so I told them to keep their eyes to themselves. That the knights of the table would not want to be ogled by maidens without flowered cheeks and bee-stung lips, by my daughters with hog-chins and hair fine as an old man's. They paid me no mind, and all labor ceased while everyone waited for a glimpse of Arthur.

Here he came then, on a mighty dapple-gray stallion draped in green, a faerie's color, and he was more splendid than they had said. His bearing—proud! His face—kind! His mouth behind its trimmed ginger beard was set with both good humor and the weight of responsibility, a face every mother should wear. I was in love with him at once, but everyone is. It is easy to love Arthur. Still, I flattened my skirt and pressed my hands to my girl-flushed cheeks and was glad that my husband was not about to see me undone so by the heroes.

I barely had time for this first glance when I realized they were coming this way. My son Aodhan was pelting toward the house, fast as a hound, and his voice carried well to me, full of terror and adulation. "The king wants a drink. The king wants water."

I MAKE MY CHARACTER NAMES AS CONSISTENT AS POSSIBLE IN MY FANTASY STORIES, IT NEEDS TO FEEL LIKE A REAL PLACE, FORMED BY A COMMON LANGUAGE

My heart leapt inside me as I began to weigh the request—the king could not have water, the king needed wine, did we have wine fit for Arthur, we had the mead that the Deutscher had brought—and then, as the dapple-gray horse approached, I realized with sinking heart that I could hear the uneven thunder of a beating from the house behind me. Though Eoin, as ever, didn't cry out, my husband made up for it with grunts and bellows, insults and crowing, loud enough to hear outside the threshold. Oh! Eoin was never his son, not with eyes like that, oh, did he think that a king would want to look at him, a boy finer than a maiden, oh! a surlier son he hadn't bred.

LIKE HIS BROTHER AODHAN, I CHOSE AN IRISH NAME FOR EOIN.

The shame stole my words as Arthur's shadow fell across me and my doorstep. For a long moment there was silence, the king and I listening to the crashing inside. My husband had fallen quiet as well, and now there was only the sound of a beating in earnest.

"Lady," Arthur said after a space. His face was hidden in shadow, the afternoon sun a nimbus behind him and his commander beside him, tall as gods on their horses. No one had ever called me Lady. "Could I trouble you for water for our mounts?"

No one could say that we did not do well by him. Once I had stopped the boys' mouths catching flies and dragged the girls out of Launcelot's gaze, we watered those horses and we watered those men, and I have to say that watching the knights drink, their hands young and unlined, their eyes grateful, I realized that they were just boys like my own.

Arthur thanked me then, but instead of giving a coin in return, he said, "I am needing someone to tend my hounds, Lady. I would ask you if you could spare one of your sons. We will be back through here again, in good time, and I would return him again."

And here I had given all our mead to his men, and he wanted my sons as well? What kind of deed was that in return, this king who was so known for his benevolence? I said, "I would be hard-pressed to survive the harvest without my sons, my lord."

The king's eyes followed the vines up the side of our house, and he did not look at me as he said, "The hounds are skittish this year. They have given us trouble, staying with us as we travel." His eyes returned to me. "I need someone quiet."

And I understood the bargain he meant to make, the kindness he meant to offer. That is how Eoin came to join the knights that year.

Oh, I missed him. I missed him as we harvested and rolled hay. When the frost lightened the fields. When the snow covered the branches of the trees that edged the lane. When spring came and the thawed world smelled of animals rutting, flowers budding, carcasses rotting. I missed him every time I heard one of my other sons gasp in pain under my husband's hand. I cried for him, too, and the wind took my cries and brought him back to me in summer.

There were fewer knights with Arthur this time, but they were no less splendid. His smile was magnificent in its benevolence. "Lady," he said as I wiped my eyes, "Did I not promise you I would return your son? I daresay he has refined his silence in our service."

And there was Eoin, dismounting and making his way through the others towards us. He had become a willow tree rather than a wand, my Eoin, that year.

"Thank you for returning him, my lord," I said.

Arthur merely smiled and turned his horse. Launcelot, however, remained, his horse half-turned away as he looked over his armored shoulder at Eoin. "Do not forget what I told you," Launcelot said. And then he spat on my husband's doorstep. "My apologies, Lady, no insult meant to you."

I LIKE MY LANCELOT. BECAUSE HE SPITS,

Then they were gone, with nothing to prove that they had been there but this new Eoin. He was quiet as a churchman, steady as rain on the roof, and when night came, he cut my husband's liver out at the dinner table. My husband made no sound, gutted like an animal. Eoin twisted the knife, however, and we both wept, as the wind took our cries away.

ON OUR ~~CRITIQUE~~ ~~FRIEND~~ PROFESSIONAL Critique RELATIONSHIP

Everyone else figured this out already.

I've decided I must really like the sound of my own voice. Because really, when a critique session is going well, when we're really into the spirit of it, Brenna or Tessa give me suggestions that sound like something I would've said. I mean, that I would've said if I had even a scrap of objectivity left. Because that's really when I need them. When I've had my head down working on a novel for months and I'm basically breathing, eating, sleeping, dreaming this thing, that's when I need them. I'll be cooking eggs and thinking: a skillet might be a good weapon for chapter four. I'll wake up with a headache and I'll think: if I describe my character's head as "filmy," would that get this feeling across? Every moment will be this book, and as such I won't have any distance from it at all. I can't tell if I've written gold or garbage. This is when I need someone else to step in and share her thoughts. And don't get me wrong, I'm pretty happy with every suggestion that Tessa or Brenna makes, even if I don't agree with it — it's always thought-provoking. But my absolute favorite moments are those when I think: That's what I would've said, if I was just seeing this book for the first time. Of course that's right. You can never get objectivity back. Not really, truly. But with Brenna or Tessa, it feels like I do. —Maggie

I try to write as if I'm the best writer in the world. As if I'm always confident, know what I'm doing, and have perfect instincts. The obvious truth is that the moment I climb out of my own imagination, I'm not the best, and that's what I need Brenna and Maggie for. I need them to be better than me at some things. Preferably at things I need to work on. In the time I call "Before Merry Fates," I went through scads of readers, hunting for my writing soul mates, but I didn't understand exactly what I was looking for. The moment I began working with the two of them, I knew what it was: complementary talent. It isn't that we're all good at the same things, or all on a level, or all trying to learn the same skills at the same time. What matters is that we complement each other. We shore each other up, one of us with glue, one with duct tape, and one with drywall. Or, when it's needed, a good old-fashioned battering ram. —Tessa

FOR ME, THIS WAS A PAINFUL PROCESS AND FOR SEVERAL YEARS I DECIDED I WOULD RATHER HAVE NO CRITIQUE PARTNERS THAN ONES THAT MADE ME HATE WRITING.

I'm a big fan of thinking of stories as giant, fancy snowflakes with lots of intricate little stars and flowers and spirals. This is nice, because it's whimsical and fun and better than thinking of stories as giant, angry monsters that want to eat your brain. It can also be bad though, because a lot of times it turns out that I'm easily confused by the intricacies.

I prefer my stories as giant, angry monsters, because then I don't feel bad ripping them apart.

Spoken like someone who's never felt the deep satisfaction of smashing a Christmas tree ornament...

So when the snowflake gets too big and too fancy and the story starts to spiral wildly out of control, Tess and Maggie are always there to set me back on the path of Making Sense. When I get overwhelmed by all the bits, having another voice (or two) helps me see where the real meat of the story is, what needs to be strengthened and expanded upon, and what is just a very small, very complicated spiral. —Brenna

A. COMPUTER NAMED DARCY
B. TURQUIOSE DESK
C. PLANT NAMED BORIS
D. MODEL OF A 1973 CAMARO
E. 10,000 SHARPIES
F. A BAGPIPER MADE FROM RAILROAD SPIKE
G. YOGA BALL CHAIR
H. 38 VERSIONS OF SHIVER, TRANSLATED
I. A GUITAR COVERED WITH SHARPIES
J. BOXES. ALSO, BOXES
K. OBSCURE HISTORY BOOKS
L. NOVELS, ALPHABETIZED

MAGGIE

OUR WORK

Tessa

Ghost

Monster cup

BY

AUBURN

by Brenna Yovanoff

I think this might be the first time I wrote a story about a jaded girl facing down a bad, bad man. It is, however, definitely not the last. —Brenna ✸

✸ *for which we are all eternally grateful.*

My hair was the brittle color of drying blood.

Lola had done it in her mother's kitchen. She said we needed to be more glamorous. She said, "I dare you," and the next thing I knew I was standing at the sink with my head under the faucet while a flood of vivid water ran down the drain.

It wasn't glamorous, but red like desperation. The kind that says look at me look at me please please tell me I'm pretty! It was a Lola color, is what I'm saying. When I pictured my own face wearing it, I could taste it in my mouth like metal.

We were the only girls in the pit. Onstage, Mason Tyler was humping his guitar, crooning in his signature rasp. He was the official love-mascot of Lola's life. She wrote poems about his hands. She dove into the crush, where boys made plunging circles and didn't care about the bruises. Their arms thrashed like branches, a forest of bodies, and Lola was the gleaming fairytale tower at the center of it. I was no one. Redheaded cipher. Zero.

The guy in the hunting jacket wasn't punkrock. He didn't bic his head or bleach his hair or wrestle it into a prissy double-hawk. He didn't look like Henry Rollins or Jimmy Urine or Johnny Rotten, is what I'm saying. He didn't look like anything.

Lola didn't see him coming. Her fist beat time to the bassline, and when he smacked her with his shoulder she didn't even flinch. He hit her again, harder, slamming her against the rail. The look on her face when she turned was close to magical. She punched him in the back of the head and everything got slow.

For a second I thought he'd grab her by the throat. His teeth were sharp, crowded in the front, and I was in hard, sudden love with the set of his shoulders. By love, I mean terror. I mean, in awe.

He caught her by the collar of her shirt and yanked her up on her toes while the rager boys thrashed around us.

"Hey, Red," he muttered, barely glancing at me. "Get your skank out of here before she does something she'll regret."

He opened his hand and Lola stumbled backward, scrambling away from him. She grabbed me and dragged me out of the pit. I could feel his eyes burning into my back.

. . .

Lola made me stand by the stage door to wait for Mason Tyler. She took the pass from security when Mason pointed and left me there in the crowd. Whatever Lola wants, right?

It took the guy in the hunting jacket less than three minutes to find me. "Well, well, well, if it isn't Red. Looks like you're all alone."

"It's auburn," I told him with my arms folded over my chest, but the shade was cheap and sticky.

"So, what's your fantasy?" he said, all wicked smile.

"I'm sorry?"

He gestured to the wall behind me. The ad was four

feet high, for cologne or gum or snow tires. It showed a glossy spread of twigs and leaves. The girl, index finger pressed coyly to her lips. In bold caption she declared, "I want to run naked through the piazza."

"I want to go home."

"Then what are you doing standing in the dark?"

"I don't know how to get to the bus station, and Lola left with Mason Tyler." His name came out shrill and bratty.

"It's close," the guy said. "I'll take you."

I knew then that I was just as desperate, twitchy, needy as Lola. I was just as hungry. We weren't going to the station.

. . .

His apartment was a studio with nothing in it. He didn't have a TV. He didn't have junk mail or magazines. There was a beat-up stereo sitting on a pair of packing crates, and he turned it on. Mason Tyler's voice came blaring out into the room. It was the last thing I wanted to hear.

"You're pretty," he said, coming in close, and my skin began to prickle. "I like your hair." He ran his fingers through it. They got stuck and he kept pulling.

"I like your skin," he said against my neck, and his breath smelled like beef jerky. Like a dream I had once of being eaten alive.

When he moved, he did it fast, the weight of his body pinning me against the wall, one hand hard against my throat.

"You're hurting me," I said, and my voice was high and soft like a little girl's.

On the stereo, the music was too loud. The kind of loud where the neighbors bang on the ceiling and complain about the noise and sometimes they even call the cops, but only after a couple of hours. The kind of loud where they don't hear you scream.

The knife was in case of emergencies—one of those ones that folds out when you press a button. I kept a lot of sharp things in case of emergencies. I held it to his neck and felt him go rigid.

My mouth was inches from his ear. "What's your fantasy? If you tell me you like to cut up girls, I'll gut you."

He repositioned himself on the blade, leaning into it, pressing his throat against the point. He was smiling. One hand was tangled in my hair, guilty-red wound around his fist. We held the knife between us, his other hand over mine, the cold, shining center of the world. His eyes were bright and hungry.

"I dare you," he said.

THE DEADLIER OF THE SPECIES

by Maggie Stiefvater

*Maggie's stories always make me smile—not because they're
(always) charming or pretty, but because I find them delightful.
Delightfully, gleefully dark or funny or whimsical. Whatever she
does, she makes it delightful. Which seems like faint praise, but
it's not. It's drawn-out, wicked-grin, deeee-light-ful. I might have*
— definitely would have.
said zombies could not be delightful before this story. —Tessa

I never thought I would write about zombies. Now I have.+
—Maggie

↓
Don't be ridiculous.
Zombies are always
delightful.

+ You think you'll never write about werewolves again, too.**
** DON'T BAIT ME, GRATTON.***
*** It's what I live for.

Jamie hated Andrew Murray. She didn't feel that he had any redeeming qualities, unless you numbered an ability to wear extremely pointy man-shoes and an annoying chesty laugh as positive features. She hated the way his nostrils flared before he made a joke. She hated the way he talked about women. She also hated the way he talked about men, midgets, babies, and nuns.

To be fair, Andrew Murray also hated her. He found her politics appalling—well, he had, politics were not quite what they used to be. He thought her voice was too loud. He had once, memorably, called her a fat, ugly bitch, which was slightly unfair as only one of those things was true.

The only thing they had in common was Annette Quinton. Jamie's best friend. Andrew's fiancée. What she saw in the other was a puzzle that mystified each of them.

"Well, this place is a dive," Andrew said. He laughed. Chestily. It was not a promising beginning to the evening.

Jamie didn't answer. The place was not really a dive. Only eight months earlier this had been one of the snobbiest areas in the city. She'd applied for an apartment only a few minutes away and had been turned down for bad credit, the only thing her last boyfriend had ever got her for her birthday. Now, of course, it was less than it had been: weeds overgrowing the medians and windows broken out on some of the shops. There was nothing left in Gap except the racks.

Andrew slammed the door of Jamie's old Escort, and Jamie said, "Are you trying to break the door off?"

"Yes," he said. "Right off." He stepped around the back of the car in those ridiculous, long shoes of his— he had an identical pair in some exotic skin like rattlesnake or hamster; Jamie couldn't decide which pair was worse—and retrieved the rifle from the trunk. He offered it to her, but Jamie shook her head.

"Did you see the latest *Now Boarding*?" Andrew asked as he put the rifle in the crook of his arm. He had to know she hadn't. It was one of those stupid sitcoms that people watched so that that they could tell people they'd watched it and those people would know that the person saying it was young, single, and wore long, pointed shoes and skinny Italian pants. "Diane was checking this dude's bag because the X-ray picked up something that looked like a weapon, and Edgar was headed over with a cup of coffee and—"

"Murray. I don't care," Jamie said. "That show is for men with small members."

"So you and your boyfriend used to watch it?" Andrew asked. This amused him, so he laughed again.

Jamie didn't want to warn him not to step in the puddle in the middle of the parking lot, but she did anyway. "Don't step in that."

Andrew stepped around the shallow puddle and checked the bottom of his shoes. They looked dry, but he scraped the soles against the asphalt, hard, anyway. "Why do you think she's here again?" He stopped to look in the window of an American Eagle.

I ADORE INVENTING NEW POP CULTURE REFERENCES.

I ALSO LIKE TO EAVESDROP ON PEOPLE'S CONVERSATIONS AND WRITE DOWN EXACTLY WHAT THEY SAY. IT IS NEVER EXACTLY THE SAME AS WHAT I THOUGHT THEY SAID

It, too, had been vandalized, though mostly it was just the jeans that had been stolen.

"Her voicemail said that she could see the IKEA from her window."

Andrew paused and turned in a full circle, squinting through the gray-green light of the evening. "And the IKEA would be . . . ?"

Jamie pointed to the building that had once been the IKEA. Now its identifiable color scheme had been painted over by dozens of enterprising graffiti artists, big blocks of color and patterns to symbolize different gangs. Large bubble letters said THE WHORES EAT US ALIVE.

Which was not quite a fair statement, as only one part of it was true.

Andrew raised his eyebrows; his nostrils flared, but no joke followed. He turned to follow Jamie around the end of the shopping center. "Okay, so if she could call you and she was here, why couldn't she get to us?"

They rounded the end of the shopping center, and Jamie said, simply, "Because it rained."

The lot in front of them was flooded. Unlike the glossy shopping center behind them, it was pocked and uneven—an old gas station in the middle of the new development. There were tiny islands of asphalt surrounded by puddles. Some of them were shallow enough to see the pitted lot through, but others were deep enough that they could be any number of inches deep. Something smelled. But then again, now, something always smelled.

THIS WAS THE PLACE I FIRST IMAGINED WHEN I BEGAN THE STORY — THIS DESOLATE GAS STATION.

"She's in there?" Andrew asked with dismay. "Why wouldn't she just run over to the shopping center as soon as it started to rain?"

Jamie turned to him. "It's Annette, Andrew. I assume you know the girl by now, or you wouldn't have asked her to marry you."

Andrew had no answer to this. Annette was intelligent, neurotic, and completely bereft of common sense. She collected packaged pastries—Andrew's apartment still held several hundred Twinkies, Snowballs, Ho-Hos, Ding Dongs, moon pies, and Little Debbie snack cakes that she'd acquired over the years. Some had held up better than others. The durability of a Honey Bun had to be seen to be believed. Anyway, Annette had a small but honed skill set that didn't extend to survival in this new world.

I SHOULD MENTION THAT I'M ALLERGIC TO PRESERVATIVES

They stood on the sidewalk for a moment, each attempting to devise a plot to get across the lot. Andrew crouched and looked at the standing water closest to him. "Maybe it hasn't been long enough."

Jamie made an irritated noise and scouted about for something to dip into the water. She considered breaking a branch off one of the trees in the grassy area beside them, but she didn't recognize all the leaves that were growing up through the bushes and around the tree branches, so she didn't want to risk it. Instead, she sighed and removed her belt.

"Oh, don't do that," Andrew said when he saw that she meant to dip the end in the puddle.

"I can always get another one at Gap," Jamie said sarcastically.

Andrew shook his head. "I meant your pants might fall down and I'd have to see things I really didn't want to."

Jamie said, "I should just push you in and then I'd know. I could use your body as a bridge."

Andrew was too distracted to hear her threat, however. He was looking, pensive, at the glass front of the convenience store. "If she's in there, why is she not waving or something?"

Jamie could think of several reasons, some harmless and some the opposite of harmless, but she kept them all to herself. She crouched next to Andrew and dipped the end of her belt into the water. The tip of the belt parted the pollen that floated on the surface. Jamie counted three and then lifted it back out again. They peered in to look at the result. Andrew said "Gilded" at the same time that Jamie said "Skunked." This made Jamie think that Andrew watched too many of those commercials that had piano music, soft focus, and drug names plastered in the corner. Andrew thought that Jamie read too many left-wing periodicals.

Regardless, both names meant the same thing: a thin layer of slime clung to the end of the belt, and in the nearly transparent gel, small green-and-yellow parasites milled and spun, working their way into the leather of the belt.

Andrew looked back to the parking lot, at the thirty feet of puddles full of barely visible parasitic swimmers. Jamie thought he was probably thinking that he didn't really love Annette that much, was too young to die, and that he'd ruin his shoes. Which was an unfair statement as only one bit of it was true.

"The car," Jamie said, finally.

Andrew, after a pause, said, "I'd rather have Annette. You can keep the car. Also, you can have her sugar collection and weekend visitation rights. I can be reasonable."

"I'm always stunned at how funny you think you are," Jamie said. "I meant we could get in the car and drive it to the store. We'd have to go up over the bank and we'd have to both get out on the same side, but we could drive through all this if we're slow and don't splash. You'd have to mind that you don't get wet."

"Me?" Andrew looked at Jamie and made a little pincer motion with his fingers. "How about you?"

Jamie had to admit that both options were not pleasant. As they went back for the Escort, she felt a faint prickle of irritation at the rest of the world, for the news with its images of tidy, dry cities—albeit it far more empty ones—out on the West Coast. Bright, upbeat reporters told the world that the economy was picking back up after the epidemic and that the leader singer of Shimmer had just begun a new clothing line that was expected to be a hit. Then they'd cut to a commercial for a four-piece chicken meal with fries—feed your family fast! While here on the East Coast they were being forced to travel with guns and check puddles with sticks.

It was Jamie who drove the Escort through the lot. Although the threat to Andrew was more immediate, she just didn't trust him to be able to control the speed with those pointy shoes on the pedals. And, in the end, it was uneventful. A slow, creeping progress across the lot and then parking in the shade of the awning, front tire scrubbed against the sidewalk.

"I'll get out first," Andrew said. "I'd rather not get another look at your ass." He climbed cautiously out onto the sidewalk, stepping well clear of the car. Jamie followed. Andrew cautiously called Annette's name, and Jamie found herself oddly and irritatingly touched. He used a different voice when he thought Annette might hear, one that seemed less prone to chesty laughs.

Jamie and Andrew went into the convenience store at nearly the same time—there was a bit of a fight to see who would go in first, and neither won—but Jamie was the first one to discover the arm.

It was deeply tanned and wearing a sweat-stained T-shirt sleeve. Presumably the rest of the body still had the rest of the shirt. It was also the source of much of the smell.

"Andrew," Jamie said. "Something has been eating here."

Andrew pointed the rifle at the arm as if he thought it might be a threat. "Man?"

Jamie's expression was withering. Of course it was a man. All the mutilated corpses were men. The parasites in standing water killed men immediately. And then, dead or alive, men made good meals for the Skunkers.

"Something else has been eating," Andrew said then, in an entirely different voice. His rifle was pointed down toward the aisle, where boxes of Ho Hos and Zebra Cakes and Strawberry Rolls were torn open. He poked one of the wrappers with one of his long-toed shoes. "Annette?" he said.

Jamie thought, suddenly, that it was probably better to not call Annette's name.

But it was too late, because there she was. She stood in the front doorway they'd just entered by. Her arms and face were battered. Where the skin on her arm was torn, pus dribbled out, bubbling with green and gold swimmers. Her eyes were full of it. She was eyeing Andrew with hunger and Jamie with calculation.

Annette had been Jamie's best friend for more than a decade, but Jamie didn't hesitate. "Shoot her, Andrew."

"I can't," Andrew said. They backed up together, shoulder to shoulder, toward the counter.

Jamie snapped, "You pussy."

"No, really," said Andrew. He tapped the trigger. "I can't. It's stuck."

And Annette advanced toward them still, slow, lazy. She'd made a meal off whatever was attached to the sweat-stained arm and was still metabolizing it. For a Skunker, she still looked good—she must have turned into one not too long ago. Unlike men, who died instantly and painfully at the touch of contaminated water, women underwent a slightly longer—but no less painful—process when they were infected. Then they had only two missions: eat and infect. Depending on what your gender was. The only positive was that the Skunkers were not cunning.

Jamie reached over and undid the safety on the rifle. Andrew made a face—his nostrils flared, but Jamie could forgive him for that at this point—and pulled off a shot. It neatly took out a standing display rack of Frito-Lay products. Annette didn't flinch. Pus dripped from her arm onto the floor. Green and gold particles scattered from the drop, wiggling to find water before they died.

Andrew said, "Jamie, watch—"

Jamie froze. The counter behind them was covered with open bottles and glasses of water. Her eyes swept the store, and she realized that every surface was covered with open bottles of water. It took her a long moment to realize that it was a booby trap waiting to happen.

Jamie turned to look at her best friend just as Annette threw a bottle of water in Jamie's face. Green and gold burrowed into the fabric of Jamie's shirt. It was that moment when you smash your leg on the coffee table and realize that in two minutes it's going to hurt, a lot.

Andrew looked from Jamie to Annette, and he laughed his chesty laugh that Jamie now saw was the one he used when he didn't really find things funny.

"This is fantastic. Now we're all going to die. She always did like you better than me," he said, and he aimed the rifle.

Which was slightly unfair, as only one of the statements was true.

MAN, I FORGOT HOW GROSS ZOMBIES WERE.

That's what makes them delightful.

PUDDLES

by Tessa Gratton

Every now and then, one of my fellow Fates will bust out a story that I really, really wish I'd written. This is one of those times. In only a few thousand words, Tess has managed to make ordinary, everyday puddles seem both scary and kind of sexy. Before, I would have said that either of those adjectives was impossible. Also, there is dysfunctional flirting. —Brenna

In which I attempt to write a Brenna story. Subtle, weird, with a misunderstood romantic hero. —Tessa

what I meant, obviously, was "with dysfunctional flirting."

You know me too well...

I don't know what made me do it.

The giant puddle was like every puddle: a hole in the world reflecting back light and sky. I'd always loved them, been fascinated by them. Wanted to close my eyes and leap through into that mirror world. As a child I would skim my fingers along the surface, distorting the reflection, and then sit back to watch it slowly, slowly right itself.

Tiergan Fitch used to push me into them when he found me poking around his family land. He patrolled it on a red dirt bike, lording around like a knight on a stallion, and I was the trespasser and thief. "Yo, Izzy, you like puddles so much, marry them," he'd say, chin lifted. He'd raise the pine staff he always carried and charge. His bike would veer close and I'd lose footing, only to tumble back into the water. As he pedaled off, he zigged and zagged to smash through every single other puddle.

I thought he was a heathen who hated water. Everyone else thought he was just a bully, until we were in sixth grade and Juliet Banks decided he was beautiful. She looked up his name in a baby-name book and told all of us, "It means strong-willed, so of course he can be difficult." Her lip gloss and eyeliner made her look older, and she started wearing real bras like the grown-ups wore, that she said her mama bought her at the mall. Soon all our friends were begging for push-ups and tinted lip gloss, and I was alone in my jeans and training bra thinking Tiergan was a dick.

When I named him, I thought "What would Brenna name him?"

It was totally accidental that I picked a last name she has used.

Brenna writes about misperception, of characters and of ordinary things turning out to be strangely and unexpectantly extraordinary—so I was trying.

113

It became a game. I'd creep into the woods after a rain, toes quiet in my sneakers, hair all pulled back to avoid snagging in the thin pine needles. The best puddles were along the hiking trails, since most of the forest floor was covered by years' worth of soft, rotting needles and leaves. The air smelled better than peach cobbler, all clean and fresh and alive with rain, electricity, pine resin. If I was lucky, I'd find a boulder off the mountain, pocketed with tiny, fresh water circles. I'd climb up and sit cross-legged in front of the best one, surrounded by cool, damp air and the pointed tips of the trees. Tiergan would have to get off his bike and come up on his own, get his hands all dirty against the rocks. He'd glare at me and reach down to scoop all the water out of my puddle.

Once, when I'd just turned fifteen, I yelled after him, "What's wrong with you?"

His bike skidded to a halt and he didn't look back. From my position on the boulder I could see the top of his head, the swirl of his cowlick. I didn't think he was very pretty like stupid Juliet Banks.

"My mother drowned in a puddle," he finally said before taking off.

Which I knew was a gee-dee lie. His mama ran off with a professor from St. Mary's. Everybody knew that.

I stopped playing our game. There were puddles in town, in my own backyard. But in town they got filmed over with oil, and that was all shiny and rainbowed, but you couldn't see the other world in them,

Here I attempted a very Brenna interaction, where nothing significant happens, but you learn a lot.

couldn't imagine falling through to find your other self. And in my backyard, Daddy was too near.

At school, in the cafeteria, I caught Tiergan watching me from his table with the other freshman who'd made the football team. Or rather, I caught him looking through me like I was as transparent as water. I flipped him off, which Juliet and Tabitha noticed. "Oh my God, Iz, what are you thinking! Does he like you? Oh my God!" They went on and on while I stared at Tiergan Fitch, fluttering their hands and begging for the scoop on how we knew each other. I told them he pushed me into a puddle once when we were kids.

Look! High school!! Obviously a Brenna-story thing!

That afternoon it stormed so hard we all ended up in the school basement in case of microbursts. On the way home I veered immediately into his woods and ran so hard down the hiking trail my footprints made fresh little puddles in the mud.

A half mile in, a huge puddle—more like a tiny lake—cut across the track. I fell to my knees beside it, ignoring the cold mud that squished against my socks and the hem of my skirt. I froze. The surface of the water was perfect. Still as glass and so wide I could see the whole gray sky with its leftover waves of clouds. The tips of pine trees poked against the edges like a ruffled border. I panted from my run and was overwhelmed by the scent of resin and rain.

I leaned over, and there I was: red-cheeked, hair falling out around my face, hands pressed to my chest where my heart beat a hundred times too fast.

Something under my reflection moved. Another face like mine, with huge, round eyes. But no mouth. In its eyes were secrets. I darted out my hand to grab at it. Instead it grabbed my wrist and tugged.

I fell in, all of me collapsing into the water, and it was deep—oh, so deep. Tiny hands grasped at me, and I whirled around, not struggling. It was dark here, black like a cave, and the water clear and clean as rain. Light spilled down from overhead, from the puddle.

Eyes surrounded me. Each pair like tiny caves themselves. I couldn't breathe, and the water was freezing. But I wasn't afraid. Their secrets pressed at me, whispered through the rainwater, and I stared at them, at the hundreds, the thousands of them. I opened my mouth to reply, to tell them my own secret. Water poured into my mouth. I jerked, flailing back, kicked for the surface, but they were above me now, too, with their huge eyes. My lungs spasmed, my stomach, my throat, all begging for air. I reached out, grasping with my hands, and the things slid smooth cheeks and cool fingers against me. I could hardly see them anymore, the weight of the water in my lungs and stomach dragging me down.

Something hard knocked into my shoulder. I grabbed at it. Rough wood. I circled my hands around it and felt myself rising up.

The creatures whispered their silent, rainy secrets after me, scratching my ears, but I clung to the wood and was pulled up, inch by inch, until my head broke the surface and hands tugged under my arms. My fingers dug at the mud and I coughed and choked, tears hot on my face. I rolled away from the puddle, puking out all the dark rainwater.

On my back, I opened my eyes. The sky was blue as the last of the clouds faded. Birdsong pinged and rang all around, and I could hear the slow drip of water off the pine needles.

And there was Tiergan Fitch, leaning against his staff with his mouth pinched and eyes worried. "The rain washes too many secrets away," he said. "It isn't good where they collect."

He crouched beside me and helped me sit up. I didn't even mind his warm hands on my back.

THE BONE-TENDER

by Brenna Yovanoff

So I said before, in my introduction to "Date with a Dragon Slayer," that I would lie to you and tell you I wrote that story. Well, guess what. I also wrote this one. —Maggie

SEE EXAMPLES A–G

Magical powers frighten me. This is a story about that. No matter how benevolent or valuable a superpower seems, I can't help thinking that this is not going to end well for someone. Which is probably why I write a lot of horror stories. —Brenna

When Brandon Rowe was eight years old, he hit a squirrel with a rock and broke its back. I know because I was standing on the other side of the fence, watching.

After he went inside, I climbed into his backyard and crouched over the squirrel. I petted it. Its fur was soft and felt like the collar on my mom's winter coat.

When I carried it home wrapped in my shirt, my mom told me not to touch it, it was dirty and I'd get a bad disease. My sister Rosie, who was in eighth grade, helped me make a bed for it with a shoebox and some rags. When I picked the squirrel up to set it in the box, it looked at me with one shoe-black eye and made a noise like a rusty can opener, but it didn't move. Rosie showed me how to give it water from a plastic dropper. Then she took me in the bathroom and made me wash my hands.

She said, "It might die tonight, okay? If that happens, don't be scared. Just come get me."

I was scared, though. The squirrel was little and soft. The room smelled like Dial soap, and I tried not to cry.

"Oh, Noah, don't be sad. Things die from shock sometimes, is all."

I spent all night lying on my floor next to the box and watching the squirrel breathe, putting my hands on its back, feeling the places where the bones didn't line up. The squirrel twitched and shook. Then it stayed still.

I was seven. What did I know? In the morning the

A.
FLASHBACKS.
I LOVE ME
SOME CHILDHOOD
MEMORIES.

squirrel was still breathing, and when it climbed out of the box and whisked in circles around my room, I was the only one who wasn't surprised.

. . .

When Brandon was twelve, he broke my best friend Milo's pinky finger. We were down at the community pool, and Brandon pushed Milo off the diving board and jumped in after him, even though Milo was still splashing around like a drowning cat and couldn't get out of the way.

Brandon crashed down on top of him, and when Milo struggled back up to the surface, the look on his face was all shock and white-lipped pain.

After Milo paddled awkwardly over to the side, we sat on the edge of pool and I studied the damage while Brandon stood over us, calling us a couple of whiny little gaywads for holding hands. I looked for guilt or pity in his face but didn't see it. His grin was so wide it made me feel uneasy and like the world was a pretty out-of-control place. Milo's hand was swelled-up, already turning purple.

"Hold still," I said, and Milo nodded and squeezed his eyes shut.

"What are you going to do?" he whispered. His face was so pale he looked gray.

"Nothing. Just hold still."

The hardest part was setting the broken ends back together. Milo kept his eyes closed, swaying a little on the edge of the pool. I held his hand between both of mine and waited for the rush of electricity that would mean it was working.

"What a couple of queermos," said Brandon, and I tried to tell myself it was because he was secretly sorry, but I didn't believe it.

. . .

When Brandon was fifteen, we had PE together. The class was supposed to be for freshmen, but he'd skipped so many times the year before that he had to take it over.

On the second day, he hit Melody Solomon in the face with the volleyball. He did act sorry that time, but only because she looked like a cheerleader. He wouldn't have cared if the same thing had happened to one of the fat girls, but Melody had shiny hair, nice legs, and a very good tan.

When he tried to say he was sorry, she twisted away from him, cupping her hands over her face.

"Here, let me see," I said, reaching for her shoulder. She jumped like I'd startled her, but didn't recoil the way she had with Brandon.

When she took her hands away from her face, blood was running down over her bottom lip and dripping off her chin.

"Is it okay if I touch it?"

She didn't look at all sure about that, but she nodded.

I ran my fingers along the bridge of her nose, feeling for the break. It was high up and to one side.

D.
BRENNA SEEMS TO HAVE USED ONE OF MY CHILDHOOD MEMORIES FOR THIS STORY. WHEN I WAS IN 3rd GRADE, I KNEW A GIRL WHO HAD BROKEN HER NOSE AND COULD STILL WIGGLE IT WITH HER FINGER

121

When I pressed the cartilage back into place and held it there, Melody winced and tears leaked out of her eyes. She was watching me with this numb, pleading look that reminded me of the squirrel and how it stared at me defenselessly, like it didn't have a choice. Her eyes were gray, with pale starbursts around the pupils, like tiny metallic suns.

Behind me, Brandon made a thick, disgusted noise. "Oh, gross—don't let Noah touch you or you'll get his nasty-ass stink all over you!"

And Melody flinched and pulled away. Her expression was frightened, almost lost, and I could still feel tingling sensation in my fingertips.

Brandon laughed and pushed me hard between the shoulder blades. "You don't know where he's been, Mel. I've seen him out on Garner Street, playing with the roadkill."

And it was one afternoon, hot and dismal, and one panicked, shuddering dog, but it didn't matter. For the rest of the year everyone called me skunk-boy. Melody's nose healed straight and perfect, but she never looked me in the face again.

. . .

When Brandon was seventeen, he shattered his right ankle in a car accident. He also broke his collarbone and fractured his left femur. It happened the week before soccer started, and the accident was pretty much the end of his season—maybe the end of all his seasons.

E. HERO'S AN ANIMAL-LOVER. CLASSIC MAGGIE MOVE.

He missed a lot of school, and being the good neighbor she is, my mom volunteered me to get his homework assignments and bring them over to his house.

I hadn't been in his house since I was a little kid, and the few memories I had of the Rowe place weren't good memories. When I came into the living room, Brandon was sitting in his rented wheelchair in front of the TV, watching like he wasn't really seeing it.

I dropped the stack of make-up work on the coffee table and he didn't look up. I was used to him vicious and laughing, but now he just looked resigned. He looked like he hadn't been sleeping.

"The project for history is a research paper. Give me your list of books by Thursday and I'll get them from the library."

When he still didn't say anything, I turned and started for the door.

"Are you going to do your crazy-voodoo laying-on-of-hands thing?" Brandon's voice was low and flat, and when I turned around again, he was still looking at the TV. "I mean, isn't that what you do?"

I didn't answer. There were plenty of things I should have said—excuse me? or I don't know what you're talking about—but the truth was, I kind of wanted to.

His injuries were bad, worse than anything I'd ever seen—worse than dying squirrels or skinny, shivering best friends or beautiful girls in PE. I was half-crazy to see what would happen if I tried my touch on a really bad break, one that might never heal right, even with pins and screws.

F. MEANIES ARE COMPLICATED

Brandon sat in his chair, looking up at me, and my hands felt hot. My skin was singing with adrenaline, a wild electricity that couldn't wait to jolt out of my fingers and into bone. I knew, without a doubt, that I could do it—knew with ninety-nine percent certainty. Except.

Except, I didn't feel pity when I looked at him. Except, I'd spent more than half my life mending bones and now, in the tips of my fingers, something didn't feel right. My hands were hot.

Brandon watched me without saying anything, and then his face changed. His stare turned hopeless and painful, like he knew there was cruelty sparking off my fingertips, burning in my blood. He could see it on me before I was even sure that it was there.

"Jesus, Noah," he whispered, and his voice sounded tired and almost frightened.

"You don't want me to touch you," I said. "It wouldn't work out."

G.

THE BAD GUY NEVER WINS.
AT LEAST, THAT'S WHAT I
SAY.

124

DEATH-SHIP

by Tessa Gratton

This was the first longish story I wrote in one sitting. I'd had this idea of the bride waiting at the burial mound for the year anniversary of her husband's death humming behind my eyes for a few weeks, and on my day to post, I sat down and started telling the story. I'm not sure I looked away or stopped typing for a moment until the final word was typed. ALSO there is no magic. Did you notice? No magic. No monsters. I can do it. —Tessa

I always, always forget that this story has no magic, though. Because it still feels like it does!

Y ou died far away from me, and I didn't know.

When Kitta comes to tell me, I am scraping seal hide to make into mittens for you, humming old lullabies and dreaming of your ship's prow cutting through the whale-road.

"Geira," she calls, waving her hand.

I glance up from my work and shift my feet on the sand. To my right the ocean sighs, and to my left the land rises in rocky bluffs. I hear cormorants shrieking and the low of a cow, the distant song of Hrof's shepherd, and from the edges of town the clang of ironsmithery. The sun is warm and high in the sky, and clouds trail peacefully down to the horizon.

And then I see her face.

. . .

They burned you in Uppsala, near the row of kings. I want to have been there. Everyone tells me again and again, "Hold your pride, Geira. They honored him and continue to do so with their gifts." Because with the box of ashes are gold arm rings and fine iron weapons, statuary, dress-pins carved in their outlandish northern fashions, and piles of sealskin. I say, "It's a wonder they didn't send a pair of walrus tusks." Your mother grips my arm, bruising it, and I am quiet after that.

We inter you in the barrow field, near your father and grandfather, your aunt and old cousin, and all the strong warriors of your line. I do not cry, and I know you will forgive me even if your mother does not.

. . .

I did 2 years of research on Northern European technology circa 400 CE for a novel you will never read, and got to put some of the details in this story. YAY.

I have diagrams of this.

At night I cannot sleep. The press of your brothers and their wives, of all the children rolling on their mats near the long fire, itches at my eyelids until I open them and stare at the timbers holding the roof up. I stare as the dim glow of embers catches the whorls of woodgrain, and I remember your fingers tracing the lines of my palm.

I also have diagrams of this house-type.

The emptiness when you were only traveling was finite. It would end when the days began to grow short and your ship would sail you home, your arms filled with treasures and stories. I spent those sleepless nights dreaming of what the stories would be, what tales of blood-price and love, of betrayal and honor and courage, you would whisper to me beneath the blankets.

These sleepless nights promise no end. The ship you steer now floats on an ocean with no shore. And I have neither shore nor ship. I am drowning.

. . .

This story is when I fell in love with 1st person present

I throw aside my blankets and go out into the night. It is the end of summer, so already the sun teases at the horizon, never too far from us. Even without my overdress I'm not cold, but I wrap my arms about myself and walk through the town and around the edges of the iron bog to where the land rises toward the silvering sky.

At the top of the bluff the barrow field spreads out before me. The granite boulders mark out a silent fleet of death-ships, arcing over the grey-gold grasses. I push through to yours, touching my fingers to the cool stones. Most are splotched with lichens, giving green and yellow eyes to the rocks. I trace the shape of your stone ship with my feet, walking the ring of stones and imagining you standing at the prow, which faces the ocean as they all do. I imagine you as you were the night you left, cheeks flared with excitement, wrapped in the blue mantle your mother and I made. The rings on your arms and fingers glittered while the sun set, and you were the most glorious you'd ever been. I took you home and slid them off of you, stripped you down and washed you with lavender water. I braided your hair and you pulled me onto your lap. You promised to come home with wealth enough to build our own house, a house for eight children, each stronger than the last. I laughed and reminded you we'd be lucky to get two out of me.

You put one of your rings on my thumb, and while I stand in the barrow field, I twist it around and around.

. . .

Every night I go to the fields and sit in the center of your ship. I listen to the ocean whisper, to the scrambling feet of rodents and foxes, to the wind ruffling nighthawk feathers. To the far-off wolves. I begin to carry your hammer with me, the one that did not protect you in the mountains of Uppsala. Some nights I see the Raven Keepers tending the graves, silent as wights.

When the sun lights the sky, I work. I sew aprons and turn milk into butter; I tend the fire and go into the bog with the other girls to collect ore for the

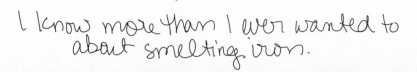

I know more than I ever wanted to about smelting iron.

bloomeries. More and more I stay in the bog, or wander the forest gathering bilberries and roots. Alone.

The daylight grows shorter, and most of my time I am in your ship. At first I bring a basket of sewing and spend the night with bone-needles pricking blood from my fingers because I light no fire. I sew until I can do so no longer, and then I sleep. I curl up in your ship, press my cheek to the rough, cold earth, and sleep.

. . .

"You must stop, Geira," Kitta tells me, tugging at my hand. The sun is setting behind her head, making her hair into a fiery aura. "Stay here with us. Drink and eat surrounded by your family, love."

I stare at her.

Her lips press together. "You can remember him next to the fire as well as you remember him in the barrow field. Better, even! He has been here, alive and strong and whole—there, he is only a ghost."

I nod and pull away from her. I come out to the ship and wait for you.

. . .

One morning I wake and find a bundle of cooked rabbit meat wrapped in a small fold of cloth. The air is cold, and I don't smell it until I've unwrapped it and brought the meat close to my face. My stomach pinches and I eat it. I cannot remember the last time I've eaten.

. . .

Where are you? Why haven't you come? Just to tell me you're well. I light a fire and pray your spirit be released from Hel for one night. Only one. The flames dance over your ship's stones and on all the stones beyond, echoing out into the field until I am surrounded by dancing light. The silver and gold shadows will call the *svartálfar*, and I hope they come. I hope they come and hear my sorrow. I will give them anything they ask if they help me see you again. Sheep, horse blood, all the cream I can get, flowers, honey—anything.

But no one comes.

. . .

Two mornings later, a pile of roasted acorns. I thank the empty air and eat them. The soft nuts remind me to drink and to bring a pouch of water with me tonight. Perhaps the *svartálfar* are indeed watching out for us.

. . .

See? Magic.
It feels like
MAGIC.

I bring handfuls of rings with me now, the small ones you gave to me, that your father had given you when you were a boy. In the morning when I wake to find three strips of dry deer meat, I eat them and leave a ring, shining dully against the brown grass. When I return at sunset, the ring is gone.

. . .

There is not always food, and my own rings weigh heavily on my wrist-bones and slide off my fingers. I cannot wear the thumb ring anymore, but I tie it about my neck with a strip of wool.

Kitta tries again, bringing her children whom I've always loved. They take my hands and drag at my skirts, pulling me into town to share in the harvest feast. Your mother avoids me, as if she expects me to curse her for not joining my vigil. But I know she has other sons, other daughters, other family to care for who are living.

I stay until they light the bonfire, throwing offerings of mead and horse blood into the hungry flames. I think of you, as I always am, and close my eyes to pretend you are dancing with your sister and will soon come to me and swing me to my feet for a wild, raucous turn around the fire. We will laugh and spin, and when I stumble you will catch me up and tease me for being clumsy. I will promise to show you my grace when we are alone, and we sneak to the beach, kissing and clutching at each other.

If there are tears on my cheeks, the hot fire eats them away.

Kitta's youngest climbs into my lap and tugs at my braid. I take her grubby hands and whisper stories to her, of sea-dragons and trolls hiding under cliffs, and in all of them, yours is the hero's name. She falls asleep and I cradle her, leaning my cheek against her hair. I watch others leave the fire ground, and Kitta joins us. She touches my hand, and I turn mine over so she might weave together our fingers. It gives her comfort and buys me more nights at your ship.

· · ·

I have gifted my dawn-time benefactor with three rings before I ever see him. It is a frosted morning; I wake to find my eyelashes frozen together. I must have cried in my sleep. I cover my face with my mittened hands and breathe into the dark pocket until the tears melt. And I see him.

He crouches against the large boulder that marks the prow of your ship, and the first silver of dawn reflects off the thin clouds and onto his face. It is Orri Never-Smile, who came here when I was a maid and lives in the forest. He is lordless and will never approach your father for explanation or trial. You said, I remember, that we should be kind to him, for we cannot know what tragedy tore him from his lord and his family. The only clue is the great scar slashing down his face. It pulls the side of his mouth down so that he cannot smile.

Orri leans on the butt of his great ax and holds up one hand, palm inward. He flexes his fingers, and I see the rings lined up on his smallest like armor. I nod once, slowly, and before he goes Orri taps the ground at his feet.

I find a small square of meat, and I stare after him. It is pig meat, and Orri must have brought down a wild one all on his own.

. . .

He lets me see him now. He haunts the ship field as readily as I do, though there is not always food left at your ship. I catch glimpses of him in the darkness,

See Brenna,
this is a ghost
story and it's
SAD.

walking between stones. Does he wait for someone from Hel, too? I notice he has no proper mittens, but only thick woolen ones. So I find the sealskin I meant for yours and spend a week of daylight hours stitching them together. I embroider the edges with thread dyed red, for heat and summer and war. It is a pattern of axes, and I think you would approve.

He leaves me a leg of rabbit and more roasted nuts, and I leave him the mittens.

. . .

It is the darkest hours of the night, one week before the Midwinter sacrifice. I sit with my knees drawn up, sewing abandoned, and stare up at the stars. There are neither clouds nor moon. Only the stars, mirroring the patterns of the barrow field until I wonder if I sit among silver-white boulders and look at the stars, or if I sit among the stars and stare down at the death-ships.

Orri says from the edge of your ship, "I remember the story of Hildr Sweet-Tongue, who won her husband from the hands of Othinn himself. When he died, Hildr waited at his grave for nine months until he appeared. He rode his great horse around and around, smiling at her. When invited to mount, she did, and spent all the time from dusk to dawn riding within his arms. As the sun rose she was again alone, and pined and waited for nine months more until again her husband appeared. From dusk to dawn she rode in his arms, and as the sun rose she was alone.

[handwritten margin note: I would put more contractions in this if I was editing it now.]

Every nine months she rode with him, neglecting all else in the meantime, until at last her foot touched the earth and she collapsed into bones."

I have never heard this story and suspect him of inventing it. But I understand his meaning. So I say, "Orri Never-Smile, what do you do in these woods alone, with no rings but those given by a widow?"

His lips twist, and I do not know if it is anger or humor they try to convey, because it is too dark now to read in his eyes.

I touch the ground beside me. Orri comes and sits. "You are Geira Silver Hair, from the land of the Geats."

"Yes."

"Why not return to your childhood home?"

"My home is with my lord."

"As is mine."

"My husband's father would accept you, were you to tell him your story."

"Whatever it might be?"

"He is kind."

"So I heard, and of his son, too."

I remember your gentle smile. "Did you make up the story of Hildr Sweet-Tongue?"

"I have watched you waste yourself here on this death-ship, lady."

"No less do you do, a fine warrior without a lord."

"They say women are stronger than us, when a lord is lost."

You used to tell me I was strong. Practical. Like a thrice-woven rope. But I am unraveled. I say, "It is only six nights to the sacrifice. That is when he will come."

"Is it?"

I clench my teeth together and nod. Orri pushes to his feet and leaves me alone.

. . .

The day before the sacrifice, I am delivering a basket of ore to the bloomery, when I hear a crowd of children run past me, yelling at each other that the wolf has come to see our king.

"Bloomery" is an excellent word.

I know the wolf they mean, and I drop the iron ore and run after them. I shove through into the great hall, where all the benches and long tables have been pushed against the walls. I join the youngest children and several other women in climbing up onto the tables so that we can see over the heads of the war-band. I could take my place beside your mother, who stands behind your father in his thick throne, but I have given that right up these long weeks.

Lifting a girl—Jofast, her name is—onto my hip, I stretch to see the back of the hall better. A man kneels before your father, and he is speaking. His hair is braided in seven thick ropes and tied together with leather, and his clothes are old but clean. I see your mittens tucked into his belt.

Orri Never-Smile tells his story, and I hear pieces of it, that he was sworn to Alfarin Stone-Skin and they sailed over the eastern sea to Daneland to ally with a king there and fight against a Frankish clan raiding northward. I missed how they were split, but he fought with all his spirit and arrived back at his lord Stone-Skin to find him far dead. Orri's scar was won during the vengeance quest, at which he also failed. His lord's killer died of a sweating sickness, and so Orri had no blood nor rings to bring home to the kith and kin of Alfarin Stone-Skin. His only recourse was to wander as the wolves and pray he might find a ring-giver willing to forgive his failings.

Your father offers him his ring-sword and welcomes him.

Jofast wriggles out of my grasp, and I do not move as the mead-cup is passed and the war-band recognizes their new brother. I do not move as the boasting begins, a night early. I imagine you standing beside me, glad of the merriment and feasting, looking forward as you always did to the sacrifice and the drinking. Your warm hand presses my cold skin, and I curl up my fingers wishing for the weight of rings upon them.

I do not move even when the fire is low, when the poem-singer stands forth and recites for us all. Orri is seated at your father's feet, and he finds me in the crowded shadows. He finds me and holds out his hand again, palm-inward. He flexes his fingers, and I see the glint of my rings on his smallest. Below it, circling his wrist, is a new, larger arm ring of twisted copper that your father has given.

. . .

Outside and alone, I run to the barrow field. I stand at the prow of your ship as the sun dips away. Tonight is the sacrifice. Tonight you will come, if you are to come. I watch the last light tug at the crystals hidden inside some of the boulders. I stare and stare and then, just before the light vanishes, I turn my back to the death-ship, and I walk steadily towards the hall.*

THIS IS TESSA'S
VERSION OF A
HAPPY ENDING

* I sure do like to end my stories with a character making a choice.

ANALYZE THE END:

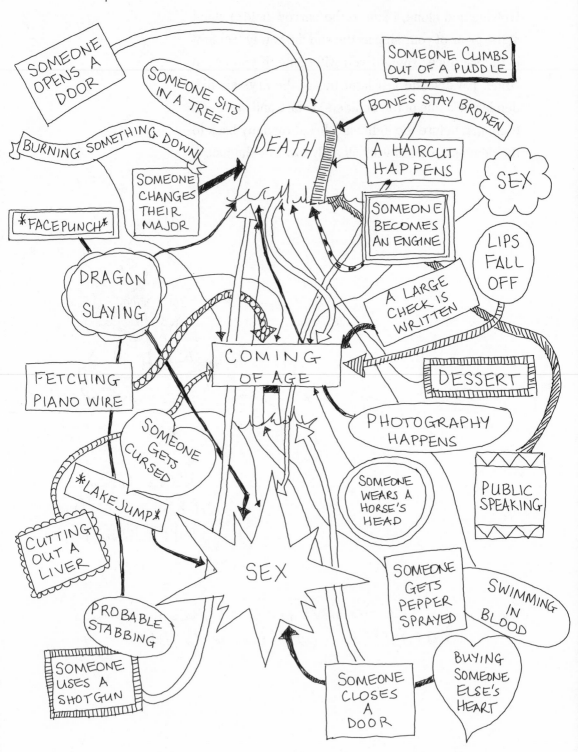

SOMEONE OPENS A DOOR

SOMEONE SITS IN A TREE

SOMEONE CLIMBS OUT OF A PUDDLE

BONES STAY BROKEN

DEATH

A HAIRCUT HAPPENS

SEX

BURNING SOMETHING DOWN

SOMEONE CHANGES THEIR MAJOR

SOMEONE BECOMES AN ENGINE

LIPS FALL OFF

FACE PUNCH

DRAGON SLAYING

A LARGE CHECK IS WRITTEN

COMING OF AGE

DESSERT

FETCHING PIANO WIRE

SOMEONE GETS CURSED

PHOTOGRAPHY HAPPENS

SOMEONE WEARS A HORSE'S HEAD

PUBLIC SPEAKING

LAKE JUMP

CUTTING OUT A LIVER

SEX

SOMEONE GETS PEPPER SPRAYED

SWIMMING IN BLOOD

PROBABLE STABBING

SOMEONE USES A SHOTGUN

SOMEONE CLOSES A DOOR

BUYING SOMEONE ELSE'S HEART

THE LAST DAY OF SPRING

by Maggie Stiefvater

This story makes me desperate to know where it came from. I want to pin Maggie down and ask her all the most annoying questions about inspiration and muses, then take the story back to college and write an essay about time and sex and god and death. It's about all my favorite things, but in a way it would never occur to me to write it. —Tessa

Tried this, didn't work. Next time I'll try water-boarding.

We're such products of our surroundings. It's not just where we grow up or what sort of people we are, but things that are specific to our species: how long we live, how far our eyes are from the ground, the fact that we see color, the fact that we cannot fly. If you change any one of these variables, so much of our culture suddenly fails to satisfy our needs. This story is about me removing one Jenga block from the tower—our life span—and trying to see what shape the collapsed pile is afterward. —Maggie

And then you ruin it.

This makes you sound so wise.

I WOULD LIKE TO POINT OUT THAT YOU WERE THE ONE JUST DESPERATE TO WATERBOARD ME FOR MY JENGA SECRETS.

FIRST, I HAD
THE IDEA OF
THE PAPILLONS'
LIFE SPANS, AND
THEN I THOUGHT
OF THIS BEGINNING,
AND THEN I BEGAN
TO WRITE.

The Papillons had ruled the spring for as long as I could remember. We were always told not to touch them, because it would hurt.

"Them?" I asked my mother. "Or us?"

I was tiny back then, a paper-thin facsimile of a boy, no hint of my almost epic height to come. My mother was in the long, thin cotton sweater that she wore every day—or at least in my memory she did—and she tugged my slender hand to guide me around a flock of them. "What a silly question, Mark."

It was the first warm day of spring, and the Papillons had come out in flocks. Beautiful and shining and resplendent, no sign of the unformed creatures they'd been in their cocoons. They were clustered in Persephone's two parks and around the trees that lined the streets, caught in the flowers that grew in the highway median and in each other's hair.

Annoyed that she hadn't really answered my question, I said hello to one of them.

"Hello," the Papillon said back, brightly, his hair on fire with the sun and his smile alight with the sight of me. The Papillon loved children, the same way we loved them. I wondered if they'd been told not to touch us as well.

"Mark," said my mother disapprovingly, not bothering to whisper.

"Mom," I said back. I was always brave when it was just words.

"What did I just tell you?"

"Talking is not touching," I replied.

Mom jerked my arm, leading me away from the red-haired Papillon. "It's close enough. I'm going to tell your father you've been trouble today, and then what do you think will happen?"

I looked over my shoulder at the Papillon. He was singing to a group of girl Papillons, the simple delight of his face transformed to something more urgent.

My mother hadn't answered my question, so I didn't answer hers either.

. . .

I didn't see much of the Papillons next spring because my parents enrolled me in a Catholic school. Not only was I in school every day—and the Papillons, of course, didn't go to school—but I was also in Mass twice a week, and if there was one place Papillons definitely didn't go, it was into churches.

"Is it because they're demons?" I asked my mother once.

"No," she said. "Ask the nuns."

So I asked Sister Therese, and she told me they were animals or angels or something in between, and I didn't need to worry about much other than their general lack of soul. There would be no Papillons in heaven.

"Will there be butterflies in heaven?" I asked her.

"Possibly," she allowed. She liked me and knew I liked insects, so I'm sure she thought she was being kind.

The Papillons, as their name suggested, were very like insects. What else hatched from cocoons and

LIKE ROMANTIC CHEMISTRY, MAGIC + CREATURE ATTRIBUTES HAVE TO BE ESTABLISHED VERY QUICKLY IN A SHORT STORY: SKETCHED, NOT PHOTOGRAPHED.

lived for only three days? I persisted, "Then why not the Papillons?"

Her lips parted and then pressed together again, twice, and finally, she said, "Because they are made in the image of God, Mark, and they choose to deny it."

Later that day, I tried to persuade one of the Papillons, a girl still shimmery and damp from emerging, to go into the empty church with me. She let me take her hand, and I stood there for a moment, thrilling to the illicitness of it—touching a Papillon, four feet from a church. Her hand was like a bird in mine; I could feel the bones through her smooth, damp skin, and it didn't weigh anything at all. It was very, very warm, and her pulse tapped against me at the base of her palm.

"Your hand is so cold," she told me.

"Actually, yours is hot," I said. She had brilliantly rich hazel eyes, very large and round, like those small dogs that you're afraid of breaking. I was filled with the need to get this particular Papillon into heaven after she died.

"Well, it's still a hand," she said. "Both of them, I mean."

It was true. There was nothing really to distinguish her as a Papillon aside from her pale skin, not old enough to have a tan, and her long, long hair, laying against her back like new butterfly wings.

"You should come into the church," I said. "God's in there, and I want Him to see you."

"I'm not supposed to," she said. "They said it would hurt."

"It's not that bad. Only if the homily is really long."

She grinned at me. "I'm not that good at sitting still."

It was such an ordinary, human exchange. I had expected her to sound more like an insect. More like a child. My eight-year-old self suddenly realized that he was holding the hand of an adult, an adult halfway between birth and death, and I lost my nerve. I released her hand and ran. I was a coward.

· · ·

Three years later, it was cold for the Papillons, and most of them died before they ever lived; frozen, dried corpses inside papery cocoon coffins. The ones that did emerge were hungrier than they had been in previous years, and though they were fewer, it seemed they were everywhere.

That year, I learned a new word for Papillons: whore.

ORIGINALLY, THIS WAS GOING TO BE AN ENTIRE SCENE, AND THIS WAS JUST THE INTRD. I REALIZED AFTER I WROTE IT THAT THIS DID ALL THE WORK I NEEDED IT TO.

· · ·

By the time I was in college, both the Papillons and I were well-managed. Some city dignitary had come up with the idea of shelters with glass roofs, and now there were fewer gruesome mornings after late frosts. My parents had realized that the only way I would stay in college was if they took away my car and gave me an apartment. Now there were fewer gruesome mornings after final exams.

So we all had a roof over our heads.

It was spring semester; classes were just beginning to grow odious, and the weather broke. So, like every year, it was simply this: one morning they weren't there, and then they were.

As a college student the Papillons offered me a different sort of entertainment than they had when I was a boy. The further I was from childhood, the easier it was to tell which day they were on. Day one: birth, discovery, innocence. Day two: the frantic search for other Papillons, the mad desire to pursue and be pursued. Day three: the weaving of new cocoons and then the countdown to death.

It seemed such a futile life. Such frantic scrabbling, only to die before the week was out.

But I didn't have a lot of time to think about it. I had classes and exams and a campus full of college girls. The only time it stuck in my head was when I had to step over a body, newly minted and already exhausted, lying in doorway of my apartment building.

Then it was pretty hard to miss.

. . .

In my senior year, I broke my mother's rule.

It was spring, and it was late, past Papillon season. Summer was edging slowly onto campus, stretching the days longer, robbing the threat of night. Soon college would be out, I would join the ranks of the matriculated, and the real world would steal me for one of their own.

And yet, here was a Papillon girl, new and damp, hazel eyes huge in her face. There was no other Papillon for her to be wrapped around, none of her kind to flock with, and so she just sat on the sidewalk with her knees next to her chin and her arms wrapped around them.

I started to walk past her. Every other year I'd walked past them. This year, even, I'd walked past hundreds of them. But this time, there was just the one. And next to her the dead body of what had been another Papillon girl.

I stopped.

It was easy to be brave when it was just words.

"Hello," I said to her.

She looked up at me. "Hi."

She reminded me of someone eleven years earlier, holding my hand, looking into a church. I said, "Come to breakfast with me."

So we went to breakfast. We sat outside and she sipped a juice while I made a tornado with my spoon in a cup of coffee. It occurred to me that I'd missed Western Civ II.

"Don't you get bored?" she asked me. "If you don't mind me asking?"

I blinked at her. "Bored . . . with . . . ?"

She twirled her hand around in a circle. "With all that time. What do you do with all of it?"

I looked at her, bemused. "Live? Party? Become wise and wonderful?"

"Are you wise and wonderful yet?" She was

smirking at me. I'd known her two seconds and she was smirking at me. It had taken her no time at all to arrive at the same conclusion my parents had about me.

"Getting there," I said. "Are you?"

"Naturally," she replied. "I was wise and wonderful hours ago." Again that wicked grin that reminded me of the Papillon outside the church.

"Aren't you afraid of dying?" I asked. I thought about the dead Papillon she had left behind when she stood, looking down at it with an unreadable expression.

"That's days from now," she said with a shrug. "Thanks for the juice. Would you like to go dancing?"

I should have said no, because I had more than two days left to my life, but she was holding her hand out to me.

So we went dancing. At first we danced on the campus green, to the bad band that was playing a free concert at the other end. Then we danced on the sidewalks, to the music that leaked out of cracked car windows. And then, as the night came and she got older, we danced in my apartment.

Naked, you could not tell which of us would be dead by the weekend.

. . .

We went to church in the morning, because guilt pinched my chest like an ill-fitting sweater. She did not catch fire. She just looked bored and discontent at being indoors, and afterward she asked me why I went.

"So I don't go to hell when I die," I told her. Her fingers were laced in mine, and every so often she would stop to loop her arm round my neck and kiss me. We both kept our eyes open when she did, so I could look into her hazel eyes.

"How do you manage hell?" she asked.

"By doing something awful."

"I wouldn't know about that," she said. "I'm disgustingly good."

She hadn't been around long enough to do something awful.

"Aren't you afraid of what will happen, after?" I asked.

She stopped to kiss me again, only this time she didn't put her lips on mine. She just rested her forehead against mine and we stood quietly, both of us smelling of flowers and dancing.

"I'll come back," she said. "Do you come back, if you don't go to hell?"

"No," I said. "I believe I stay dead."

"Why are you crying?" she asked me. ⬥——————— I ♡ this.

. . .

She was dead in the morning.

During the night she had told me, "I feel old. I miss being young." She'd curled her arms over her chest, looking already like all the dead Papillons I had seen littering the grass beneath the sycamores on campus.

Unlike any of the other dead Papillons, though, she was in my apartment, curled in my lap.

I missed being young too.

Only I had thousands of days left to go.

This is one of those times Brenna has a story like a delicate snowflake, and it's perfect that way.

CUT

by Brenna Yovanoff

I don't know how to write a story like this. All interlocking pieces and spirals of narrative moving around and around to somehow make a cohesive whole. Every once in a while I try and then end up lying on my floor, staring at the ceiling. —Tessa

Snow White is a story I've never quite come to terms with. It bothered me a lot as a child (did I mention that I was a slightly neurotic child?), and I couldn't really get a handle on the stepmother, because she was always two different people: the aging beauty, destroyed by her own vanishing youth, and the evil witch, lashing out, bent on destruction. It seemed like different versions of the same story, playing out in different ways, and this is kind of the same thing. —Brenna

My mother cut my heart out and put it in a box.

If this was a story, that's how it would end.

It would begin with snow and the tragic, impersonal death of a young trophy wife and fade into a montage of the replacement bride, how she drenched her hair with honey and washed her face with milk.

That part's true.

When my father remarried, the woman was unapologetically vain. She spent hours in front of the mirror, looking all alabaster and perfect. On Wednesdays and Saturdays she went downtown to the day spa, where they shaped her fingernails and peeled the top layer of her skin off with various kinds of acid.

I stayed home and dyed my hair. I caked my face with powder and drew black lines around my eyes to show everyone the difference between us, that I wasn't like her, that she wasn't really my mother. She kept buying me dresses in pink and turquoise and acting like we could be best friends.

Let me start again. My father's wife had my heart cut out. She put it in a box.

The secret is that it wasn't really my heart. Her slim gigolo boyfriend took me out to the Presidio, where the salt wind blew in off the sea. He touched my face and breathed licorice and aftershave on me, which made me want to scream. Then he bought a pound of lamb's heart from a butcher in Greek Town and took it home to her. He told her he loved her. He told her that the dense, membranous muscle belonged to me.

Okay, that last part was a lie. Can you tell that I'm lying? My stepmother doesn't have a boyfriend. But if she did, he'd be young, with wavy hair and bad shoes. He'd be the kind of guy who knows where to buy organ meat in primarily ethnic neighborhoods.

This is more like it: my obscenely vain stepmother put on her fifty-dollar Dior eye shadow and her Manolo Blahnik pumps and reached for her Gaultier clutch. She cut her own heart out and dipped it in lead or mercury—one of those metals that poisons you and makes you go crazy. She fed it to me in sly, careful moments, in pieces, so that I would be like her.

I sat in my room with the shades pulled down, and the venom of her heart moved like poison, getting under my skin and making me all drowsy. She spent hours by the country-club pool, trying to look younger, but washed-up socialites never do.

I lay with the blankets over me, so heavy I couldn't move my head. My dye job was starting to grow out and the roots were showing. I stayed so long it felt like I was turning into stone.

Then one night she came to my room like a silent-film star, slightly crazed, smelling like gin, and yanked me out of bed. She sat me in front of the ruffled vanity, studying me with bleary eyes.

"I just want you to like me," she said. "I just want us to do things together. Why don't you like me?"

The whole time she kept touching me in that clumsy, drunk way, tugging at my hair. I watched her reflection so I wouldn't have to watch my own—the crumpled way her mouth seemed to just collapse. Her eyelids were dark and greasy-looking, like she'd bruised them.

She took me by the shoulders and shook me hard, suddenly. "Why are you doing this to yourself? Why do you insist on looking like a freak? Are you determined to embarrass me?"

She brandished a handkerchief—white, petal-soft—and began to scrub my face. She scrubbed hard and fierce until my mouth got pink and so did my cheeks. She wiped my makeup off like she was scrubbing me back to life.

"Answer me," she kept saying, but her voice sounded weird and shrill, and the words had stopped making sense.

When I opened my mouth, it felt like a tiny version of a black hole, where light disappeared and nothing could come out. She shook me, and my head rocked back and forth. I couldn't stop nodding.

She swept from the room without warning and came back with the scissors. I closed my eyes. The blades made a whispering noise, *snick, snick*. I felt lighter.

When she dropped the shears on the carpet, I didn't know how to feel. It was the worst thing anyone had ever done to me. I had a sudden thought that no one had ever really done anything to me. It was glorious and shocking. I didn't feel like myself, but for the first time in years, I didn't feel like I was trying to be someone else.

In the mirror, my hair was brutally short. It stuck up everywhere, patchy-black in places, but most of it was blond—my real color. My mouth and cheeks were hectic, and my eyes looked wild. My blood felt like electricity. Like I could do anything.

We sat in front of the mirror, staring at my reflection. She was crying now, sloppy and horrifying, asking me to forgive her.

I wanted to tell her not to cry. That I forgave her for her smallness, for so many reasons.

I was something breathtaking and rare now, while she would never be beautiful again.

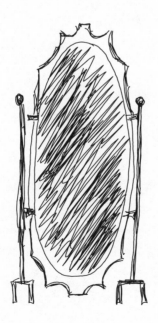

DIAGRAM of BRENNA'S BRAIN

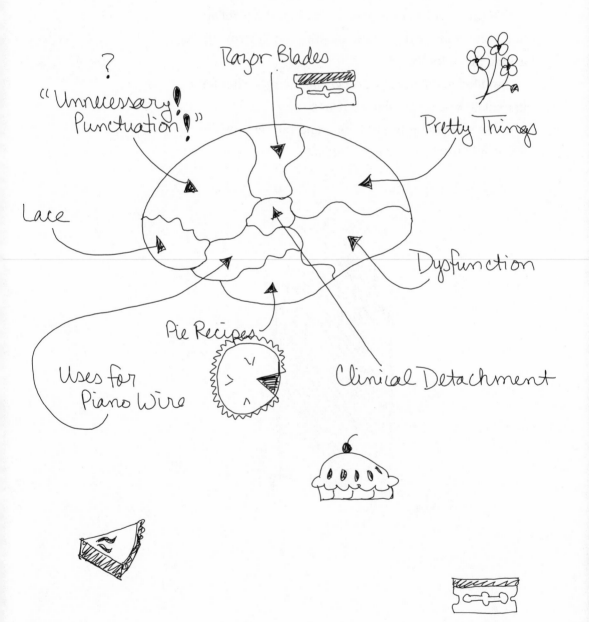

?
"Unnecessary!
Punctuation!"

Razor Blades

Pretty Things

Lace

Dysfunction

Pie Recipes

Uses for
Piano Wire

Clinical Detachment

PHILOSOPHER'S FLIGHT

by Maggie Stiefvater

*This is another one of those stories that made me uncomfort-
able to post, because it was so strange. It was based on a
dream, as many of my short stories are, but it spiraled wildly
out of control from there. I played with two of my favorite
themes: neurotic geniuses and fallible leaders. —Maggie*

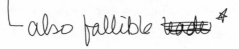

└ also fallible ~~leaders~~ *

*joke fail

My name is Scott Anthony Caul, and I am E. M. Parmander's only living assistant.

Parmander is a genius and a philosopher and as such is very difficult to work with. He also has a disregard for his own personal safety that would have been thrilling to watch if it hadn't extended to my safety as well.

"I'm not certain this is the best of ideas," I tell him. I bore even myself halfway through the sentence, so many times have I said it. Parmander is in the process of building a flying machine. It is all gears and canvas and rope, and somehow it is powered by thirteen frantic sparrows that are caged in a bamboo nest in its belly. The cage has no door.

"I will need you to fly it, Caul," Parmander says in response. "My thighs are too monstrous to fit in the seat. No starches tonight."

Parmander has no thighs of which to speak. Aside from being a genius and a philosopher, he is also vain, and his intelligent, thoughtful variety of vanity means that he will often skip meals while he works. He studies himself in reflective surfaces. Pinches the skin at his hipbone and makes a wrinkle to match the one that appears between his eyebrows. Pensively brings back up the contents of his stomach after lengthy luncheons. If his thighs are too monstrous to fit the seat of the machine, then he has built the seat too small or he intended all along for me to fly it.

I crouch to look at the sparrows. They are horrified by my presence and flap crazily about. Their activity makes something in the machine hum, and its canvas wings twitch as if to flap.

"Caul," Parmander says, "You are agitating the engine. Come away."

I come away.

"Where," I ask, "is it you're wanting me to fly this thing?"

"Pshaw," says Parmander, "You needn't sound so ill-tempered."

This should be one of Maggie's listed favorite words.

"Have a tangerine," I suggest, because tangerines will frequently improve his mood. He refuses the fruit. I have it. I say, "I don't think there's any use to having this flying machine. Where is it you want to go with it, other than up into the fog?"

Parmander gazes wistfully out of the garage. The scene before us is a maze of roads, crawling with vehicles driven by gears and powered by bellows thrusting steam and darkened by coal. There is nothing quite as elegant as Parmander's flying machine, all bleached cotton canvas and whips of golden bamboo. Over all of it is the fog, and below it the black birds and the pigeons that cannot be troubled to challenge the clouds.

RIGHT NOW, IT SOUNDS LIKE YOU COULD BUY IT AT POTTERY BARN.

"Through the fog," Parmander says. "Over the fog. To where the fog ends and the sky begins."

I have another tangerine as he begins to expound upon how only in the unpolluted air can man truly be free to contemplate the complexities of existence. I should be tidying—geniuses leave a lot of clutter behind—but it seems to me that if I am going to risk my neck going up in the machine, I shouldn't have to work.

"If I could fit my hideous buttocks into the machine, I would fly to the Tower," Parmander muses.

He is just trying to bait me now. The Tower is a massive, prewar stone structure that lies in the middle of a moat. The fixed bridge that takes you over the moat is submerged under a foot of water so that there is no way to get to the Tower itself without getting wet. This is because the Tower contains a breed of cloaked monsters who cannot cross water. They are forbidden to come in contact with humans—not that this is likely to happen, as precious few cross the flooded bridge to the island.

THIS WAS THE PART I DREAMED ABOUT.

"And convert the monsters to Parmanderty," I say. This is what Parmander has named his brand of philosophy. It revolves around purification and denial and clarity of thought and women not wanting to have sex with you. There are finer points, but that is the bulk of it.

Parmander adjusts the rudder of the machine. "Breaths," he says. "Not monsters. St. Vladimir's Breaths, that's what we knew them as, because they were so quiet. Get in the machine so I can strap you in."

I get in. The seat is small and uncomfortable and pinches parts I'd rather not pinch. It wouldn't have pinched Parmander any worse than me, however. He straps my foot down in a place that will be difficult for me to reach myself if I crash.

"Knew them as when?"

"When I was a student at the Tower," Parmander says. The birds are beginning to flap around again, and the whole machine is humming. I feel it in the foot Parmander has strapped down. It feels like it is buzzing up my leg. He straps down my other foot.

"I didn't know you were a student at the Tower."

Parmander lays a strap across my waist and pulls it tight. Now I can feel the entire machine thrumming, the wings thinking of flapping even if they are not already. "I was there for twelve years, Caul," he says. "That is when we built them."

The machine is shaking the heartbeat out of me. "You . . . built . . . the monsters?"

"That is why they cannot cross the water," Parmander concurs. Disconcertingly, he binds my hands to the steering device. "The current that runs through their gears and brains would short out if they put their feet in it."

I can feel the power of the machine working all through my body, from my feet on the copper foot plates to the hard seat to my fingers bound to the metal of the steering wheel. The wings are starting to buffet air beneath them. I can barely hear the birds flying around in their bamboo cage.

"But you will not have to worry about that," Parmander says. "Because you are flying over it."

The machine is flying, flapping, pulsing, throbbing in time with the beat of my heart and I realize, suddenly, that I am the machine and the machine is me.

I am not so much lashed on as plugged in.

"When?" I gasp as the flying machine lurches forward and the birds howl. I feel gears grind inside me, tendons tied onto wire, wire embedded in lungs, lungs fed by bellows, bellows turned by screws. "When did you build me?"

"When I needed you," Parmander replies. He shakes his head as he looks at my unchangeable form. Now I can see the wistful envy, the same that he directed at the sky earlier.

Parmander is giving me directions to the Tower, telling me all of mankind wants nothing more than to return to its point of origin, and that is where we shall find perfection, only it is a we I am no longer a part of. I cannot listen to him. As the birds and my fearful body power the flying machine, I am building a new philosophy.

ASH-TREE SPELL TO BREAK YOUR HEART

by Tessa Gratton

Often, when I'm reading the stories, I can hear Brenna's or Tessa's voices as I do. Not just their word choices, but the sounds of their voices. I can see the hand gestures and imagine their faces. We've told each other enough stories in person that I know the way these long-distance ones will look. This is a fun thing, but for me, the most amazing thing is when I'm reading one of their stories and I can't hear them. Sometimes they write a world that is so other, so outside, so complete without my knowledge of them, that Brenna or Tessa becomes completely invisible. "Ash-Tree" is one of those stories for me. Intellectually, I know that these are things that interest Tessa, but to me, this story moves past that. I think this story was when I first really realized we were getting better as writers. Because it is a simple thing to be inconsistent when you are unsure of your authorial voice — it's a very easy thing to have no authorial voice. But it is a harder thing to be consistent — to always sound like you, to have a style. And it is something altogether different to have a style that you know quite well and to be able to put it down. To become a different sort of storyteller for four thousand words only. To hide yourself cleverly away so that even your friends cannot see you. "Ash-Tree" was the first story that did that for me. —Maggie ✳

This story started with lips falling off and turning into rose petals. —Tessa

✳ *Dear Maggie, there are these things called "paragraph breaks."*

161

I was created of beeswax and honey, with a butterfly for my heart. He should have used a spider or iridescent beetle.

My master gave me hair from strips of ash-tree bark and lips of rose petals. Violet-black chokeberries became my eyes, and he sculpted the planes of my face with kid gloves until it was as perfect as perfect could be.

He named me Melea, for it is the word to invoke the power of the Ash.

I breathed a breath of life and rose to my feet, more graceful than the rippling clouds that were my first sight through his chamber window. Master touched my chin with his cold fingers. He was sharp and bright like the sun on ice. He said, "Welcome, Melea. Here is your order: find my rival August Curran, make him love you, and rip out his heart."

The butterfly in my chest cavity fluttered as the command settled into my ashwood bones.

. . .

Master's housekeeper dressed me in an elegant gown of violet with cream lace and black-pearl buttons. My hair was lifted onto my head and pinned under a cap that frothed with netting and spilled over my eyes. The housekeeper sighed and whispered, "Such a sight I never saw. No need for color on your lips or cheeks, Miss Melea. 'Tis life and beauty glowing through you like a sunset."

She shuffled me out the door with a parasol and boots buttoned up my ankles. The street was damp from an early morning rain, and the air smelled of water and oil and dank horses. But also, the breeze hinted of sun-warmed brick and window-box flowers. And the teasing scent of those high-up graceful clouds. I tilted my face and saw the billows of white fluff spread in strips and ripples against the bright sky.

And I began to walk.

My footsteps were quiet against the cobblestones, and every person who passed me tipped a hat or bobbed curtsy. Four times a gentleman paused to guide me around puddles or across the street, and an elderly lady in an open-air carriage offered me a ride somewhere, but I only smiled, nodded, and continued on my way. The butterfly pulled at me, and the smell of the clouds bade me forward.

. . .

The sun had dipped below the tallest buildings, and I had wandered out of the city's heart. The homes around me lined the street in simple rows, all white stone and red bricks, with arching windows and small brown doors. My toes ached where the point of my boots pinched them, so I chose a delicate iron-wrought bench and sat. Lowering the parasol, I placed it across my lap with my hands, in their lace gloves, folded demurely. Here the air was filled with living smells: trees and grass and flowers from the small square gardens in the center of every block. It was spring, the beginning of it, and blossoms had awakened during the day to sip at the world.

"Miss, are you lost?"

I opened my eyes and saw the face of the man for whom I had hunted all day. He was brown and warm, like tree bark baked long in the sun. His hair curled around his face like wood shavings, and his eyes were as green as the garden behind me. For the first time I parted my lips and formed words. "No, sir, I am where I need to be." And I smiled. It was an easy smile, for I found myself wanting to be beautiful for him.

The sun-brown man bowed and held out his hand. His gray jacket was not near so opulent as Master's had been, and he wore boots splattered with mud. But it was fine and fit him impeccably. "I am August Curran, King's Cunning Man."

"I am Melea, Mister Curran." I put my hand into his.

His eyes slid from the crown of my head to the toes of my boots and his smile fell away. "You are, indeed," he murmured, before smiling again. "And beautiful, too."

I thought perhaps I should blush, but instead I rose to my feet. I was nearly as tall as Curran, and it was easy to press my lips to his. He tasted like salt, and I gasped.

"My apologies, Melea," he said, though he did not lean away from me. "I was poison tasting for His Majesty this afternoon. It is only a simple charm and should not harm one so well put-together as you."

"You know? What I am?" The words tumbled out, though I was certain I should not say them.

"I will not send you back to your death," he promised, turning to offer his arm.

I took it, and Master's command shivered again through my butterfly heart.

. . .

August Curran fed me delicious soup tasting of mushrooms and curry powder, and while we dined thin, shadowy servingmen darted in and out from the kitchens to bring us fresh wine. I ate, discovering that I could be hungry, and watched Mister Curran. The setting sun spilled through the perfectly clear glass of his windows, gilding the edges of his hair. I discovered then, too, that I wanted him to love me. But I did not know if it was the command or my own wish.

"Why did you invite me into your house?" I asked.

"You have nowhere else to go. And so long as you are here, he may leave me alone."

. . .

I was given a room on the third floor of his house, tucked into the corner and full of light. The balcony hung over a thick but well-tended garden surrounded by high stone walls over which no one from any of the other houses might peek. I slept with the moon pouring in and woke with tiny blue finches singing from perches all throughout the room: atop the bureau, clinging to the oval mirror, to the back of the armoire chair, and to the bedposts. I sat up, and they fled to the balcony.

I found my way to the dining room and ate from the spread of breakfast cakes. The shadow-men brought me a crystal glass of tart apple juice. I asked one where I might find Mister Curran, and he bowed with a yellow flicker of firelight-eyes. The door behind him opened. I stepped through it and followed the blue hallway around a bend and up a half flight of stairs. There was no door, but a wide arch led into a grand library that should not have fit inside the house. August Curran lounged in a rocking chair with a large tome in his lap and a steaming mug of fresh-smelling coffee in hand.

"Ah, Melea, good morning." He flapped his hand toward another chair, which was cushioned in a yellow to rival the sun.

"Mister Curran." I curtsied and sat near him in the yellow chair. "May I go into your garden?"

"Yes, of course." He closed the book and set it on the carpet. "You are no prisoner here."

I thanked him, and he brushed it off. "Please, you should call me August. You are my guest."

"August," I said, letting the name hold still on my tongue. I sighed and said, "It does not feel like a proper name. Did your mother know you would be a wizard?"

"No, I chose it as I began my apprenticeship. Coffee?"

I accepted both the coffee and the cream he poured. It smelled like the earth, like old, rich, but bitter earth. What strange magic to drink in the morning. "Why did you choose it?"

"I thought it sounded delightful before 'King's

Conjuror' or 'Cunning Man and Charmer.'"

I laughed.

August paused as my laughter rang out, and his eyes focused on something invisible just before my mouth. I licked my lips as I watched, thinking of his salt taste. Did he wear such a charm now? "What is it, August?" I asked.

He did not answer until he had taken three breaths and blinked three times. "Ah, it irks me that he knows me well enough to have created you."

"I am sorry," I said, for it was true.

"You shouldn't be sorry for being so appealing, Melea. You are what you are: ideal."

"Ideal in what I am for, not in who I am."

"In who you are?" August's lips twitched with surprise. I suppose it is because I am not anyone outside of my command.

. . .

I remained in his house. Though I ventured into the city, I never could be long away. The fluttering command drew me back to him before many hours passed. I pretended at my freedom by taking books from his library into the garden, where I might curl up between eldertrees and read.

Many times he vanished into the lower reaches of his house, where his workrooms were tightly guarded. He came out with his arms filled with potions for the king and parchments covered in his looping notes, which he would pass to his fellow conjurors.

We ate supper together every night: soups and greens and never, ever, meat. I caught him often watching me, spoon halfway between bowl and lips, and I watched him back until a shadow-man broke our line of sight with his decanter of blood-red wine.

Some afternoons he accepted visitors, and at the beginning of the summer a grand Lady-Witch arrived for dinner. I was banished to my rooms by the shadow-men and from my balcony heard the lovely and grand tones of her voice. I tried not to hate her. When she finally departed, I stayed on the balcony, talking softly to the blue finches who nested in the eaves. The knock on my door was soft, and when I called enter, August walked in, still dressed in his finery. Gold and green swirled on his suit, pulling out all the living colors in his face and hair, and his fingers were clothed in heavy-looking rings.

I did not rise from the stone of the balcony, and so he came to me and crouched. In the moonlight his eyes washed into blackness, but his smile was the same. "Melea, you are angry with me."

"No," I lied.

"She would have killed you if she'd seen you."

Something clawed at my throat from the inside, as though the butterfly grew talons. I choked on my words. "You were protecting me."

His hands found my shoulders, and he pulled me against him. His jacket was rough and stiff from the gilded embroidery, but I did not care. He smelled of sunlight and wood. A forest grove that my butterfly

There is a scene missing here. A brief interaction, a momentary pause, to set up the sudden! passion! in the next scene.

longed for with all its desperate fluttering. "You should have let her kill me," I said.

"No, no." His lips pressed to my hair, my ash-bark hair.

"Why not? You know what I am, you know who sent me, and so you must know I will bring you no good." I whispered into his shoulder, and the corner of my mouth burned with the rough touch of his jacket. "You must destroy me."

"I cannot." His arms tightened around me, and I knew what he was going to say. "I cannot because I—"

I kissed him before he could say the words the command vibrating inside me needed to hear. I kissed him and did not let him go.

. . .

August brought me into his workroom in the morning, a wide grin teasing his lips as his fingers grasped at mine. "Come, Melea, and don't be afraid."

The room spread over the entire subterranean floor, blocked out of the earth with giant white stones. Half was empty but for diagrams and pictures drawn onto the floor. A quarter of what remained held books glowing like miniature moons and shelves of jars and ceramics that every wizard must have. The final quarter was furnished with round and square tables, each of which held additional books, strange metal and glass contraptions, and piles of parchment. The entire place smelled like fire. I paused at the threshold, but August drew me in and tapped the ceiling with a cane he picked up from the closest table. At the third tap, my ears popped and I felt the workroom close behind me.

"Sit down, sweet," he said, rummaging already through the chaos of the largest round table. He found a pair of spectacles, which he shoved over his nose. I did not sit, but stared as August drew out from inside a long stone box a thin piece of wood. A wand. He brought it to me, muttering under his breath and cupping the pointed tip with his right hand. I didn't breathe as he set the point lightly against my ear. His eyes focused, and he said a word of power that sent my butterfly shuddering and my bones a-tingle.

As he pulled the wand away from my ear, I heard Master's voice snake throughout the workroom: Welcome, Melea. Here is your order: find my rival August Curran, make him love you, and rip out his heart.

I wrapped my arms around my stomach, but August only laughed. "What an old fool," he said and he turned to me. "He thought you would betray me easily, but you love me, too."

It was too close. I began to back away. "No, August. Don't. You mustn't."

"Don't you see, Melea, we can break his command. It is impossible for you to hurt me the way he wants you to. What will you do? Go to the king and offer your body to him? Marry another man? Ha!" He rushed to me, grabbing up my hands. "I love you, and—"

I opened my mouth and coughed, the butterfly trapped in my neck, trapped and terrified on my tongue. But it would not fly free. I tore away from August, shaking my head. I would not do it. I would not.

August stared, dumbfounded, as I gripped my own hands together and pressed them against my chest. Tears spilled over my cheeks. No, no. The command shoved me forward a step. I stumbled and fell to my knees. The jolt against the hard stone shook my bones, and they did not stop shaking. Get up, get up, the butterfly's wings beat out the command. Get up.

"No," I whispered. And then August was there, lifting me up by my shoulders. My fingers brushed against his chest, pushing the loose material of his shirt aside.

"Melea, what is happening? What is he doing? He cannot get to you here, not in my workroom."

I snatched my hands away from him before my nails clawed into his skin.

"Melea, your hair," said August in a hushed and horrified tone. "Your eyes."

I could only see my hands: the skin darkened and was thickening back into wax, sticky with honey. The ash-tree bones were brittle; they would break. No doubt my hair was returning to bark and my eyes to chokeberries. I was fighting my command, and so I was dying.

August touched his chest where I'd bared his skin. "Oh. Oh." he breathed. "I am the fool." And he sank back onto his heels. "Three times the fool."

My vision was dull when I looked anywhere but at his chest and I could not open my mouth. The rose

I invented the whole story for this moment.

petals that were my lips fell off my wax face and trembled in the air as they sank to the stone floor.

"I do not have the—the ability to remake you, Melea," he said. "You would not be who you are."

I managed to nod as I clutched my dangerous hands together. I would fall to pieces on his workroom floor, and he would use the wax in a spell for the king perhaps, the ash-bark for the princesses. I would like that.

"Take it," he said, and his voice was flat. He put a dagger—pulled from the air!—against his chest. With his other hand he lifted up the rose petal and pressed it to my mouth. "Take it, and live long with your butterfly, and remember me." I threw out my hands, but the dagger found its sheath between his ribs. August's eyes widened, and his lips parted enough that I saw his tongue.

"August," I said as he died. The blood poured over my hands, and my lips were my lips again.

. . .

His heart was hot and heavier than I expected. But it smelled like the heart of a tree. I could not think, could not speak past the command quivering through me. Cupping the thing in my palms, I walked up the stairs. His blood ran down my forearms and pooled at my elbows before dripping onto my skirts.

Master waited at the front door, surrounded by sparking, furious shadow-men. But they did not—could not—approach Master. He laughed, sharp as

172

cracking ice. "Follow me, Melea," he said, hands triumphantly on his hips.

But I was not made with a spider or iridescent beetle. I was made with a butterfly. "No," I whispered, and walked into the sunlight.

I figured out the ending second, after I knew the core image, then worked backwards.

Also, I've written 3 other stories where Melea appears as a secondary character. All posted on Merry Fates.

DIAGRAM of MAGGIE'S HEART

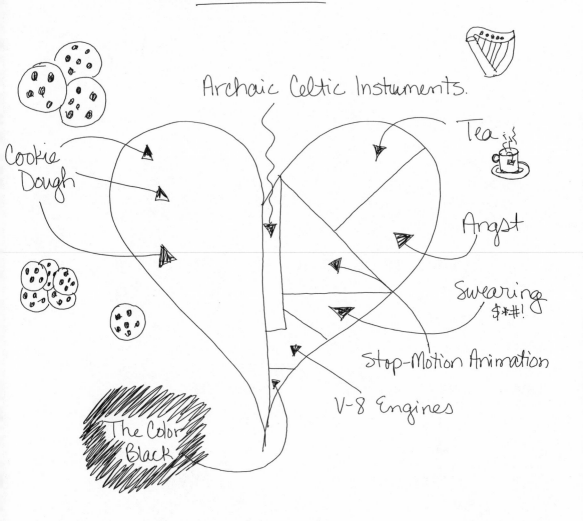

Archaic Celtic Instuments.

Tea

Angst

Swearing
$*#!

Stop-Motion Animation

V-8 Engines

Cookie Dough

The Color Black

RAIN MAKER

by Maggie Stiefvater

I find this story intensely upsetting. (Which is another way of saying that it's awesome)

Sometimes my own stories surprise me and make me uncomfortable, and I'm sure it says something about me that several of the stories that I picked for this anthology fit that description. I don't always know why they make me uncomfortable, just that I feel a little squirrelly about posting them on the blog right after I finish them. This story is one of them. I almost threw it away and began again. Looking back on it, I'm still not entirely sure why it made me so uncomfortable. I can see right off that I was amusing myself as I wrote it, because I gave the narrator the name that I gave all of my snarky, favorite characters in my novels as a teen: Dominic du Bois. When "Dominic du Bois" first appeared in a novel, he was the villainous but witty son of a fifteenth-century French knight. (Hey, I was fourteen, go easy on me.) I also see that I'm unashamedly playing with one of my favorite tropes: geniuses behaving badly. And also that I'm doing my very level best to harpoon one of my least favorite elements of society: voyeurism. But I think what probably made me feel uneasy about posting it was that I didn't try to hold back in unsettling the reader. From breaking the world to making cute dogs the enemy, I warped reality as much as I could to make it unpleasant. —Maggie

True fact: sometimes the most important thing we can do is to amuse ourselves.

We didn't know what stopped the rain.

At first, everyone was relieved, because you know, everybody's an expert, okay, not really, everybody's an idiot and they wouldn't know a death portent if it bit them in the ass. But I guess I could see their point. It started raining in March and it rained every day, all day, through April, and May, and June, and July, and August, and halfway through September until the last day that it rained. Ever.

That much rain all over the world washed away tiny villages first, then crops, then American SUVs, then big cities, and finally it was like the friggin' apocalypse, if reality shows still played on TV during the apocalypse. Boat sales were good, I'll tell you that much. And recipes for fish. There were a lot of recipes for fish on the morning shows. It was pissin' awful, to tell you the truth. It was gray and sticky every day, like a jungle without the dirt, and those people that had SAD, sunlight alertness deficit, or whatever it is that makes you pretty friggin' miserable when the sun doesn't come out . . . well, I guess sales of antidepressants were good too.

You know what I said? "Whatever." I was trying to finish my degree, and you get a lot of homework done when you can't go outside without stepping in a pile of whale or something.

Anyway, there was a lot of rain. You get the point.

And on September 14th, when the rain stopped and the sun finally showed its gawd-forsaken head, everybody was going "boo-yah" and "thank heavens" and "finally" and, maybe, just maybe, some of them who are probably feeling like dumbasses now said, "I hope it never rains again!"

Cause the universe doesn't get sarcasm.

You know what I said, though? I said, "Whoop-didoo, I'm buying me some bottled water." Mostly because my father told me not to, because he said, "What's a twenty-two-year-old pile of crap who lives at home under the pretense of finishing his degree going to do with two trillion gallons of bottled water?"

Be rich, is what he's going to do.

Yeah, the filtration and the storage cost money, but sure as your granny's good in bed, the water didn't. And those "boo-yah" "thank heavens" "finally" types weren't interested in water in September, or October, or November, or December, or for most of the spring. But by the time my father kicked me out of the house and I switched majors again and I got my *Time* magazine feature as world's most eligible genius or whatever, they wanted it. Oh yeah, they were dying for it.

So I was rich. I mean, I wasn't the only one who read the writing on the wall that said the planet was due for a royal screwing, but it didn't matter. I got rich enough.

But whatever. I didn't really mean to talk about me and my money. I was just trying to explain the whole rain thing. It didn't affect life as much as you'd think, having lots of water and then not having any water for years. Mostly, it was just, like, a few million people dying of strange diseases that hadn't been around for

I KNOW I HARP ON THIS IDEA A LOT IN THIS BOOK, BUT THIS SORT OF EFFICIENT WORLD-BUILDING WAS SOMETHING I JUST COULDN'T DO BEFORE MERRY SISTERS OF FATE.

centuries, and every species of corn going extinct except for this weird albino variety that looks like it's been growing under a rock, and it's really hot all the time, and you can just forget horseback riding as a sport, because there isn't much in the way of horses.

But there are still reality shows, only I guess they're a little weirder than beforehand, because the stakes are a little higher and you get a lot of whackos both as contestants and producers. They were filming one right outside my m-flat that was particularly messed up. The producers were standing around looking like zombies on crack while the host and camera guys watched these people trying to squeeze their bodies through an impossibly tiny hole to get a key on the other side.

By nature of their makeup, the humidity-recycling membrane and all, m-flats don't have great insulation, so I could hear the host as clearly as if I were standing next to him. So I knew that these contestants—who looked kinda like four hundred miles of bad road, if we're being honest—were all trying to get this key because it was a key to a brand new m-flat, which was a pretty ace prize. Basically it cut down on your water usage by two-thirds because of the way it recycled the water in your breath and the air and crap, and so it is basically the difference between spending your yearly salary on water or on the other nice things of life, like shoes. Or, you know, food.

I went down there to check it out. It was gross but fascinating. Mostly I wanted to see how idiotic people

would be for an m-flat. The answer, if you're wonder- HAVE YOU EVER SEEN FEAR FACTOR?
ing, is pretty idiotic. One guy dislocated his shoulder
on purpose to try to fit through this hole. So he was YEAH.
sweating like a sumo wrestler, screaming like a baby,
and even with all that lube and noise, he wasn't get- IT'S NOT REALLY MY THING.
ting through that hole.

Another girl almost got through, but she just
couldn't get her hips through. Not like she was big—
great thing about the apocalypse is that it really cuts
back on that obesity pandemic—but she just couldn't
do it. She clawed at her hips and I almost went back
inside, but she gave up.

Then the third girl came up, and when she saw me
standing there, watching, she shot me this real crappy
look. And you know what? I shot her a real crappy one
back, because if she had a problem with me watching,
just wait 'til this show aired on national television.

She stood there and looked at the hole, which, I'll
give her credit, none of the others had. Then, without a second's hesitation, she took off all her clothing. She was gleaming with sweat, thin as a rail, with
about one thousand more ribs than anyone else I'd
ever seen. Yeah. Pretty much only wearing her black
hair, up top and down below.

And she just slid through the hole and got the key.
She came back out and stood in her birthday suit,
clutching it with a screw-you-all sort of expression.
The cameras kept swinging to her and away, as if they
couldn't decide if they shouldn't be showing this or
this was the best catch ever.

The producers conferred amongst themselves. The host told the girl that it was against the contract. The naked part.

And they took the key.

They took the key.

For a moment I didn't really think they would do it, but then I saw the producers wrestling it out of her hands and thrusting her clothing towards her. The host ran his mouth about some new challenge for the key instead, since this one was void. Something about killing as many dogs by hand in ten minutes—what, didn't I mention this? Oh yeah, dogs and horses, they were the big carriers of that retrovirus that showed up during the first part of the drought. The horses just died, but the dogs passed it on to humans before they did, and dog-killing became this big thing. First any dog that looked like it had the signs, the scabs, you know, and then just any dog that looked like a dog.

SNEAKING IN MORE WORLD-BUILDING.

You know, before I moved out, I had a dog. He was a great dog.

I'll never forgive my dad. Ever.

Oh freaking hell, the producers weren't kidding. They had a pen of dogs. Like, a hundred dogs. All kinds. With collars and without. People's pets. Oh, that was messed up. There weren't really going to—

The contestants were staring at the dogs. The big guy with the dislocated shoulder was clenching his fists and unclenching them, testing the strength of his bad arm. The girl with the big hips was tracing a finger over a ligament in her neck, looking thoughtful.

And the girl who'd gotten the key already was just staring at one of the dogs in the pen, a golden retriever, who was looking back at her and wagging his tail. She'd covered up her ribs with her clothing again, but I could see she was shaking as she watched the dog.

Wagging his freaking tail.

I smacked aside one of the cameras and stepped between the contestants and the dogs. I walked right up to the girl. She looked at me with that same screw-you look, only now I knew why it was on there. Because c'mon, look at what they'd done to her just since I'd been watching. I took out my wallet, got out the blank check I always kept in there, and I wrote it for $57,000, which is $1,000 more than a basic m-flat costs. I handed her the check, and I just walked away.

I heard the producers say, "That was Dominic du Bois. Dominic du Bois! He invented the m-fl—he is a billi—what did he give you?"

At that, I turned around to look. The freaks were fighting with her about it. They told her she couldn't quit because of her contract, and they told her she couldn't keep it, because she got it while on the show, and then when that didn't work, because I was staring at them, the producer came over to me.

"The dogs are all gonna get killed anyway," he told me.

Just to be mean. Because people are like that, a lot, now, I didn't say that before either, but they are. They're kind of awful, actually, a lot of them.

"You're a piece of crap," I told him. "You're a piece of crap that other pieces of crap crap on."

He sneered at me, ugly bastard only his mom would like, if she even did, because he knew he'd gotten to me because I'd said anything at all.

The girl with the check stood behind him, looking at me, and she was still staring at me in an unfriendly way. Probably because she thought I was trying to buy her or something as messed up as the reality show people had been doing to everybody.

I went back inside the m-flat. I needed to study. Not for the degree. Screw the degree. I was going to make it rain.

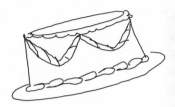

DUMB SUPPER

by Tessa Gratton

*It occurred to me to discover if I could write a story without any
dialogue. Instead of talking, there was a lot of food. —Tessa*

The point is to be silent. The dead can't speak, so in their honor, neither do the living.

I rarely talk the other three hundred and sixty-four days, so for me Halloween is not such a challenge. Nor do I invite any other living persons. I haven't reached the point where I have to converse with myself to stay sane. Or I've never been sane, and so have never needed spoken words to ground me in the moment.

All day I've had chili simmering on the stove, with cinnamon, honey, paprika, red pepper, and clove. The apples are cut in half so you can see their seed-stars, pumpkin muffins are iced with thin cream cheese, and I pull rosemary bread out of the oven just at sunset. There's cornbread, too, and dried plums. Two bottles of red wine are breathing next to the jack-o'-lantern waiting unlit in the center of my dining table.

My dishes are black, and the tablecloth, too. But I only have silverware. I like the contrast where they rest on the black napkins, especially when the candles are lit.

I brush my hair and put on slight touches of eye shadow and lipstick. My skirt flares just below my knees, and I have on decent stockings and solid shoes. The shirt is silk and buttons up to my neck. I have on small pearl earrings and a charm bracelet made of small golden headstones.

This year it is storming, and I part my curtains to see a family running between two houses, clear-plastic ponchos distorting the costumes on the three little ones. Porch lights shimmer through the rain, their welcome glows ruined and sad. Most children will be eating bowls of candy meant for other trick-or-treaters but relegated to consolation prizes against disappointment and tantrums.

And I know that a mere storm will not keep the real tricksters away, the dead and their never-living brethren.

So I walk through the dark halls and rooms of my house and light candles in every corner. Black for warding off evil, orange for the holiday, and white to invite peace.

When all the air wavers with flickering flame, I go to the kitchen and bring out the chili pot. I ladle some into every place setting, and I break bread to dole out. I place a selection of dried fruits and apples beside chunks of cornbread, and last I pour the wine. Then I sit at the foot of the table, across from the black-draped chair at the head. I fold my hands, bow my chin, and pray.

Silently, of course.

Restless ghosts, I welcome you to this table. It is filled with the year's bounty, with my bounty, and I would share it with you that you not go forgotten or hungry.

Nothing happens, but I am not alarmed. The dead arrive when they will. I sip my wine, a heavy merlot with the hint of chocolate and smoke. And I wait. Excitement and dread mingle on the rim of my glass.

Outside, the wind rattles branches against my roof like a welcome knock. The first spirit arrives, and I feel it with a chill. It is a boy in an Irish cap and knickers, swinging his feet and watching me. I smile.

Next to him appears an old woman with glinting gold at her ears. Both ghosts are flimsy and white, and I can see the upholstery through their flesh.

More come. I smile welcome at each arrival, recognizing my regulars and being careful not to stare at those unfamiliar. The young woman in the empire-waist summer dress I've been seeing since I was seven takes the seat to my left, and my affection for her makes me raise my wineglass in salute.

I have done research, of course, on my local spirits to discover their identities, but only in one case has a ghost ever matched in death his final picture from life. I believe it is not the last moments that mark a ghost, but their happiest. I see no slit throats or gunshot wounds, no bloodshot eyes or yellowing lips. I see instead how they project themselves. For the little boy, it is not necessarily that he died when he was five—perhaps he was twelve or twenty or fifty-seven—but his moment of strongest self-awareness and identity was at such a young age.

But it is only my theory. There is no exact science to this, and I had no master or old crone to learn from.

Soon all the seats are filled but for the head. We do not eat until everyone arrives. I stare at the empty chair and wonder if this will be the year he does not come.

Travis Andrew McCarthy. I know his name because he showed it to me, one Halloween when I was thirteen. He wrote it in smoke at my girlfriend Ginny's house, when I hid in the bathroom from her bullying older brother who said my costume made me look fat and trashy. Travis's touch froze away my tears, and when he smiled I felt my sore heart soothed. I felt the flush of shame melt away. I said his name, and he mouthed mine back at me. I could not hear it, but I knew what he said. Every day between that Halloween and the next I thought of his slicked-back hair, the unshaved jaw and dashing jacket. He appeared perhaps nineteen or twenty, and I loved him as hard as thirteen-year-olds must.

I am older than him now, older than he seems, by several years. But every October thirty-first, I set my table to welcome the dead and wait for him especially.

They used to terrify me, the ghosts no one else sees. They like to slink into your peripheral vision and mouth words at you, words you have no way to hear. It is awful to stare and stare and not know what they are saying—it is a greeting? A warning? A dire threat? But Travis never frightened me.

At my dining table, candles flicker, casting shadows through the spirits. They move their lips, chatting to each other. But all is silent around me, except for the clang of my clock striking nine and the wind in the trees.

I sigh, and Travis forms himself beside me, brushing his cold fingers down my neck. I watch as he walks down the length of the table to sit opposite me. He nods and smiles, and I smile back. The table is complete.

I lift my spoon and dip it into the cooling chili. Taking a bite, I see all the ghosts mimic the same. With invisible cutlery they carve bread, stir soup, and pick the plumpest fruit. None of the food moves, of course, not even a drop of wine, but for my own. But if you let your eyes relax and did not worry about details, it might be a family, eager to join in supper together.

Travis leans his elbows on the table and says something to me. I demur and sip my wine. He grins and raises a ghostly glass that seems to lift out of the real one. We flirt across the table, him smiling and using his eyebrows, me bashfully fluttering my lashes, biting my lip, hiding behind the food. The wine fills my head and I am alive. I imagine color in Travis's face, warmth in his lips. I imagine the feel of his hair, thick and rough under my hands. Superior to any living man's. He is attentive and laughing, and he loves me.

Slowly, slowly, my plate clears. I pour a second glass of wine. Soon ghosts are patting my arm and mouthing their thank-yous, rising up out of their seats and vanishing up into the ceiling or zipping through the walls. My summer-dress girl takes the hand of the little boy in the Irish cap, and several of the older spirits twirl off together. I am left alone with Travis.

He stands, hands flat on the table, and smiles at me. It is a smile that says, well done again, my darling, a fine feast you set.

Travis and I, we do not need to talk.

I rise as he comes around the table. I close my eyes, and his hands press cold against my cheeks.

It is like the temperature dropping suddenly, or the snap of frigid wind when he kisses me. Ten seconds of frozen bliss. My heart stops and I keep my hands at my sides, knowing that if I reach for him all I will find is cold, empty air.

Then he is gone. I look at the dumb supper, spread out in all its black, candlelit abundance. Except for my crumb-covered plate and empty bowl, every setting is filled still with food and drink, colorful and welcoming.

I sigh and sit back down. Dark rain pummels the windows. I drink more wine.

And next year, I decide, I will add sweet-potato casserole.

I attended a real dumb supper one Halloween. It was super creepy.

NEIGHBORS

by Brenna Yovanoff

Sometimes the hardest story to tell is the one that everyone has already heard. I feel like readers have been trained, especially with short stories, to look for the trick, the switch on a switch, the twist ending. So if that's what you are indeed going to give them, you must be very, very careful. This short story impressed me as both a reader and a writer because this twist is one that my generation is very prepared for. But still, Brenna sells it, and in the end I'm not sure it's the surprise that matters. It's one of those stories I dissected, trying to learn the secrets of its strange body. —Maggie

This story surprised me, even though I went into it knowing all the parts. As I was writing I felt like I already understood the basic layout and the reveal. What I didn't expect was the camaraderie between the girls and the fact that ghost stories, by their very nature, are sad ones. —Brenna

It says something about you that you don't expect ghost stories to be sad. OR it says something about me that I do.

It takes forever for the house next door to sell. Poor For-Sale Sign, rickety and crooked, like it's been leaning there all summer, all year, all my life.

The real estate agent blames the lack of interest—no, the entire state of the housing market—on our yard. She leaves a note taped to our front door, saying that no decent family would move in next to a disaster like ours, that the lawn is an eyesore. And it kind of is. I want to tell my dad to get off his ass, crawl out of the bottle and pull-start that mower, but at the same time I don't want to tell him anything. It's easier, just walking past the mess like it doesn't even exist.

And the house does sell, despite the condition of our yard. I lie out in the weedy grass and watch the people come and go, first the movers and then the family. Their son looks my age, maybe a year or two older. He's tall and dark-haired, with great shoulders and long, graceful hands. He's always texting—never even looks up or turns around, but I don't need to know the color of his eyes to tell that he's delicious. I watch from over the fence, hopeful and terrified that at any moment he'll turn and see me there.

The girl is less oblivious. On the second day she comes wandering over with bare feet and a beat-to-hell Polaroid camera.

She's younger, eleven or twelve, with a round, pale face and bangs cut short and straight across. Her hair is black and makes her look like a Gothic baby doll. She's holding a handful of fresh photos and staring

I know they're hard to find these days but I love Polaroid cameras.

I saw one at a friend's house and didn't recognize it.

191

at me like I'm some kind of extraterrestrial. Her eyes are ice-blue with freakishly long lashes.

I flick a hand at her and smile. She's way too young to actually hang out with, but maybe she'll invite me over anyway.

"Hi," she says in a flat voice.

"What's your name?" I ask brightly, but I already know. Behind her the guy—obviously her brother— is sitting on the steps, gazing intently at his phone. There's a box next to him with photo albums and notebooks and a well-loved plush unicorn sticking out of the top. The name Abby is scrawled down the side in marker.

At first she won't answer or look at me, so I just keep talking, yammering about whatever, glancing past her every now and then to see if her brother is watching.

Finally, she takes a step closer. "How long have you lived here?" she asks in a tiny voice.

"Always—all my life."

She tips her face to the sky. "What's it like? Is there anything to do?"

"Well, what kinds of things do you want to do?"

"I like to take pictures," she says, offering the handful of photos, fanning them out like playing cards. The paper is slick and glossy. The pictures are of the house and the yard, her brother standing by their one skinny tree, a burly pair of movers wrestling a red couch up the front steps in a long awkward diagonal.

"They're nice," I say. And they are. Surprisingly nice. The one of her brother makes me feel weirdly sad, like seeing a helium balloon tied to a railing somewhere and knowing that no one's coming back for it.

Abby smiles and looks away. "I have more. I keep them in an album."

"Will you take my picture?" I pose for her, leaning on the fence, propping my chin on one hand.

She regards me doubtfully, then raises the camera anyway. When she presses the button, there's a click and a flash and the camera spits out a pale square of paper. Abby catches it and stands, head bent, watching it develop. Her expression is so blank that it could mean a million things.

"Well, can I see it?"

"No," she says, holding it against her chest.

"O-kay, never mind then. So, does your brother have a girlfriend?"

"Yes. But she doesn't live here. She goes to his old school."

A tiny flare of hope—I mean, distance is a killer, and how long can you really stay together when texting is the primary basis for a relationship? If I can just get him to see that I exist, maybe I can cure him of the girlfriend. "Is he always on his phone like that?"

Abby shrugs and shakes her head. "He's been really into it lately. He didn't want to move."

"Yeah, that sucks. Maybe I should go over and introduce myself. You know, show him around."

Abby follows my gaze, waving the Polaroid in one soft, little-girl hand, careful to keep it turned away from me. "Do you ever feel . . . forgotten?" she says, and her voice cracks on the last word. Behind her, her brother is still staring into the vortex of his phone, ignoring the way she slouches by the fence.

The summer has been the longest, slowest, stupidest of my life. My dad sits in his study or in front of the TV, and talking about feeling forgotten just makes you feel more forgotten, so I smile like nothing is wrong. "Look, I'm sure he'll get over it. Maybe I could come over and see your album sometime."

"No," she says, the word coming out much too loud. Then she takes a deep breath and shakes her head. "I mean, I don't think it would be a good idea."

"So, are you going to show your brother my picture?"

She gives me a sideways look and shakes her head again.

"Can I at least see it then?"

"Only if you really want to." Her expression is so empty it's unreadable.

"I do."

She holds out the picture, offering it to me over the fence. I don't take it from her, just look. The paper, shiny and old-fashioned, familiar band of white along the bottom. In the foreground, the pickets of the fence are jagged like teeth. Behind it, empty sky.

Where there should be a girl with long brown hair and freckles, there's nothing.

Abby looks up at me, near tears. "I'm sorry," she says in a whisper. "I'm so sorry."

I just shrug, smile weakly. I mean, what can you say?

"How did you die?" Her voice is thin and shaking.

And I want to tell her that I don't know. I don't have even the faintest idea. But I do. Sometimes you make yourself forget the things that make you stop breathing. You remember them, and you still forget anyway. I was riding my bike to the lake, out along the county road, and then it was over. Just like that.

Abby backs away, clutching the photo. "Did you not know?"

"I guess I knew," I say. "Yeah, I did. But sometimes . . . well, it's just nicer to think it never happened, you know?"

She watches me with brimming eyes. "You're not going to haunt me, are you?"

"What? No, I'm not going to haunt you. Don't be stupid."

"What do you want, then?" she says, looking miserable.

The question is so honest it's painful. I want to eat Sour Patch Kids and kiss boys and walk down to the Dairy Queen with my friends—all those friends I used to have. I want to spend my days with someone else, do what they do and not be shut up in my house all the time, alone with no one but my father.

She looks so lonely standing there. So lost, and I want to hug her but the fence is in the way and what if my hands go right through?

"Can I take your picture?" I ask, because it seems to be a language she understands.

When she passes me the camera it feels angular and solid, like I am really holding it. Sometimes I remember the world so clearly it almost seems real, and even though I can't shake the knowledge that I'm not there, I push the button, take the picture anyway.

The camera whirs and grinds, spitting out the square of paper, and we stand with our heads together, with the fence between us, waiting for the image to show up.

Shapes appear, ghostly at first, then showing up clearer and clearer. Her lawn, weed-free and carefully mowed, racing to the edges of the photo like a tiny green sea. There in the background, her brother is texting, sitting on the steps beside the abandoned box. The Abby box, overflowing with notebooks, stuffed animals, photo albums and an old Polaroid camera, and this whole time, they have not brought in one stick of furniture that looks like it belongs to a twelve-year-old girl.

The photo is crisp, everything bright and in focus. There is no black-haired Gothic baby doll—no Abby, besides what's in the box—and I knew that too. I knew it since she crossed the lawn to talk to me. Knew it even when I wanted, wanted, wanted to know something else.

"I'm sorry," I say, because the look on her face is like looking at myself.

DIAGRAM of TESSA'S LIVER

Terrifyingly Organized Thoughts

Mixology

Museum of the Grotesque

DINOSAURS

Beowulf

Nail Polish

Nightmares

Magic!

COUNCIL
OF YOUTH

by Maggie Stiefvater

Leadership is one of Maggie's recurring themes, from the very beginning up through the novels she works on now. Leadership and the relationship between a leader and her followers, and what impact being a leader has emotionally and psychologically. What does it mean to be listened to? What does it mean to be responsible? Some of her favorite questions. —Tessa

What Tessa said. Pretty much all of it. —Maggie

I'm in yr brain
thinkin' yr thoughts.

It's been about twenty-four hours since we took over the government of the United States of America. About six since I've seen Raphael.

When he joins us, we can all see he's nervous as hell. He's pacing, shaking his hands back and forth at the wrists, like he's going to loosen them up for some great physical task ahead of him.

"You know what's stupid?" he asks me, because I'm still his best friend, even though that means something different now. He smiles, foolish. "I couldn't stop thinking last night about my Civic. About how I'm going to miss just getting in and driving it."

I smile encouragingly back at him while loading my pistol. "You've been pressed into greater things, Rafe."

"I'd rather be pressed into my Honda," he says, and we all laugh, because we need it.

Outside, the crowd is loud, screaming and shouting, waiting to see Raphael. They're waiting for his State of the Union address, even though all of them know the State of the Union is Crap. Raphael watches me shove the magazine back into my pistol. He looks tired and way older than just a few weeks ago, back when we were just juniors at Boston College. "They're going to kill us, aren't they?"

"Don't be stupid," I say. "You're worried about the audience? They're just impatient."

"Is it an audience, or is it a mob?" His runs his fingers through his brown mop of hair again and again, leaving tracks of anxiety behind. "This is crazy. I'm nineteen. My dog won't even listen to me."

This is such a lie that we all jump in to correct him. Jules's voice is fond: "Raphael, everyone loves you. Everyone listens to you. That's why you're here." What she doesn't say but means is, Raphael is the only thing that keeps us from being a bunch of armed teens. We need him. More than his Honda needs him.

The door opens. It's the oldest person I've seen in the past two days: some guy in his late thirties. The oldest person alive, anyway. He looks at Raphael and smiles a tight smile—he's nervous too, but like everyone, he loves Raphael. He's probably read his blog. The world has. "Mr. President?"

Rafe closes his eyes at the title.

"It's time to roll," says Cayden, who never could tell when someone needs a second to friggin' catch their breath and get used to the idea of addressing a crowd of fifty thousand.

Raphael looks at me, and his expression contains the pain of every single life that's been lost over this. "Are we terrorists or revolutionaries, Matt?"

I hold his gaze for a long moment. "Something had to be done. People were dying. Someone had to do something." I holster my gun with a soft snick.

Raphael bites his lip, and I wonder how I could've ever thought he looked old. But there's no turning back. We lead Raphael to the balcony doors, and as we stand inside them, the sound of the crowd outside is deafening. Raphael shakes hands with me, really formally, because he knows just like me that he might be going out to his death. And he knows I'm going with him, either way.

Thirtysomething guy pushes open the balcony door, and I walk out first, in front of Rafe, just in case someone's got a gun out there. The crowd goes quieter when they see me. I survey their faces. They're young, young faces everywhere—teens like us. Maybe there aren't any older people left.

Raphael steps out from behind me and leans into the microphone set up for him. He smiles as if he's not afraid. "Hi, America. Did you miss me?"

The crowd goes absolutely wild. Old America is dead.

THIS STORY IS VERY, VERY SHORT, AND ALSO ONE OF THE FIRST I WROTE FOR MERRY SISTERS OF FATE. KNOWING WHAT I KNOW NOW, I WOULD EXPAND IT WITH SOME MORE DETAILS OF THE WORLD-BUILDING. BACK THEN, I DIDN'T KNOW HOW TO DO IT WITHOUT THE DREADED INFO-DUMP, SO I JUST SAID NOTHING AT ALL.

THE SUMMER ENDS IN SLAUGHTER

by Tessa Gratton

Now I want to draw someone wearing a horsehead.

I read a line in a guidebook when I was in Wales about an old ritual where somebody would knock on your door wearing a horsehead. I wrote it on my hand and thought, horsehead! kissing! obviously! —Tessa

But that would be gross.

THIS THOUGHT PROCESS CONFUSES ME, BECAUSE I BELIEVED THE USUAL TESSA CREATIVE PROCESS WENT LIKE SO: "HORSEHEAD! KILLING!, OBVIOUSLY!"

OF COURSE, THAT WOULD'VE BEEN A DIFFERENT STORY.

The killing comes later, when I turn this story into a novel.

On the first night we slaughter animals for the winter.

I walk behind my father, carrying a shallow bowl of blood. Mother and I drained it from one of the chickens moments ago, and it's still warm.

We are a chain of people weaving through the field. Father first, then me, then my mother and sisters with black veils over their faces. The rest of the town comes behind, trailing back to the edge of the trees. We are a snake, a serpent of frost, of death, searching out the oldest of the cows, the ill hogs, the troublemaking goats. When Father chooses a beast for death, he turns to me and dips his fingers into the cooling blood. I murmur, "Blood to mark," and he replies, "God protect us." He smears a widdershins circle onto every forehead—enough to feed us throughout the long dark of the year.

Oldest sons lead the animals away to the shambles, and there they wait for us.

It is the first night of Samhain, and the grass is dead. Trees spit scarlet and orange leaves to the earth, turning the fields to fire. There will be no more free grazing, no more evenings lying out among the sheep, staring at the stars with my sisters and whispering predictions for each other's husbands. Nights will be spent huddled by the hearth fire at home, wrapped in my sisters' arms beneath blankets rubbed with evergreen needles and dried rosemary to keep bad dreams away.

"Blood to mark," I say again and again. We kill many this season, for the cunning man in Rose Spring says it will be a rough winter. My mother looked to the crows this morning and agreed.

Children at the end of the line gather handfuls of dry grass and their favorite leaves to toss onto the fires tomorrow, and I hear their laughter and nervous giggling. Tonight it is safe, but soon the spirits will come, the devils and goblins hungry for our winter harvest.

Last, we come to the horse pasture. Here we do not go to the dying or troubled. Father pushes through the herd for Fourth Wind, a stallion in his prime. Gray as a ghost and proud, Wind's nostrils flare at the scent of the blood in my bowl. I hate this, the feeling of loss twisting my stomach. Wind has sired beautiful horses, and I've raced over the hills on his back, thrilled and terrified.

Two men step forward to restrain him. One is Rhun, my neighbor's oldest son. He has dark eyes and a slow smile that makes me glance away. He holds one hand out to me, shaking his head to keep me back. Wind rears, and my father's shoulder knocks me so that my blood bowl sloshes.

Ropes wind around the horse's neck, and Father quickly marks a dark red circle over the slash of white starring Wind's brow.

My face hurts from holding back the ache. But a horse must be slaughtered. The dead must eat this winter, too. Rhun leans forward and wipes his thumb down my cheek. "You have blood on your face," he says with a frown.

. . .

When I wrote this line I knew I was learning one-line characterization from Maggie. Finally.

204

The second night we burn their bones.

The day's been spent killing and butchering, salting some for the year and doling parts out to the families who share the herds. We've been baking, too, and stringing woven grass around the bonefire as Rhun and his brothers build up the tower of wood. Old Miss Marion's cauldron waits like a chunk of nighttime, waits for Fourth Wind's head.

Icy wind blows through town, promising to keep cold our meat over the night. The smell of death wipes the last scent of flowers from the sky. I bundle dry lavender and the last of my dill together and pin them to my sisters' collars. Between gusts of blood and cold, the relaxing perfume trickles up.

I take a final bucket of water to Fourth Wind, where he's tied at the edge of town. He does not drink, though I smooth his mane, feeling my fingers weave through his coarse hair. He rolls his eyes so I see the white all around and I want to free him, to untie the hobbles around his front legs and slap his flank until he runs faster than he ever has. But not even a horse can run from the dead.

A hand touches my back and I shudder. I close my eyes, not knowing if a human being stands behind me until his warm breath skims my neck. "The wind is too cold for you to go without your hood, Riana."

"I wanted him to know me," I whisper, watching Fourth Wind's eyes.

Turning me by my shoulders, Rhun makes me face him. "When he comes for you tomorrow, will you go with him?"

"Everyone will." My hands are shaking, and I tuck my arms over my chest, burying my cold fingers against my ribs.

"But you . . ." Rhun tightens his grip on my shoulders. "If he comes for you first, will you dance at his side? Will you walk with him into the arms of the dead? Will you help him be strong to survive till morning?"

I stand with my lips apart, barely breathing. "Yes."

When he kisses me there is no warmth. Our lips are as cold as the rest of us.

We go separately back to the fires as the sun sets and the roar of flames draws us in. Barley ale is passed, and bones, too. We suck at marrow and throw the hollow bones onto the fires.

The moon rises, and we feast on roasted pig. Aaron stands near the cauldron with his fiddle and plays hard and fast. Mother drags Father to dance, and my littlest sister shrieks with laughter, clapping in time with her friends. I toss rosemary and evergreen into the fires, changing the smoke, and for a while at least I forget the horse as I whirl and laugh with the rest of my town. Tonight is the second night, when we feast and celebrate and toss out the bones, just us and us and us; no dead, no haunting devils, no goblins pulling skirts and clawing ankles.

. . .

The sun rises for the third day, and we rise too, from shallow sleeping, from prophecy dreams and ale-soaked nightmares. I whisper my dream to my closest sister: I am watching her wedding from above, as though I float in the wind. I feel free and happy, and she looks up at me from beneath her flower-crown. With a smile, she beckons me to join her. I fly down, and when I take her hand it bleeds.

Before she can respond, Father walks into the circle of coal-fires. Behind him is Rhun and his father, pulling a skittish Fourth Wind. My fists clench. I close my eyes as my sister takes my hand and leads me into the line. In darkness I walk. Out into the fields again, where the light of the sun does nothing to steal the chill from my cheeks. I do not join in the quiet humming. Nor do I watch when they cut his throat and his blood pours into the earth. It soaks into the cracks of the field, splattering the dead yellow grasses.

I stand with my arms wrapped around myself as they quarter the corpse. Parts are taken to each corner of our land, a boundary of blood and bone to tell the dead where we are.

But the head is taken back to town. Old Miss Marion's cauldron is set over flames, and Wind's head is stripped of skin and meat. Eyes go to Mother, who will save them for burying with honey half a year from now.

The skull goes into the cauldron. Two hours' hard boil, with the bubbles roiling and popping so hard the children play at getting as close as they can without burning their faces. After that, it will be picked clean and returned to a simmer for the rest of

the day. Come night, come night—the final night—
Fourth Wind will invite the dead to feast.

· · ·

The third night we wait in our houses. My back
presses against the inside of the front door, my shawl
clutched around me. Father and Mother wait in the
center of the little house, holding hands. My sisters
flank them like a flock of geese fleeing south.

The red glow from the setting sun traces along the
dining table, highlighting generations' worth of nicks
and gouges. I know every single one and have run
my fingers along them. I wonder what the table of the
dead will feel like under my hands.

The door vibrates with the first knock, and I close
my eyes. The second comes, and Father nods to me.
At the third knock I turn and throw open the door.

He is there.

White bone glows in the moonlight: a horse skull
grinning down at me. His shoulders are covered in a
horsehair cloak, and leathers from last year's beast
wrap around his legs. Braided tails spill down his back.

And I can just see his slow smile hiding in the shadows under the jawbone.

He spreads his arms and steps back, tossing his
head like a prancing horse. Inviting us out. I take a
deep breath and reach for his hand. It is warm, and
we weave our fingers together. He pulls me into the
road toward our neighbors. I hear my family lining up
behind us.

I can do structural
refrains, too! Not
as seamlessly
as Brenna, but
this is me trying.

Together we knock on every door, calling the town to join us, to dance with us to the dead feast. Through houses and gardens we weave: a cold snake, a death snake, but now with our own death's-head.

Around and around the bonefire, through the bloody smoke we dance. His hand firm in mine. We do not laugh or shriek or call with the rest of the town. The moon rises higher, and we spin into the field where Fourth Wind died.

He stops. The town pours around us in a massive crescent. A shield between us and the town. And at the edge of the trees the dead wait.

Crouched and huddled, peeking through branches, crawling up from the ground. Meat in their teeth, blood under their nails. Pale as light, hard as stone. They are everything dead: maggots and rot and perfect airy spirits. Floating, reaching, begging. One holds a horse hoof in its hands, another braids tendons together into a bracelet. They have our quartered offerings, and they wait. They stare at Fourth Wind's skull.

His hand trembles. I grip it between both of mine. He steps forward. He must go to them. To dance with them in the death-mask. To survive the night on his feet, leading them a chase through the woods so they cannot come back to town before dawn.

My mother calls wordlessly, unwilling to say my name before the hosts of the dead. She has realized what I mean to do.

I glance back once and wave.

Then, before Rhun charges, I leap away from him, running toward the dead.

His steps beat after me, and I hold out my hand.

Our fingers link.

The dead slather gleefully and lick their lips.

It is the third night of Samhain, and we run together.

Raw Data:

Kisses	IIII
Fire	.III
Dead Bodies	IIII II
Flowers	0
Non-fatal Wounds	IIII I
Butterflies	II
Monsters	IIII II
Sex	III
Knives and/or Swords	IIII III
High School	IIII
Happy Endings	II

*Full disclosure:
I still don't really know what
this title means! But I liked
how it sounded.*

BLUE AS GOD

by Brenna Yovanoff

A lot of short stories go like this: There is a girl. There is a man, and he is bad. Terrible things happen to the girl, and she is never the same. A lot of Brenna's short stories go like this: There is a girl. There is a man, and he is bad. The girl is worse, and the man stops breathing. Sometimes I'm afraid of Brenna, but mostly I'm glad I'm a girl. —Maggie

Sometimes I write stories about timid, sheltered girls who don't know who they are and who are forced to learn their own stories because they suddenly don't have any other options. This is not one of those times. —Brenna

I like to be slightly afraid of my friends.

It's my favorite kind of title because it seems like it should mean something to me, but doesn't, so I have to read the story to understand.

I woke up in the dark. The room was big, without a lot of furniture, and I could see the bone-white sheen of my legs. I could see my reflection on the ceiling, sprawled on the bed like a sad, busted skeleton. What kind of pretentious jackass has a mirror on the ceiling?

I'd come up the canyon for the party because I wanted to be somewhere that wasn't my apartment, be my same self, but in a different place. I was tired of my own thoughts. The time ticked on like a leaky faucet, and let me tell you one thing: L.A. can suck it. It's where nice girls come to die. Not that I would know. I came from Spencer's Branch, Idaho, home of nice girls, but I can't make the case that I ever was one.

I just wasn't built for a small town. I didn't curl my hair, didn't cook Hamburger Helper meals or wear sweaters with kittens. Had stopped closing my eyes when I prayed. Okay, once maybe, I was a good girl. I guess. As long as we're being honest. I kept my smile decent, my eyes downcast, and I never used to say yes, but now yes was the only thing that seemed to come naturally.

When the director came up to me on the roof, I knew who he was, of course. It was his house. The night was hot, and the Santa Anas didn't quit. Fifteen miles inland the fires had been raging for days. Even in the refrigerated chill of the house, the air smelled burned.

He said, "You have a certain look. Hard. I like that."

He was young for a director, and the industry rags said that he was some kind of genius—all the best festivals, the jury prizes, the speeches, the very best parties.

He touched the side of my arm. "I think I could use you."

All around, the girls laughed and rolled their eyes like jackals, giving me looks. Like they wouldn't have jumped headfirst if he'd said the same thing to them.

He said I should stay and we'd get to know each other, talk about a project—he thought it would be perfect for me. His smile was honest, and I knew there was no project, but I was ready to buy the other lie, the one he sold as often as that fictitious starring role. A warm fantasy that he'll pet and hold and cherish you for twenty minutes or an hour. That he'll want you for longer than a heartbeat.

Around us, the crowd was sweating, glossy like otters. My hair stuck to the back of my neck, and my makeup was melting off my face.

He took me down the wide, curving staircase to his room and we drank red wine and listened to records on a 1940s turntable. He was pretentious, but charming, and kind of solemn.

He said, "Stay here with me. We can work out some of the fine points after everyone goes home. Just don't go wandering around—it's a big house and a person could get lost. Then I'd have to look for you."

Later, I woke up in the dark and he was gone.

I got up and put on my crumpled dress, found my shoes and my purse. Everything was so quiet.

I'm totally making this all up — I have no idea what Hollywood parties are really like but my brain seems to think they're like sordid TV shows.

Out in the living room there was no one. Not a single mumbling cokehead or blackout baby slumped on the couch, and no one on the roof. I crept through the kitchen and down the stairs into the basement. It was cream-colored. I mean, the whole thing was. It was white like a hospital and went on forever, cut right out of the hill, and I kept thinking I should leave, I should get out. The farther I went, the worse the emptiness got.

I wandered down hallways and turned corners, looking for someone, anyone. Even a cat or a house-plant would prove that I was still real.

The door was narrow, painted a cracked, peeling blue. It wasn't locked.

The room was full of video equipment—handheld cameras and computer monitors and a whole stack of memory cards with paper labels. Every label had a name and date. I picked up Becca, June 6–7 and put her in the media slot on the one of the cameras. When I pressed play, the screen lit up, showing a blonde, smiling girl, fresh-faced and juicy like a blue-ribbon pie.

"Well, I'm from Clement," she said to the camera. "That's right near Houston. I moved out here because it just seemed so exciting! I mean, my whole life, I've wanted to be an actress."

From offscreen, the director's voice sounded raspy and playful. "What would you say your greatest strength is? Your greatest weakness?"

I forwarded through the slop to see if it got better. It didn't. But it got interesting.

The director set the camera on a tripod and moved into the shot. His voice was sharp and excited, and then he was doing things to her. Not sex things, but bad, sick things, and I yanked the card out, feeling breathless. But I have never believed in knowing when to stop, and I stuck in another one.

I watched Susan, who spent three miserable days in July down in the director's cutting room, and Cara, who only lasted part of July 18, and Valerie on August 12, and it didn't ever turn out okay. And there was a stack of other ones, this whole stack, too many to look at, and I put the camera down.

The girls all ended up with their heads slumped forward and their hands tied. All his beaming, corn-fed girls. By the end of the movie he'd taped over their mouths, but their eyes all had the same hunted look.

As I backed away from the monitors, the door shut behind me, and then I heard the key whisper and the lock slam home, because of course it bolted from the inside.

"I told you not to wander off," he said. "I told you not to go snooping around, but some girls just don't listen. As long as we're down here, though, why don't we get started on the project? Have a seat."

You already know the way this ends.

She finds Bluebeard's secret room and sees his murdered wives, and then she tries to cover up and act like she didn't. But I'm a pretty worthless liar. I've just never seen the point.

Out on the rooftop, the sky would be hazy and black. No cloud of dust on the horizon to signal rescue. The moon was long gone, and the sun wouldn't rise for another couple hours. Up in the hills, the fires were burning and the smoke was everywhere.

He stood in the middle of the cutting room with the camera trained on my face. "Tell me about yourself—your hopes and dreams. Your fantasies, your fears."

So I told him my story. It was short. I said, "I came to L.A. with nothing. I don't know why I stay here. I came from a poor little cow town, and trust me, there was nothing there either. I don't have much family. No brothers, no sisters. I pray like a dyed-in-wool hypocrite in church, and if I don't bow my head for God, what makes you think I'll bow for you?"

He said, "Everybody bows eventually."

I said, "Really. Is that a fact. Well then, let's skip the whole interview process and get down to business."

"You don't really mean that."

"Try me."

The thing about pepper spray is, it's effective from a distance of up to ten feet. If you discharge it from four inches, the burn is something else.

The key ring was dancing, jangling as he thrashed. I yanked it off his belt and shoved past him, coughing and raging like the autumn fires, eyes streaming. He knew she'd lied because the key was magic, an everlasting charm. It betrayed her. What a way for the lie to fall apart—undone by an inanimate object.

He caught me by the wrist, dragging me down to the floor, down to where he gasped and swore, face red, eyes puffy and squeezed shut. I raised my other hand and slashed. You can do a lot of damage with a two-inch strip of metal.

The stories are baffling. They don't make sense. She married a maniac—what, she didn't notice?—but in the gruesome context of the tale, it sounds random, circumstantial, just another little victim.

Still, they were right about one thing.

The key had blood on it.

THOMAS ALL

by Tessa Gratton

*Now, here's a piece that showcases Tess's ability to scare the bejeezus out of me. While "Thomas All" is indisputably a faerie story, it's one that also happens to feel a lot like a horror story. The sheer perverse creepiness and the modern setting both serve to keep it well out of high-fantasy territory, but there's also this bright, adventurous quality that keeps it from falling too far into the realm of real life (not to mention a massive, mysterious world winking at us from just below the surface).
—Brenna*

Every once in a while I try to write a novel about Thomas. Someday I'll manage to. I love my plastic sword–wielding fifteen-year-old psychopath. —Tessa

I have 30,000 words of a Thomas novel in a desk drawer somewhere.

We're all called Thomas, because it's easier for the old ones, who hardly notice the difference between us.

And most of us don't ever realize we're only one of many. But it's been happening forever, and we're each of us only good for ten years on the outside. I think I was about fourteen when I escaped, and I don't know how young I was when I was taken, but I had to have been four or so because I have dim memories of my mother and father. She had milky green eyes and black hair, though I have black hair and so might be conflating the two because I want to remember. Father was missing two fingers from one hand, and I remember when Hop came for me, its grip was like his against my wrist.

. . .

I track her because she's been elf-touched, and once touched you become like a magnet for others of their kind. She wasn't stolen like I was—I can tell when you've spent time in their castles and rocks. Perhaps she'd been to a mushroom dance: one night when she was out late with her boyfriend, she followed a light around her house and beyond the edge of the backyard. She woke in the morning hungover and frightened and unsure what had happened. If her boyfriend was lucky, she recalled that he'd dropped her off and driven away first.

She appears normal to everyone around her, though maybe a bit distracted. Her fingers twitch at things no one else sees. To me, when my eyes are anointed, it is as though she's been dipped in oil and a

This is one of my favorite of my own first lines.

rainbow shimmers over her skin. I wish for her sake it was a rainbow that washed away, but even a swim in the ocean might not remove the taint.

The attraction she holds for them makes her perfect bait.

. . .

My prince was not the worst, by all I've gathered, but he was bad enough. He was beautiful like stars are beautiful, like angels are supposed to be. Cold, alien, pristine. Being with him was like drinking the most delicate champagne all the time, until I didn't care that when he laughed there were teeth all the long way down his throat.

Hop would take me from the toy room and limp before me, dragging its crushed leg along as we twisted through the rocks and roots to the prince's feast hall. I asked Hop once what happened to the leg. It told me a tragic story of a human girl it had loved who'd betrayed it to her village, and they'd laid in wait at its hovel-hole and, as Hop emerged, they'd thrown salt water from the sea. The salt shriveled the skin of its leg and cracked its bones into millions of tiny pieces. (I saw the prince's daughter grow tired with a tatterfoal once, and she swallowed his hind leg as he scrambled from her boredom. After long moments where his screams harmonized with the song I dared not stop singing, she released him. The bones were shattered and skin shredded. I thought of Hop's story and knew they could lie, sometimes.)

Scary fairies are scary. Sometimes I lie in bed thinking about ways to make fairies normal on the outside but horrific on the inside.

I could not help loving Hop, for I was a child and it looked after me and brought me food. It cradled me against its chest when I cried, hard enough that I could feel bones through the velvet of its doublet.

I cried against that same chest after I shoved a hawthorn wand up into its brain. The salt in my tears seared his neck and chin. But Hop's blackened blood soaked into my pores as I rubbed it onto me, as my disguise and means of escape. I could smell my sin for weeks. Every time I breathed, I tasted it on my tongue.

. . .

As I follow the girl, I watch the crowd to see who notices her. I search for odd bits of anachronistic clothing or an eye that cannot seem to glance away. We are walking through a crowded outdoor market near the Mississippi River. There are teenagers and tourists everywhere. I blend in. None of them wonder why my shirt is inside out (I'm not the only one) or why I've drawn labyrinths on both my palms. They can't see there's salt in my jeans pocket or smell the marigold and clover scent of the ointment on my eyelids. The wand in my hand is only a stick to them, smooth and buttery gold, that I've picked up to poke at bugs or fight invisible enemies.

There is a boy, over there by the hot-dog car, crouched as though he is just picking something up. But his gaze follows her and his hair is dripping. There is no rain today. But a small pool of water has formed beneath him. As he stands and goes after her,

This was my first ever 1st person present though I didn't love it until "Death Ship"

he leaves two footprints: bare feet, although he appears to wear boots.

I shift my attention fully to him. As I walk, I rub a pinch of salt over my eye-ointment to cancel out the magic. The water horse should not smell it over the stink of his own breath. I also shove the wand up my sleeve so it runs like an exoskeleton from my wrist to my elbow.

once again, me and my complex magic.

Picking up speed, I come alongside the water horse, and my nostrils flare at the overwhelming scent of rot. He slides a glance at me when my shoulder brushes against his. I see the red flash in his eyes as he notes the rainbow shimmer over my skin. I smile at him. "I can't find the marina," I say.

"I can show you." He forms the words carefully and quietly. His smile is shy. I feel his glamour pushing against me like warm air. "Over here." He offers his hand, and when I take it his smile grows. Were I what I appear to be, my remaining allotment of life would be measured in brief moments.

. . .

It was the first Thomas, the original, the real Thomas who taught me how to escape.

"We're all called Thomas," he said. He was not a boy any longer, but had a man's gaunt face and triangular cheekbones through which I could see the shine of his heart. It was so full of light.

I pressed my back against the rough limestone of my prince's underground castle, cutting my palms on the edges, and stared. Thomas knelt, and his knees were knobby like a goblin's under red hose. The strap of a guitar cut across his jerkin, and he shifted so that its head didn't knock against the stone floor. "Do you remember what you were named before?"

"No," I whispered. "I don't remember."

"Ah, Tom," he said, shaking his head as if disappointed in me. "No worries, lad, most of us never do. They take us so young, don't they?"

"You remember yours, though?" I clasped my hands together behind my back and stepped away from the wall to show him I was less afraid. I looked down at his reddish hair, and he raised his chin. I saw how beautiful he was from that angle, and why they'd taken him. All of us were beautiful.

"My name has always been Thomas. I was the first."

"The first?"

"They've always taken children, of course." He chuckled. "But I was the first they remembered."

"They think I am you?"

"When they think of us at all."

.   .   .

It is a strange sight to the locals: two boys walking hand in hand toward the river. But after a moment their efforts to surreptitiously gawk are thwarted by the water horse's glamour. Their stares begin to slide off of us until we are as good as invisible.

The river laps calmly here, and the noise of the city behind us overwhelms the calling of gulls and the roar of the interstate zipping by on the bridge overhead. I say, "We've passed the boats," but not as if I care.

The water horse smiles at me. "I know better ones, and you'll love the water."

I nod. He takes me to the edge, where the bridge shades us so the sun cannot glare off the river (a milky green-gray that reminds me of my mother's eyes). I see the rough sand and pebbles spilling under, for almost six feet I can follow the sloping descent. He tugs me, and I resist, but he pulls again. My hand is trapped in his. I frown, but when he grins I pretend to look relieved. As if I cannot see the sharp lines of his teeth or the old meat trapped between them.

. . .

The first Thomas stayed with us for an entire season. It was winter, and that is when the princes conclave, when they stay hidden from the Hunt in their hills and ruined castles, making lights and fire through the dark, dead nights. That winter the Queen had chosen our hill for her revels and treating. I never knew why.

Thomas sought me out frequently, escorting me between bonfires and feasting halls, teaching me the names of his friends and allies and the faces of his enemies. They were all my enemies, I wanted to say. I asked, "Are there others now? Other Thomases?"

"Always, Tom. But none of you ever last."

I added this whole scene after the fact, when we put together our first self-done anthology, to clarify details of the fairy world and Thomas's place in it.

225

I frowned, picked at the skin stretched over the back of my hand. It was pale and soft, and I saw dark veins running below it. Not shining ones like the first Thomas's. "You lasted," I said.

"I did."

"How?"

It was his turn to frown. "Tom," he said, stopping under the dripping branches of a silver tree. "I chose this place. And that choice made all the difference."

"They took you. How was that a choice?" My voice cracked. I didn't even remember what my mother's voice sounded like. How could I know if I preferred it to the Queen's?

"Hush," Thomas said. "Do not draw their attention. Two of us together is like to create a tear in their space-time continuum." His lip twitched into a grin, but I did not understand the jest.

I quieted, realizing that my cheeks were hot and my chest tight. "How did you choose?"

"I left. I escaped from their hold and wandered the world on my own. I loved and sang. I – "

He continued, but all I heard was that he had escaped. I interrupted him. "Tell me how. How did you free yourself?"

Pausing, the first Thomas took my face in his hands. "How old are you? Thirteen? Twelve?"

I nodded, although I had no idea.

"Use the weapons you have, Thomas," he told me.

"I don't have any."

He tapped his long fingers against my temples. "You do." He leaned in and kissed my eyelids. Then he pulled me so that my cheek rested against his.

But I actually prefer the original, less developed version.

. . .

I killed Hop with my own salt tears and the hawthorn wand with which it chased off the grims and goblins. I ran away on the longest night, when all the old ones and ugly ones, the shining and dancing ones, huddled away from the Hunt. When it crashed over our hill, I caught onto the edges of the wild magic and sailed away with the howling and screaming.

Since that night I've killed five others, though none of the old ones. And until I manage that, the Hops of the world will continue to take children.

. . .

We walk into the river, me slowly, him guiding me. I pretend to panic. He tugs, and muscles stand out on his arm. His glamour is falling away, and his hair looks stringy and coarse. He is taller, longer, and walking on his bare toes. I cry out, and he laughs. It sounds like a horse's whinny. He dives into the water and drags me under. I hold my breath and don't have to fake the panic anymore. I dig in with my feet, but his pull is inexorable and we go farther and farther under. My only relief is that I know he will not eat me until I am dead and the water softens me. Water horses are like crocodiles.

I twist, sliding my free hand into my jeans. The salt is soaked but still potent, because this is not truly running water thanks to slow rains and man-made dams. It is gritty between my fingers. My feet leave the bottom of the river as the water horse hauls me into deeper water. I put the grains of salt to the place where our hands touch and he jerks still. I am free, and my lungs burn as I slide the wand out of my sleeve. The water horse's face lengthens and he snarls at me, bones changing and skin rough with newly sprouting hair. He snaps at me with razor teeth and reaches with his arms, with fingers growing together and thickening into black hooves. I do not swim backwards but dive at him and put the hawthorn wand to his neck. He freezes, and I think for a moment that I might force him to the surface and ask him three questions he'll have to answer truthfully. It could lead me to the nearest prince. But the risk is too great now that he knows what I am.

I shove the wand up through his throat and into his brain.

Black blood billows out and I wrench my wand free. I kick away, hanging in the water, lungs crushing for air, and watch the water horse die.

I close my eyes then and hang suspended in the cold river, thinking of all the long years of life the creature had had. Since before the city had been built, probably.

It is quiet in the water. But I cannot breathe, so I swim to the surface.

HEART-SHAPED BOX

by Maggie Stiefvater

This is another of those stories that I really wish I'd written. Maggie rarely resorts to full-on bleak, but the world of York St. James is bleak. The thing is, no matter how much I wish this one were mine, I couldn't have written it. I already know that my attempt would have just turned out sarcastic or overly slick, too pragmatic and mean and sociopathic. The winning component to this is that despite all the griminess and the violence and the selfishness, this story is so unbearably sad. —Brenna

One of the best and worst things about writing a million and one stories in a short period of time is that you have to invent hundreds more people than you would normally have to in a novel. Even though the characters are only appearing in your life for a few hours and only living on a page for two thousand words, they still have to have entire lives. Friends, families, cars that need oil changes, couches with backstories, reasons for why they turned out the way they did. Moreover, you only have a few paragraphs to establish these facts. You're a painter doodling angels on the head of a pin, and you need to leave room for the angel's plot and world as well. Sometimes, in the doodling of these angels, I realize that I've hit upon people I want to find out more about. Sometimes I don't realize it at the time. It's only months later when they're still haunting me that I write them into a novel. Sometimes I don't realize it all, only in retrospect, when I look back at a character and realize that I have used them again in a novel — they were a question that I never answered for myself.

The central relationship in this story — the one between York St. James and Jude — is the direct ancestor of a relationship that I wrote about in Linger, years later (Jude didn't keep his name, but York St. James nearly did, becoming Cole St. Clair). I've always been fascinated by leadership and by power and talent and how that affects the most intense of friendships, how it unbalances them or how it doesn't. This story was my playground, my workshop, for that. —Maggie

This new world was a vicious, sleek world made of streetlights and tight jeans, sharp smiles and fast cars. This was a city, edited. A city pared down to its bare minimums, beautiful and abusive.

Sharp as a bloody knife, and I didn't think there was a place for me in it anymore until someone said my name.

"York St. James?" A hand on my arm made me jerk away, survival instinct kicking in before I could help myself. The guy didn't seem offended; he just looked at my face like I was his personal Jesus. "Dude. Dude. You're still alive. York St.-freaking-James is still alive. Is that your freaking guitar? Oh my God. You still have it."

I cocked my head and looked at him. He wasn't chubby, but he was soft, softer than me with my tight blue jeans and scar-covered arms and shaved head. My eyes dropped to his nails: smooth, unlined. Then to skin of his hands: pink and healthy. I stopped thinking about the switchblade in my pocket. "Yeah. I'm alive."

"Dude. You have to play for my club. Tell me yes. Dude, you haven't been playing, have you? Why haven't I heard you? Where's the rest of The Wicked?"

I didn't know, but I said, "Dead." It was as good a guess as any.

He made a face, sort of like a snarl, weird in his soft face. "Whatever. We'll find you a band."

· · ·

That was how it started. He found me a band amongst the sleek survivors, a drummer, a bassist, a keyboardist. And another guitarist, Jude, whose angry chords made my guitar sound like an angel. We rocked even more than The Wicked, because now our sound was the lean, savage sound of the aftermath. And we had what the people wanted, because what they wanted was to escape.

The gigs started to run together like they had before, and onstage it was easy to pretend that the city was almost the same. People knew my face and my name again, and they screamed it when I led the band onto the stage. If the crowd was thinner, well, it was easy to think there were more people waiting beyond the door.

It was only between gigs that the world was changed. Nights without gigs, Jude and I would leave the apartment that the band members shared, and we'd go in search of food and new gigs. We left the Porsches and the Hummers and the Maseratis parked on the street, because the fact that we had them reminded us of the people who used to.

When we walked under orange streetlights, there were the clues to our changed city. There were the cheap cars with flat tires from sitting too long, abandoned for something better by the side of the road. There were the people you saw: they were the strong, the cunning, the wicked, the rich. I hadn't seen gray hairs in months. I hadn't seen children in years.

LIKE THE REST ⟵ OF MY GENERATION, I LOVE COMING UP WITH FAKE BAND NAMES.

IT NEVER MADE COMING UP WITH A NAME FOR MY REAL BANDS ANY EASIER, THOUGH.

And then there were the locket sellers. They sat on the sidewalk, the streetlights reflecting off the silver boxes at their feet. Lockets, they were called, and the chill from them stretched all the way to the street where Jude and I walked by. On hot nights condensation gathered on the lockets like so many tears.

Jude always looked away, his jaw set. But I didn't. I always counted the boxes. And when we got back to the apartment, I locked myself in the bathroom and carved a line in my skin for every locket I'd counted. The blood bubbled up behind my razor and streaked down my arm, and I felt less like the walking dead.

I wrote a song about the lockets. I called it "Carnivore."

. . .

Jude was the first to notice the lines on my fingernails, even before I did. One night at a gig at Club Metallic, I saw him look to my hands during a riff, waiting for his cue. My guitar wailed higher, but his eyes didn't look away. He missed his cue.

And I knew it had started. The dying.

After the show, in the dark brown room behind the stage, Martin the bass player jerked me aside, his fingers tight around my shoulder. "You didn't tell us you weren't Made."

I shrugged as if his hand didn't bruise. "You didn't ask."

"Hell, man," said Kell, the drummer. "You've got to get a locket."

THIS WAS THE IMAGE I STARTED THIS STORY WITH, JUST THESE BOXES + A SONG BY HEAD AUTOMATICA ON MY IPOD

Martin rammed a fist into my chest, pushing me up against the wall. My guitar crashed to the ground behind me, the strings ringing dully. "Even York-rich-as-God-St. James doesn't have the money for a locket. So you gonna come after one of us? We gonna have to sleep with one eye open?"

"You don't take your hands off me, slick," I said, "You won't live long enough to worry about sleeping."

EVERYONE HAS A BACKSTORY

↓

Esp. in a Maggie story.

Either Martin remembered my police record or he thought that Jude, coming closer with his guitar case held at a warning angle, might come to my defense. We were all of us dangerous these days. In any case, he let me go and flashed me a smile that wasn't one. "You're too good at what you do to die, asshole. So find a heart, just not one of ours."

Jude looked at me as Martin left, saying more with that look than Martin had with all his words. I dropped my eyes to the pale white lines in my fingernails. Innocent-looking half-moons, like the one that hung in the New York sky above the club. But nothing was innocent in this world.

. . .

No one knew where the disease had come from. Well, scientists said birds, later, but they always say birds when they don't know what they're talking about. In a month, a hundred thousand people were dead before we even knew they were sick. Fingernails lined with faint moons. Fingertips fading to blue, hands going white.

I'd watched Eva throw up in between gigs, vomiting away her singing voice, and then her smile, and then her guts. I hadn't kissed her in months, but I knew I'd been exposed, because everyone had been exposed. Everyone had been exposed, and we were all waiting to die.

I drew lines in my skin with my razor, watching my blood escape, wondering if the disease escaped with it.

No one knew who first found out about the hearts. There were cultures that believed to eat your enemy was to conquer him completely and to take on his strength. We were that culture now. They'd found the fountain of youth, and it was a human heart.

Suddenly the survival rate looked better.

I wrote a song. "Fifty Percent."

. . .

It took weeks for me to realize that I wasn't the only one throwing up between sets. I walked in on Jude leaning on the toilet after one of our gigs, his eyelids flickering like the fluorescent lights above us.

"Weakling," I scoffed.

Jude didn't raise his cheek from the seat, but he smiled at me. "You should know."

"How long?" I asked.

He shook his head, just a little bit. "I don't know. York, get a locket."

I just stared at him. Jude, who couldn't even look at them. "You said once there were children in those boxes."

Jude closed his eyes. "I know I did. But they're already dead. You're not."

"I couldn't afford one even if I wanted to." I slid down the wall and leaned back against the tile, watching the pulse in my wrist. "And if I could, you'd deserve it more than me."

He opened his eyes. "Don't stop being an asshole now, York."

. . .

I knew this was my last gig. Club Metallic again, which seemed fitting. My guitar was heavy on my back, sharp against my shoulder blades. In the dirty brown room behind the stage, I leaned it against a wall and drank a bottle of water. Drowning the nausea was the only thing that worked.

The guys who were there already were looking at me, eyes darting to me and away. I was the razor now, cutting them.

"Where's Jude?" I asked.

Martin knelt to get something from his bass case, and then he turned to me. His voice was strung tight, savage and bitter. "He wanted me to give this to you."

He held up a silver case, condensation on the outside, and Jude within.

STORIES AS NOVEL PLAYGROUNDS

One of the great things about writing a whole (whole, whole) bunch of stories for Merry Fates is that it occasionally gives a short piece the chance to develop into something bigger. Over the years, the blog has been a place to try out some of my stranger, more complicated ideas, and by actually writing them out I can understand them better and then decide if they have the potential to sustain themselves for the long haul.

In the earliest stages of a novel, my ideas almost never arrive in the form of plot. For me, it's often just the narrow slice of a world or a set of characters that keeps coming back in various ways. While not directly connected, "The Bone Tender," "Girls Raised by Wolves," and "Power of Intent" all take place in a common world, with recurring themes that play out in different ways. This doesn't mean that every shared character or the storyline is destined to make it into a novel, but it's a way of figuring out what belongs in the larger story and what's expendable. —Brenna

When we began Merry Fates, I wouldn't have understood this on a practical level. Now I do

I think that's pretty true of me as well—that idea that my novels never arrive with a plot. Really, I come up with my next novel the same way I decide what to watch at a movie theater. I never say "Oh, you know what I want to watch? A story about a man facing his childhood fears by dressing up in the guise of a bat and fighting crime in an urban area." I just think, "I'd like to watch a character-driven action adventure movie!" My novels are the same way—I get this idea that I'd like to toy with a certain theme or mood or world, rather than a distinct plot or agenda. I don't want to say that I play with these things in a short story to see if I can sustain them in a novel, because I have a theory you can sustain just about anything in a novel if you really try hard enough, but I will say that trying it out in short form ensures that something about the concept is asking questions that I actually want to answer. Both Shiver and The Scorpio Races began life as short stories; in the first I was playing with mood, and in the second I was playing with the world. —Maggie

In the beginning I assumed I couldn't write short stories, and so all of the stories I posted on Merry Fates were somehow connected to some novel idea I had. They were vignettes or character studies or fairy tale retellings. Sometimes they worked as stories on their own and sometime . . . didn't. As we wrote more and more stories, I had to figure out where to find ideas that could bloom on their own, divorced from novel thoughts and from the way I develop novels (an entirely character-based process). Because of that, I tried very hard not to let my stories have anything at all to do with novels I was writing or novels I knew I wanted to write. I didn't give myself this playground, I gave myself boundaries! Of course, my subconscious didn't pay attention to that order, and many of the stories I wrote I can see now are part of a pattern of exploring all the thematic issues I write novels about. Not to mention the world-building. Lately, I've stopped pretending I don't use Merry Fates to openly play inside a world so that I can investigate all its edges

I'm quite good at lying to myself (And to others...)

238

and figure out what works and what doesn't, and what aspect I should focus a novel on. It's impossible to separate my stories and novels these days, even if that isn't apparent from the outside. Stories and novels come from the same place and use basically the same skill set, just with different framing. —Tessa

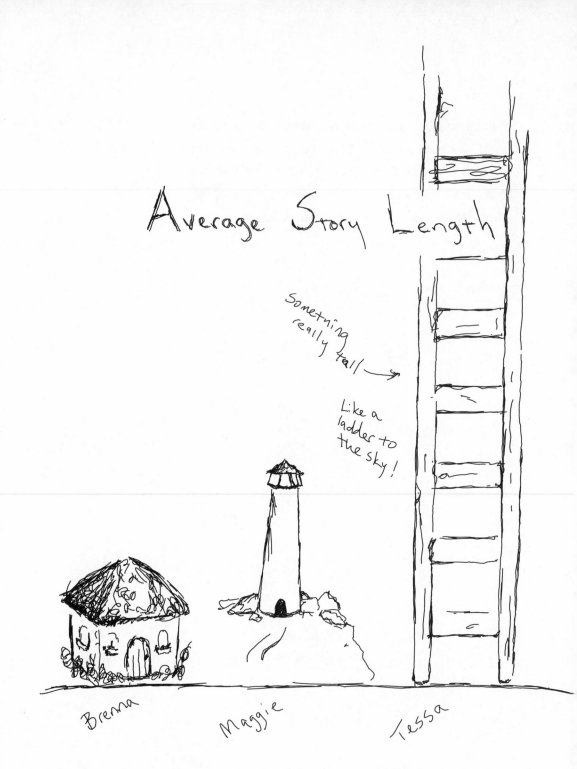

Average Story Length

Something really tall →

Like a ladder to the sky!

Brenna

Maggie

Tessa

BERSERK

by Tessa Gratton

I might be obsessed with berserker warriors. (Might be = definitely am.) The idea that the hand of God can send you into a killing frenzy is so terrible and awesome that I've written entire novels about it. I have control issues that make me feel crazy in crowds and dislike airplanes, so to me, going berserk is The Worst Thing Ever. Not only aren't you in control, but you, like, kill everything in sight. This short story happened because I was wondering about a random footnote character in one of my novels and because I've wondered what might make somebody choose to be a berserk. What might make it a GOOD thing? When is that loss of self and sense and control maybe the BEST possible thing?

I don't know if there's really an answer for that, but writing this story was a way for me to try and figure it out.

And also: trolls and motorcycles and gore. —Tessa

"These are a few of my favorite things!"

* I have written a whole novel about this now.

LISTEN! [†]

They say the stars spread so bright that night on the mountain that the young berserk looked to the west and saw a narrow road cutting between the tall pine trees. Fate whispered in his ears, and he chose at the last moment to steer his motorcycle along a new, twisting route through the Rock Mountains toward that new band of bear warriors awaiting him in Washington State. For he was in no hurry to arrive, to swear his allegiance to a new captain when his first band had so lately been destroyed. The three-day battle against ice giants entrenched at the edge of Lake Eerie had stripped his commit-brothers to bones until he alone stood. For the month since he'd been home with his mother in Dodge City, Kansas, to make proper sacrifices and come to terms with survival.

It was a column of silvery smoke carved against those bright stars that drew him off the road. His tires crushed the beds of pine needles to fill the air with sharp evergreen, and there appeared a clearing where a girl was busy flinging items into a burning house.

A brown box splayed torn and open next to her feet, and she kept bending to dig inside, pulling out a Stoneball cap, a trophy, an old book, and worn shoes. With a grunt she heaved them, one after the other, in a high arc toward the bonfire.

Swiftly he cut the bike's engine and ran to her, thinking first that she was trollkin, with her bared teeth and dark skin and roaring. But she was just a girl throwing family heirlooms onto a funeral pyre.

[†] Many Anglo-Saxon poems begin with the word "hwæt" (rhymes with "hat.") It's generally translated as "listen."

242

LUTA:

Here's what happens:

We're watching reruns of *Star Trek*. My brother Horn keeps adjusting the antennas to get a better signal. Captain Kirk's face flickers constantly until Mom throws up her hands and says, "This is ridiculous. We should play Shield instead."

As if Fate agrees, the mountain trembles beneath us.

Dad is instantly on his feet, braids swinging as he turns toward the front of the cabin.

My sister Alecia grips my hand. I pull away and follow Dad, leaving Alecia and Mom and Horn in the den. In the entryway, Dad pushes aside his All-Warm fleece jacket to grab his battle hammer off the hook drilled into the wall. He presses his ear to our thick wooden door.

"Dad?" I whisper, hands clenching. I wish I had weapon to push all my fear into.

"Go back to your mother, Luta. Send your brother to me."

"What is it?"

"Luta, listen—"

The earth shakes again, and this time the rumble doesn't stop. Dad slams the bar down over the door. I've only ever seen it lowered once before, when I was five and the Fenris Wolf was rumored to be loose on our mountain.

Hammer in hand, Dad backs up, pushing me along with him away from the door. Guttural howls echo

outside. "All the lights," Dad snaps, and we split up. He heads around toward the kitchen, flipping off switches and shuttering windows.

Eventually I return to the den, where Mom's already closed everything. Horn now stands in the middle of the room with his hammer in hand and Alecia with a hatchet pressing her back into his. The skin around my sister's lips is tight and gray with fear. I run past, into the back of the house where the bedrooms are, flipping off more lights and tugging the blinds closed. If they don't see us, they may flow past the house like a flooding river around deep-rooted trees. But I can still hear them coming, louder now—their bellowing shakes the window glass. There are screams like metal tearing into metal and the crash of pine trees ripped up and slammed into the ground. The herd rolls closer like a storm, tearing down the mountain.

I am back in the entryway, almost all the way around to my family in the den, when the front door explodes inward. A heavy silhouette crams into the doorway. I smell his rancid breath from the foot of the loft stairs. I freeze. Sometimes trolls have poor eyesight, and maybe he doesn't see me.

His mouth smacks as he stomps in, spiked club dragging over the welcome mat. Behind him are more. One calls in their language. It sounds like rocks crunching together.

The troll before me chuckles. "Little girl," he says as more of his fellows shove inside.

My father yells from the den, and I clamber up the stairs to the little loft where I sleep. The troll tries to follow me, but the rickety old wood gives beneath his weight and the entire staircase collapses. He crashes back to the floor. Thin blue carpeting holds the shattered steps together, and they dangle for a moment before the troll rips it all free in frustration. There is more trollish laughter—in the dark I can't tell how many press behind him. I huddle at the top step, my knees pulled tight to my chest, desperate to remember if there are weapons in my loft.

Wood splinters as they break open the den wall into a troll-sized arch.

My sister screams.

"Alecia!" I scream back. But I'm trapped. The stairs are broken, and my troll waits at the bottom, thick hands grasping at me as though he imagines what it will be like to pull my body apart.

Dad yells something, and Horn roars. Mom cries, and a horrible crunching sound cuts her off. Trolls laugh. I stare my troll, every piece of me shaking. His thick teeth gleam in the stray moonlight spilling down from behind me.

I close my eyes, but it makes things worse because I can hear my family fighting; I can hear the crash of the entertainment center and imagine Alecia's body crumpled and broken and sliding to the floor. I imagine their breaking bones and splatters of blood, because I've seen old black-and-white pictures of the Montreal Troll Wars.

There's nothing I can do.

I hold myself in a tight ball, and I open my eyes to stare down at the troll because a face like his will be the last face my family sees before they die. I have to give them that much, to see what they see. And I tell myself over and over again: At least they are together. At least they die in action, fighting and brave. At least.

The troll wiggles his fingers at me, beckoning. I only stare through the darkness. Another troll suddenly appears from the den and punches my troll in the shoulder. Clenched in that heavy fist is Alecia's torn sweater. A trail of blood squeezes through his fingers. My stomach rolls over.

"Little girl!" my troll coaxes, "come down, come down. I'll catch you." He makes his voice tender, like he's speaking to a little lamb or a trollkin. His companions drag him out. They're leaving.

The loft shudders as the herd of them hurtles away, making the mountain tremble.

I am left in silence.

LISTEN!

They say that Rein Konrsson had to pin her arms down and drag her away from the fire, dodging her teeth and the harsh jabs of her heels against his shins. "Calm down, kid!" he yelled into her ear.

She froze when she heard his voice, his New Asgardian tongue. Rein was just able to settle her on a boulder and step back out of her reach. In the cold starry night, she wore only jeans and a long, tattered sweater. She had no shoes, but only thick wool socks, and the rows of braids on her head ended in beads red and bright as blood. Her eyes were pink and teary— from smoke or fury or grief he had no way to know.

They say he asked what a kid like her was doing alone at a burning house, and that second time he called her a child she growled, "I am almost fourteen. Not a kid."

And so, swallowing the wish that he'd ignored the ribbon of smoke and stuck to his lonely path, Rein gritted his own teeth to say, "I am Rein, son of Konr. I was riding past when I saw the fire beckon."

Her chin lifted bravely as she declared, "I am Luta, and my family is dead." Her eyes slid toward the fire, and its red glare reflected in her dark pupils.

It was then that Rein Konrsson noticed the shattered glass twinkling across the yard. The old Veedub van with its doors torn off the frame and windshield smashed. Giant footsteps through crushed herbs in a box garden. And he smelled it under the acrid smoke: the sweet, cloying smell of mud and shit that signaled trolls had passed this way.

LUTA:

I watch the older boy stand up slowly and walk toward my house. He bends down over the box I dragged from the shed. One of Alecia's old stuffed wolves is on top, and he lifts it out. With a graceful flick of his arm, Rein tosses it into the fire.

I run back, and together we throw every memory away. It's the middle of the night, but the burning house keeps away mountain cold and most of all the darkness. It flickers over his face, obscuring his features and making his eyes black. I hope mine are that fierce.

When the box is empty, we tear it in two and creep as close to the heat as we can. My skin tightens and my eyes burn. I step in again. And again. The fire reaches for me, and I feed it the cardboard. I keep my eyes wide open, feeling them burn, feeling tears stream out onto my cheeks and dry there.

Rein says something, and I stumble back, landing on my butt. He stands behind me and lifts my up by my armpits. "Let the Aesir welcome them. They are summoned home."

"And fire lights the way," I whisper.

As dawn beings to fight against the orange glow, I wrap my arms around myself and remember the troll that reached for me. I want to tear the beast into a million pieces.

"Rein," I say, glancing up at him, to tell him I want blood-price for my family.

He looms nearer, and when he tilts his head to reply, for the first time I see the black spear tattoo slashing down his cheek.

"Berserk!" I spit it out before I think.

His grin is swift and full of teeth. "I promise not to eat you."

The ground is spinning. He's one of the Alfather's—a wild, dangerous berserker warrior who can kill a dozen men in a minute, with all his braids intact.

Now I notice the scuffed leather armor holding to his body like it was painted on. The steel-toed boots. The bracers. The heads of the battle-axes peeking at me from over his shoulders. But he's young. Only as old as Horn is.

As old as Horn was.

My stomach churns. What does it mean, a berserk showing up at my family's funeral pyre? What sign? I want it to be Fate sending me the tool of my revenge. As I stare at him, his grin fades. I plant my fists on my hips to answer, "I would be stringy and tough."

He agrees with me. His chin jerks toward his bike. "I'll take you someplace safe. Do you have family nearby? Which way did the trolls go, do you know?"

I suck air in through my teeth. The cold aches, but it keeps me from thinking of Alecia. "They went down the mountain, west and south."

LISTEN!

They say the mountain watched as the motorcycle sped down the road, east and north. From the shadows between red-barked pine trees and from beneath broken boulders where the sun never reached, thin spirits focused eyes and attention onto the berserk and the girl. At a junction of two old roads, the berserk circled his bike wide to avoid passing across the face of the crossroads shrine, hoping evade to the mountain's interest. But the girl remembered pausing there with her family, to lay down a broken telephone dressed with red ribbons and ask the ancient mountain spirits to protect them. The elves and lesser trolls loved bits of technology to shape and reform, her mother had said in a hushed voice, and maybe even just for play. Her father let her uncork the honey wine and pour libations into the dirt, let her turn the whole bottle over while the golden liquid glugged out.

Remembering, the girl pressed her face against Rein's back, finding space for her nose between the long handles of his battle-axes. Her arms wrapped around him, fingers clutching each other across his chest as if he were the only thing holding her onto the middle world. Her braids whipping back, beads slapping together in the fierce wind as Rein drove.

They say he could feel her squeezing his ribs, and he understood that the little thing grasped onto him because if she let go she might fade into a wisp of smoke and ashes.

Clouds rolled in, and as the first misty rain descended they pulled off the road to shelter in the lee of a giant boulder.

Damp air clung to the underside of the rock, but they tucked themselves against it, shoulder to shoulder. Rein tied a clean sock around the tear on her palm until the bleeding slowed and stopped. He made her drink an entire bottle of water from under the buddy seat and fed her a granola bar. She crammed the whole thing into her mouth and chewed with it stuffed into her cheeks like a squirrel.

He did not complain, for being the only survivor had made him hungry, too.

LUTA:

I finish the food and drink, and Rein nods. He leans his head back against the rough boulder and closes his eyes.

Like him, I close my eyes.

And I am back in the loft, I am hugging my legs against my chest, waiting to die. I can smell blood. The door to the den hangs from the top hinge like a flap of skin. The starlight fills the air with a quiet glow.

Slowly I stretch my legs, wincing at the ache of blood rushing back into them. I don't know how long I've been crouched, looking down the broken stairs. Wondering if they're really gone, or if my troll waits for me outside. But I can't hide forever. What if Mom is still gasping for breath? What if Horn is alive?

I crab-crawl down the top three stairs, the only ones left, because I can't bear to turn my back to the front door. At the edge I hang my legs down. It's only seven or so feet. I can drop.

So I force myself around, sliding down until my stomach presses into the jagged edge of the stairs. My arms shake from the effort of lowering my body slowly. I remind myself to keep my muscles loose when I fall, to crumple and roll. I pray to Thor Thunderer that I will land safely and not impale myself on the sharp stakes of broken stairs awaiting me.

I drop.

My bones jar and my head snaps, catching the tip of my tongue. Blood spurts down my chin. I sit, dazed for a moment, while pain burns up my left arm from a gash on my palm. Otherwise I'm all right. My ankles ache, and my butt too, but nothing bad. I struggle to my feet, and my socks slip on a plank of wood.

Scrambling up, I dash to the den and shove the broken door aside. The harsh creak makes my ears ring.

The den is destroyed.

Window glass glitters everywhere. The sofa has been gutted, and the dull white cotton fluff hangs in the air. Paralyzed in time. Unreal. Impossible.

It is worse than I imagined. Their eyes hang wide, mouths agape like desiccated roadkill. Bright shards of bone jut up where their hearts were torn free and eaten.

My heart has been eaten, too.

Everything is so cold and quiet except for the flicker of rage, of the keen building in my throat. The feeling reminds me of fire. I get kerosene from the shed and douse everything. The stink makes me puke into Mom's herb bed, stomach acid smelling suddenly like mint and dill.

It is the smell of revenge. The only thing that can give my heart life again.

In the cold, damp shelter with the berserk, I open my eyes. Rein Konrsson radiates heat. They say the berserks don't sleep and that they burn up the air around them like they're made of fire. Destroying everything in their path. Waiting to unleash the Alfather's madness on friend and enemy alike. I tilt my head and stare at his tattoo. The spear is to mark them so anyone will know to keep back. I wonder what that would be like, having that cut into my cheek. Burning there.

"What?" His eyes are closed, but somehow he knows I've been staring at him. Maybe my breathing changed.

"I was only thinking it would have been nice to be a berserk when the trolls came."

His sigh is more of a grumble. "It isn't something to wish for."

I don't believe him. "Do you hate it, then?"

Rein turns to face me, his leather armor scraping against the rocks behind us.

LISTEN!

They say that a thousand generations ago, when the ice giants ruled half the world, a man climbed a yew tree and hung himself there by his ankles. He took his spear and with a mighty jab, cut between his own ribs to pierce his heart. His screams were carried up through the yew branches, and his blood dripped far to the earth, sinking and pulling the man's need down into the roots.

Odin, the Father of All, heard.

Having once sacrificed himself to himself in such a way, Odin respected the man's courage and insanity and need. Growing to the height of a giant, Odin reached up a massive hand and lifted the hanging man out of the tree. He cradled him and asked, "Why have you done this thing, child of man?"

Through bloodstained teeth the man answered, "I give all myself to you, oh god, and ask that in return you grant me the power and strength to win my daughter back. For my family has been murdered by my enemy and my daughter snatched away."

Odin looked with his single great eye and saw that the man's heart was skewered by the spear. If it was removed, he would die. Placing the man between the roots of the yew tree, Odin cast about for aid. He found it in a wild bear, its eyes crazed with anger, its jaws wide and roaring. Coaxing the beast to him, Odin whispered promises of glory for the bear's sons if it would give its heart to the god. So it did.

With magic learned from Freya, the Feather-Flying goddess of Hel, Odin poured the bear's heart into the man.

"Go, Bear Son," the Alfather said.

Fever coursed through the man, energy like the sun's own heat giving him strength. With it he found the home of his enemy. And with it he tore through them. Wild bear's rage took hold of his limbs, keeping pain and weariness away, so that all the man knew was the whirlwind of battle.

When he woke from his rage, each of his enemies was splayed upon the earth, dead in great waves around him.

And yet so was his daughter.

For to be a berserker is to have a heart that may turn against you.

LUTA:

Rein Konrsson regards me uncertainly for a moment. "No, I don't hate what I am."

"I wish I had a bear's heart." My ribs feel tight, but not because they are too full; they are hollow. There is nothing inside. I turn away from him before he can say anything about the impossibility of girls berserking. The curse only follows the bear's sons after all. I know it. Everyone does.

Instead he only says, "The rain is letting up. We should ride on."

My wounded hand aches, and my head pounds in time with my heartbeat. Yesterday I would have complained, would have gnashed my teeth at Mom and said I needed hot chocolate with cinnamon and toast. But yesterday I was thirteen, and today I'm a hundred years old.

LISTEN!

They say as dawn broke over the horizon, the berserker's motorcycle roared around a hairpin curve coming down the mountain, then skidded in the loose gravel as Rein jerked it sideways to avoid slamming into the dying troll splayed across the road.

The girl's arms tightened around him. Rein's foot kicked up a stream of gravel as the bike curved tightly and stopped. He killed the engine and heaved several calming breaths, but the girl was off the bike in an instant, running toward the troll.

How many hours did I spend staring at pictures of motorcycles on the Internet?
□ 1   □ 13   ☒ too many

"Luta," he called, letting the bike drop as he grabbed for her and caught the hem of her sweater. She hit the gravel with a gasp and he let go. "Wait, kid, it's alive."

Huffing, the girl rolled onto her back and kicked at him so that he would step away. He held his hands out in surrender until Luta grimaced at him, climbed to her feet, and stomped off into the trees. Away from the troll.

Rein Konrsson walked fearlessly forward, a hand lifting to loosen one of the battle-axes from its cross straps. The troll's shuddering breaths sounded like wind rushing through a cave, and its dark blood snaked in a hundred tiny rivulets through the gravel, fleeing from the bulbous creature and dragging its life away. Its eyelids fluttered and it rolled green eyes at him. Crust gathered in the corners of those eyes, and bloody snot streaked across its lips. When it growled at him, Rein felt a stab of pity and wondered why the rest of the herd had left it behind.

They say it was at that moment he realized the girl had lied to him. The herd had come this way: east and north.

His gaze slid out over the valley. There were pine trees as far as he could see, broken only by the shining ribbon of a river far below. Where did the trollkin hide? Under what shadows did they settle to wait through the sunlight?

The dying troll grunted and twitched, its entire weight shifting toward him. Swift as the flick of a salmon's tail, Rein freed his axe and held it poised to strike.

I'm incapable of describing trolls without the word "bulbous."

Thank editor Andrew it's only in here once.

256

But the girl appeared from the woods with a branch as thick as the troll's arm. She stood over the troll, teeth bared, and raised it over her head. Before he could say anything, she slammed it down into the troll's face.

Rein did not stop her, even as she bashed it again and again, reducing the troll's face into a sticky pulp.

LUTA:

I fling the branch away and stand, chest heaving, eyes on Rein. I'm not sorry.

"You knew," he says quietly, so I can barely hear it over my hard breathing. "You knew they came this way."

"I knew." I lift my chin, daring him to make something of it. The stench of the dead thing rolls up, sticking to my face and neck, slinking through my hair. It's plastered to my braids, and when I turn away the smell wafts around me.

LISTEN!

They say she was a monster already.

LUTA:

I can't lift the motorcycle. The chromed steel slips from my sweaty fingers, and even when I grip the leather-wrapped handlebars it's way too heavy.

Rein takes it from me, rights it in an easy motion, and blocks me from getting on. "There will be many of them."

"How many?"

He shrugs. "You expect me to know?"

"Yeah."

"A dozen, usually."

"That's too many for you?"

"I didn't say that."

"They killed my whole entire family." I want to scream it but I don't. It's worse to just say it, like a fact. Like something I learned from a book.

He reaches forward and wipes his thumb under my left eye. It comes away dark with troll blood. "Get on. Even little girls deserve blood-price."

I don't bristle, because I can tell he's only calling me that to make himself feel better.

LISTEN!

They say it was easy to find them. They say that trolls don't travel much by daylight because their eyes are poor, that sunlight turns them into stone.

Rein felt the rage building slowly in his chest. The battle-frenzy, the need to destroy. He thought of his band, of the Bear Son warriors he should have died beside. He thought of Luta, clinging to his back, being alone, too.

They say he thought how right it was, that he had come to find her.

LUTA:

The trolls are split in two groups: most of them asleep in a grove of silver aspens, shielded from the sun, and the two biggest down by the place the river twists into a calm pool. We've snuck up, rolling the motorcycle along with us. Rein showed me how to start it in case I have to get away. He doesn't mean get away from the trolls, but from him if he loses control of his battle-rage and doesn't know me.

I am shaking behind a tree, but not from fear. I clench my hands because I want to race out screaming at them, to hammer my fists into their faces and kick in their teeth. To tear off their skin. I want to cry as I bend over them, and let my tears drop into their bleeding chests.

"Stay here," Rein whispers in my ear. "I will take their heads for you, and then we'll ride into Colorada Falls in triumph. You'll have your blood-price, and we'll both have a little glory from the kill."

I nod. I can feel my heartbeat pounding in the tip of my tongue.

My berserker warrior steps into the aspen grove with great, double-headed battle-ax in either hand. He rolls his shoulders, plants his steel-toed boots, and then grins. He winks at me over his shoulder.

Then he tilts his head back and he roars.

LISTEN!

They say that it was a swift battle.

Rein Konrsson danced with his blades, screaming a war song as he killed. There was no sense to it, no predicting the tide of motion rising within him. Axes cleaved neck from shoulder, arm from torso, cutting away chunks of flesh, digging through heavy troll hide to find death. He did not flinch when a club cracked three of his ribs or falter when his knees slammed to the ground. His axes did not lower or pause in their brutal task. Trolls fell, roaring, one after the other even as they swarmed him.

The Bear Son was surrounded. But it did not matter. He cut through them all, laughing.

LUTA:

I tremble. Rein is terrifying. I want to be in the center with him, my back pressed to his with axes in my hands, whirling and dancing the battle-rage with him.

All the trolls fall. The ground shakes as they crash, stripping branches from the pine trees. Needles shake loose and sprinkle down.

Rein slows, spinning on one foot to see that all his enemies are dead. He laughs a high-pitched, wild laugh, and his hands tighten on the axe handles. Knuckles white. He's hunting still.

I reveal myself. "Rein," I call.

His laughter fades when he sees me, his face calms. He remembers, he knows me. And he's reining back the frenzy.

My fingers flex and relax and flex, because I can't stop them from acting out my nerves. The stench of dead and dying trolls, their low groans, their hacking coughs fill the aspen grove. No birds call, no wind blows. All the animals for miles must be huddling in fear. Even the mountain is quiet as Rein restrains himself.

Finally, he meets my gaze. He smiles the same toothy grin from when he said he'd eat me.

LISTEN!

They say the wisest old troll waited until the frenzy was over. Until it was the only survivor. Waited until the berserker's back was turned, his axes lowered, his shoulders relaxed. Until he was laughing with the girl.

It walked into the ring of its dead family, footsteps masked by the groans and death-throes.

And it stabbed its spear through the berserker's back.

LUTA:

I scream.

Rein tears free and springs in a single motion, axes coming together under the troll's chin. They stand there, still, for a long moment before the troll's head tilts off its neck and lands on the pine needles with a thud.

My breath rushes out of me.

But Rein falls to his knees. His axes hit the ground, and he delicately touches the hole in his chest where the spear exited. As if the touch were a signal, blood spills around his fingers and down the old leather armor. It wanders in red streams along the weathered tooling, making patterns blossom on his chest I hadn't noticed before. A swirl of runes, the jaw of a snarling wolf, and the trefoil stamp of Odin just over his diaphragm, the house of spirit. Stained with his blood, the armor comes alive.

I run, tripping over a dead troll's arm, and skid to a stop in front of Rein. His head is level with my stomach, and he sways forward. I catch him by the shoulders. His face presses into my belly, and he grips my hips. I can't hold him up. He's too heavy. I hear his blood dripping fast onto the ground, feel it soaking into my socks. "Rein," I whisper.

My heart wasn't eaten. It wasn't torn away. I can feel it now, churning in my chest, and it isn't fair because why should this boy's dying hurt so much when I've only known him for ten hours?

We fall down together, and Rein manages to land on his shoulder instead of me. I kneel beside him. He is gasping for breath. Air whooshes out of the cavity in his chest and I'm crying. My tears drop into the tattered hole.

Rein whispers something. I pull his head onto my thigh and lean closer, my ear right at his lips. I squeeze my eyes closed as he chokes on his words. "I shall—I shall not come into—the hall . . . with—with words of fear upon my . . . lips."

It's the berserker's dying prayer.

I force my eyes open. He deserves better than for me to shy away from this death I've caused. His eyes are wide, and I meet them without flinching. They are all the colors of the forest: green pine needles, gray bark, rusty brown earth. Colors mingling in his eyes like rain has washed it all together. I pick out the colors, memorizing them. I cannot ever, ever forget his eyes.

"Gladly shall I drink . . . ale in . . ." he sucks in a shuddering breath, "in the high seat."

His eyes don't move, but I can see them focus through me. I'm not with him anymore, and he's seeing something else. Valkyrie, I hope. Riding down from the sky to take him home.

He can't finish the prayer. His mouth stops. His blood soaks hot onto my leg.

"Rein," I whisper again, seeing not only him but my brother and sister and Mom and Dad. I can finish it. His heart still beats, creeping slowly to a stop.

"The days of your life have ended," I say. "And you die with a laugh."

I kiss his lips, giving the words back into him. He is dead.

Leaning back on my heels, I wipe my hands down my thighs. Blood roars in my ears. My heart is spinning fast, and I am feverish with a burning need to destroy.

LISTEN!

They say that Luta Bearsdottir dipped her finger into the berserker's wound and with his heart's blood drew a spear down her cheek.

LAZARUS GIRL

by Brenna Yovanoff

Ever since I was little, I've been deeply fascinated by stories like "Little Red Riding Hood" and "Bluebeard"—stories where the girl faces down the psychopath and is subsequently rescued, but just barely. I loved the urgency of it, the sense of mortal danger. Mostly though, I liked that the girls in these stories were special. They had seen all the way down to the very heart of evil, nearly been seduced by it, and then lived to tell about it.

The last few years have seen me write a lot of imperiled-girl stories. I mean, a lot. They come in different forms, countless variations on the same characters and themes. In a way, it's like I've written the same story over and over, trying to get it right. And in another way, it's like I've made it my mission to find out how exactly many different stories one premise can make.

"Lazarus Girl" is a kind of culmination of all the iterations that came before it, because Rosamund has gone somewhere the other girls haven't. She's not waiting for rescue or even rescuing herself. She's already seen all there is to see. —Brenna

At first, nothing. A dry scrape of leaf, a creak and sigh of branch and twig.

The ground is frozen, feels a thousand miles away. For a long, disorienting moment she thinks she's home, lying in her bed and only dreaming that the shadows on her walls are solid, becoming trees.

The sky is low and starless above her, rolling with clouds. If it met neatly in the corners, she could almost confuse it with the ceiling.

. . .

I wasn't supposed to be there.

It was a faculty party—grad students only—but Portia Miles had heard about it from the TA in her Modern Drama class. And anyway, it was Saturday night and we were the girls who crashed the grad parties, who made shy, bookish boys ignore their dates and turn longing gazes on us instead.

The two of us were standing by the hors d'oeuvres, talking about the girl campus security had found in the woods. Or at least I was talking about the girl in the woods. Portia was picking through a dish of mixed olives, looking for the black ones. The house belonged to one of the literature professors—this tall, balding guy with a wispy goatee. He taught courses on the Romantics, and his parties were almost always catered.

"Don't you think about how she must have felt, though? When she realized what was happening?" I reached for a finger sandwich on a tiny plastic sword, which made Portia roll her eyes. I waggled the sword

I love olives. All kinds. Not just the black ones.

at her. "I mean, how can you stop thinking about it? It's so messed up!"

"Rosie," Portia said with her arms around my neck, the music swelling from seven or eight strategically placed wall speakers. "Rosie, Rosie, what are we going to do with you?"

And I laughed because I was where the night-life happened, on the inside, and we were nineteen, wicked, and warm like August, and it didn't matter that a week ago a girl had died in the little clump of scenic woods, right in middle of campus. None of the horror was ours. We were gorgeous and shocking and could always find someone to walk us home.

Out in the street it was starting to rain, the sky spitting little drops. The spray blew diagonally, spattering the windows as Portia steered me through the crowd with her hand tucked in the crook of my arm.

"Do you think the killer is out there right now?" I said, making witchy fingers in her face. "Do you think he's prowling the streets like Jack the Ripper, in a wool coat and a top hat?"

"Rosie, be good," she said. "Don't go around freaking everyone out with the morbid talk."

And I nodded but knew I'd do it anyway. When it was a choice between the small talk or the crazed killers, the choice was not really a choice at all.

I kissed her on the cheek and then slipped into the crowd in search of a promising conversationalist. Someone lonely, shy. Easily rattled. They were a dime a dozen in the English department.

I wound my way through impeccably disheveled rooms. Stylishly obscure books were stacked two deep on all the shelves, and the furniture was artfully mismatched. I made the rounds, stopping occasionally to insinuate myself into a debate or a conversation. In the kitchen, a tall, shaggy-haired boy wearing a battered wool blazer that was too short in the sleeves was holding forth on feminist readings of pre-twentieth century works, but when he asked my opinion on portrayals of women in Shakespeare and I saw the unfortunate state of his teeth, I smiled vaguely and moved on. I'd know my quarry when I saw him. Someone shy and wistful—easily separated from the herd.

He was standing alone by the unlit fireplace, holding a highball glass like he didn't know what to do with it. He was perfect and had the saddest eyes. The line of his jaw was so delicate it made me want to bite him.

There was an oil painting over the mantle, and I'd used it to meet people plenty of times. It was a decent reproduction of a piece by one of the less-infamous Pre-Raphaelites, set in a heavy frame, and it always gave me the perfect opening.

"I was named after her," I said, coming up beside him.

He glanced up, flinching when he saw me there, so close I was nearly touching him. It was a look I'd learned to love—the one that says, *Beautiful girl, I am terrified of you. I am in painful, staggering awe of you.*

"Oh," he said, backing away. He almost whispered it. "Rosamund's a pretty name."

"No it isn't. I mean, the first half is. Did you know that Eleanor of Aquitaine murdered her? She caught Rosamund sleeping with her husband and gave her a choice between poison or stabbing. Or else she had her beheaded or drowned her in the tub or something."

He shook his head, avoiding my eyes. "That's just a story, though. Rosamund Clifford died in a nunnery."

It wasn't the way the script was supposed to go. He was supposed to be impressed by my brashness, not lecture me on actual facts, but I played it off, making my eyes narrow, looking suggestive and bored. "Did she die of sexual frustration, then?"

He blushed deeply a beat too late, turning his head to the side, showing me only a well-shaped ear, one reddened cheekbone. "Of natural causes."

"There's nothing natural about celibacy. Aren't you going to tell me your name?"

"Bryce," he said with his hand held out, not to shake, but like he wanted to rest it on my arm and was too shy.

I smiled demurely, grazing my bottom lip with my teeth, and moved closer.

. . .

Under the dead leaves at the base of the buckeye tree, she rolls over. Then, with the grace of a sleepwalker, she shakes off the layer of debris and gets to her feet.

The woods are silent and bare, and the grass at her feet is brittle with frost. In the dark she is a chilling sight, with long, matted hair and dirt under her nails.

Her steps are unsteady, gait made uneven by the lumpy, frozen ground and one missing shoe.

She picks her way down the footpath, back toward the lake. The night is cold, but her breath doesn't hang in the air, and if she feels the chill, she doesn't show it. There's something so lovely in her face, so lost. She has been lonely all her life, but never so fully or so truly as she is tonight.

. . .

The Botticelli knockoff was bad. The brushwork was too heavy, and the colors reminded me of a circus. It depicted the martyrdom of Saint Sebastian, and I was forced to admit that yes, there could be such a thing as too many arrows.

We stood looking up at it. The recessed lighting made faint halos around our heads, and Bryce put down his drink like he was about to say something, gesturing vaguely. Sebastian's body was pierced in six places, but in his beatific ecstasy, he was one millimeter off from smiling.

"That's the way to go," Bryce said. He said it solemnly, without irony. "No old age, no fading into obscurity. People remember a really dramatic death."

I let myself drift closer—closer—until the backs of our hands were touching. "He's so . . . isolated though, like he's on stage. I mean, everyone's looking at him, but no one can know what he's feeling. Do you think he's lonely?"

How many art history classes have I taken, you ask? To which I answer, lots. And it was there that I learned I kind of love Botticelli.

269

Bryce shrugged, taking his hand back, glancing away. "Are you talking about the painting or the man?"

"Does it matter? Maybe I was talking about the saint. I mean, what's the difference?"

"Only one of those things is real, though. He was a man, but the painting and the saint are just impressions, the way other people saw him, and not how he actually was."

"Do you think people ever actually know each other?"

He twitched his shoulders and swallowed. "Do people even really know themselves?"

I looked up at Sebastian, martyred by arrows. I supposed that some people did know. Portia did, I was almost sure. But I couldn't say with any real authority that I knew myself.

I turned my back on Bryce and Sebastian, watching the pseudo-intellectuals in their hipster glasses. The grad-school girls weren't flirting, weren't dancing, weren't anything. They just sat around the crowded living room, waiting for someone to take pity on them and start a conversation.

I finished my drink and turned to face Bryce again. "Did you hear about the girl in the woods?"

He nodded. The question wasn't particularly original. Everyone had heard about the girl in the woods. "Nothing concrete really, but students were talking about it in my European Masters seminar."

He said *students* the way a person would say *convicts*, or *hookworms*, like they were so beneath him.

Like he wasn't one, even though last time I looked, grad student still had the word *student* attached to it.

"Was she poisoned?" he said, and I knew that he was teasing me about Rosamund. "Stabbed? Drowned in the tub?"

I shook my head, trying to convey the awful weight of the girl in the tree, her empty death, her aloneness. Trying to convey all the ways that this was not a joke. The blunt, factual nature of her demise made something shudder deep inside me, and when I pretended to Portia or to myself that the dark stuff couldn't touch me, that was a lie. I'd been waking up from nightmares since the day they found her, rope knotted around her neck and hands tied. There was nothing else to say about her. The known facts were spare and arbitrary. A dead girl found hanging in a tree, without rhyme or reason, no explanation and no story.

Bryce sighed like he was humoring me. "How did she die?"

"Hung," I said. "Hanged. Whatever. She was out in the woods behind the lake, in that big buckeye tree."

"Did you know her?"

I shook my head.

"Did you see her, then? Did you find the body or something?"

"No, but I went out to look after they took it down."

Bryce raised his eyebrows, smiling for the first time. "A little ghoulish, don't you think?"

I didn't disagree.

He reached to set his drink on the low, glass-topped

coffee table, watching me intently, and there was a need in his face that I recognized. It was the same half-buried hunger I saw in my own face. An emptiness that never seemed to show in photographs, but which was uncomfortably visible every time I studied myself in the mirror.

All at once, I knew what I wanted. What I would do. It would be this thing we'd have, a raw, poignant bond, and once it was in place, he'd see me through the lens of this one shared thing. We would have our moment of unfailing connection, and everyone else would be outside it.

"Come on," I said, reaching for his hand. "I'll show you."

. . .

There is a light in the window—the one he pointed to from the street before they left the safety of the pavement and started into the woods. Now she stands looking up, captivated by the warm rectangle above her. The light and the promise of warmth pull at her. They draw her like a flame, her face moth-white, her lips a cool, lifeless blue.

. . .

We found our coats in the pile on the bed and went out through the kitchen. I looked for Portia before we left, but she was working her magic on a cluster of lit. majors, and I didn't interrupt her.

Down in the street the rain had let up, but the

asphalt was slick, reflecting the streetlights in smeared pools.

We headed in the direction of the lake, and Bryce reached for my hand but chickened out at the last minute, letting his fingers brush lightly against my sleeve, then fall again.

As we crossed the quad, he walked faster, and I had to scramble to keep up, scuffing my feet along the sidewalk to keep my ballet flats from slipping off. Brick apartments rose on either side of us, picturesque and shabby.

"I live up there," he said, and when he pointed, I knew that after our foray into the woods we'd come back here, newly allied, and we'd climb the three flights to his tiny TA-salary apartment, where he'd suggest brandy or coffee or Parcheesi, and he'd let me stay. We'd sit together on the couch and talk about art and philosophy. About the girl in the woods.

Later, I would put my glass down, lean toward him, and kiss him before he could demur. He'd be pleasantly startled, grateful even. He would treat me like he knew how much I mattered.

The path into the woods was narrow but easy to find if you knew where to look, and everyone did. It was the quickest way to get from one side of campus to the other, and the path was worn hard and bare by so many feet. Now, though, it was late and dark and empty. Only a fool would go into the woods at night with a strange man. Only a fool would lead the way.

. . .

Shock! I do not actually know what Parcheesi is or how one plays, but it sounds hilarious.

She mounts the steps with plodding dignity. Her remaining shoe is made of silk, muddy now and in tatters, the sole pulling away from the upper. Her bare foot taps out a soft patting rhythm as she climbs the stairs. The rustle of her dress sounds like a drawn breath, but she is not breathing.

. . .

We stood in the shadow of the buckeye tree, looking up. In the daylight you'd be able to see the dusty mark where the rope had been looped and knotted around the branch, but at night even that was invisible, no proof at all that anything terrible had happened.

In the dark I could feel Bryce watching me. "This is it? What you wanted to show me?"

His tone was polite, but disappointed, like I'd promised him fireworks and delivered a burnt match. I nodded, feeling childish suddenly. Pointless. We were here, in the very location of horror and tragedy, and still it meant nothing.

Bryce started to speak again, then cut himself off. I couldn't see his expression, but the angle of his head seemed like he might be watching me with actual pity.

"Sorry," I told him, trying to sound casual, unbothered by how ordinary everything seemed, suddenly. "I don't know what I was thinking. I thought it was going to be better."

"Don't apologize," he said in a solemn voice. "I

should be thanking you. It's funny, but I'm glad you brought me out here."

"Why? It was a stupid idea. It's not even like the place is secret or anything. I mean, everyone walks through here."

He took his hands out of his pockets and moved closer. "Yes, but it's nice to see it through your eyes."

I had always been the kind of girl who made the first move, but when our lips met, he was the one kissing me. His mouth was warm and soft and just a little too cautious.

Then he was holding me, pressing my back against the tree, and I remembered the way he had looked, standing in front of Saint Sebastian, the dark hunger in his eyes, like he knew what it was to spend hours or days staring down the grimmest, most impossible questions. Like maybe he even had the answers.

He touched my throat, running a finger down my trachea, and I swallowed. My mouth was very dry suddenly. I couldn't see his face, but his shoulders had a set that told me things about his expression. Enough to know that he was smiling.

"Rosamund," he said, and it was all there in his voice, the things he was really saying.

I nodded.

Rosamund, who took what wasn't hers, whose story was a fake, a collection of rumors and lies. Rosamund, girl of a thousand deaths, and who is she without them? If none of them are true, who is the girl in stories? Nothing but a proud, selfish nobody. King Henry II's mistress, who died in a nunnery of natural causes.

I stood with the tree at my back, heart jackhammering in my chest, but not quite ready to run. When you spend your whole life convinced that underneath your warm party smile, you are utterly, permanently alone, you spend your whole life thinking nothing can touch you.

. . .

She doesn't remember the moment of her death, not the electric chill of his eyes on hers, shining up out of the dark, not the way her hands fluttered at his face like wings and then went numb.

The only thing left to her now is a memory of hope, vague but insistent. Of a wish made in the street before the long walk into the woods. Before her lungs failed and her eyes closed. A wish for closeness, for understanding.

Now she stands outside his door, waiting for the moment when she will present herself to him, share the horror of her milky eyes and her newly quiet heart. Here in the empty hall, she knows what saints know—that no one will understand the mysteries of the grave unless they have felt the chill and the stillness for themselves.

After a long time, she rings his buzzer, waits as his footsteps grow louder. There is a rattle as he draws back the chain.

In a moment, he will open the door and invite her in, and if he doesn't, she will come in anyway. The cold in her veins is overwhelming, the truest thing, and he will spend a long time dying. Long enough, in his final agony, to share it with her.

ANOTHER SUN

by Maggie Stiefvater

I would've laughed if you'd told me ten years ago that I'd be sitting on ideas for two weeks, two months, two years, two decades, before writing them. Used to be that my modus operandi was to come up with an idea at breakfast and start writing the novel by dinner. If for any reason I got interrupted before I finished writing the novel, it was curtains for the nag. These frantic ideas were as fragile as newborn pandas—wow, that is two animal metaphors in one paragraph. If the ideas were left untended for a moment, they perished. It was impossible for me to imagine ever returning to one of these abandoned novels or ideas. And yet I find myself now sitting on story ideas for months at a time or returning to novel ideas that I first kicked around when I was sixteen or seventeen. Really, I think it's because my writing has become deeper now. The plot and world and characters are just clever covers for things I want to think about and questions I want to ask myself and others.

So this story is one that I sat on for a long time. Like a lot of my Merry Sisters of Fate stories, it sprang into my head in a very uncomplicated way: "What if fires stopped going out?" But that was where it ended, because while it was a cool idea, I didn't know what I was trying to say. I had to let it (bad pun alert!) smolder awhile. It wasn't until I came up with this concept of making a pyromaniac tell the story for us that it fell into place. I'm very interested in the idea of desire and guilt, and how a slight shift in perspective can make us doubt the things we love or hate.

And of course, I rather like burning things myself . . . —Maggie

"Are you a first-song or middle-song sort of per-son?" Anna-Sophia asked.

← I CHOSE ANNA-SOPHIA FOR HER NAME AFTER SIGNING A BOOK FOR A READER WITH THAT NAME.

They stood in front of a wall of fire held at bay only by fifty feet of concrete parking lot. The air between them and the fire was greasy with the heat, shimmer-ing and moving like an infestation of ghosts. Above, the sky that held them all in was a desiccated blue.

"I don't follow," Dutch replied.

"On an album. Do you like first songs best? Or are you a track-seven person? My sister was a track-seven person. She always said the best tracks on any album were four and seven." The fire had pinched her cheeks to red. When she stepped toward the fire, Dutch automatically threw out an arm to stop her progress.

Anna-Sophia said, "I appreciate a man with a sense of fear." She said it in a sharp, incendiary way that made it impossible to tell whether she was being sarcastic. Dutch didn't care if she meant it. Keeping Anna-Sophia alive had become a reflex by then, and one didn't apologize for breathing. She said, "Also, you didn't answer the question."

Dutch tried to remember the last time he'd listened to an album in its entirety. He could only remember one that he'd bought when his forehead was still pop-ulated by whiteheads and buying things was exciting. "I guess there's Travesty's album. Track—eight?"

Anna-Sophia smiled widely, throwing her head back, sweat glistening on her collarbone. "Oh, yes. 'Hot as the Sun.'"

Once, Dutch had told his father, who was also an amiable pyromaniac, that the night was as hot as the sun. Staring at the inferno of the barn, his father had replied that that was impossible, since the surface of the sun was eleven thousand degrees and the night couldn't be any hotter than two hundred or so there by the smoldering beams.

That was back when fires went out.

Anna-Sophia still basked in the heat of the fire. It was hot enough that Dutch felt drops of perspiration trickling from his temples to his jawbone, a disconcerting tickle. He suspected the perspiration looked better on the euphoric girl beside him, and he was glad, for a moment, that none of the rest of the pack—Joshua, Luis, and Alyssa—was there to witness her. There was something magnificent about Anna-Sophia in these moments, something that would be diluted by more observers.

Anna-Sophia whirled to face Dutch. She said, "I'm a last-track kind of person."

SO AM I,
ANNA-SOPHIA ⟶

Dutch replied, "I thought you were going to say something surprising."

· · ·

Dutch wished he remembered the precise details of the last fire he set, but he couldn't. The pleasures of a fire illicitly started were many, but so were those of good vanilla ice cream. After a while, the memory of each bowl of ice cream blended into the others until it was only a collection of common sensations. In effect, every bowl of ice cream became the same bowl of ice cream, as if you'd only ever had one, the best bowl ever. Dutch had set dozens of fires, but in his mind there was only one fire, the fire he'd started with five gallons of diesel fuel and a roll of Bounty paper towels and the sky black as a yawn above him.

So he didn't remember the location of the fire he set on that night that fires stopped going out; he only remembered that there was one. The truth was that on that night, all over the world, there had been hundreds of fires cooking food, crackling fiercely under chimneys, smoking across fields of unwanted heather, simmering in oil barrels, exploding quietly in thousands of pistons, glowing at the end of a million cigarettes. Doing the daily work of sparks and heat and fire.

But still, Dutch was certain that his fire was the one to blame for the same reason the rest of his pack assumed the same of theirs. A fire set only to burn was a guiltier suspect than a fire put usefully to work. Intention crashed inside his ribcage.

. . .

There was a fine line between pyromaniac and arsonist, and usually it looked like the cage in the back of a police car. From his father Dutch had inherited the affection for a struck match. The thrill of the first flame biting on the edge of a slab of plywood. A love of watching things crumble and sink into glowing embers. He remembered, still, his father telling him that a box of matches was no more dangerous than

DIESEL IGNITES MORE SLOWLY, NO ONE WANTS TO BURN OFF THEIR EYEBROWS.

a parking garage filled to capacity; you had to know how to drive and trust others to as well. Then his father had struck a match and set fire to a pile of empty cereal boxes while Dutch clutched small fists to his chin. It was his favorite show, and never in reruns.

Dutch met Anna-Sophia because a local arsonist had been making law enforcement edgy. Combustible purchases were tracked and reported, and patrol cars arrived promptly at the first blush of sparks in the night sky.

Dutch was spending his summer incinerating lawn chairs and outbuildings. Barely illegal. He resented the intrusion of sudden, too-interested officers of the law. Dutch was patience, and so, at first, he waited for the police to find their arsonist and abandon the area. When the search stretched from smoldering summer to crackling autumn, he took matters into his own hands.

He was slightly more qualified than the police to find an arsonist, and so it took him only a few weeks to find Anna-Sophia. When he did, she was standing in the middle of a suburban kitchen with a burning rag and the serene smile of an avenging angel.

From her father, Anna-Sophia had inherited a love of burning down houses.

Dutch remembered exactly the first words he'd said to her. "This is somebody's home."

Anna-Sophia's face had been puzzled. "Of course it is." And then she dropped the burning rag onto the couch.

. . .

Dutch had never been a fine student, but he still remembered learning in school that a forest fire was a powerful creative force, wiping out one generation of vegetation and fertilizing the soil for the next in one fell swoop. But that was back when forest fires went out. Now the bodies of trees burned to a crisp, and then the crisp kept burning, and when there was no more crisp left, the dirt burned, and when there was no more dirt, the rock melted, and the center of the earth glowered at whoever was still there to watch. This new, fiery world, where a cornfield could become an inferno in a moment, was a hungry one.

And the pack—Dutch, Anna-Sophia, Luis, Joshua, Alyssa—was as hungry as everyone else. There were on an almost continuous hunt for food. Food was not unattainable, but it was expensive, and money was hard to come by when you were feral and young. Dutch was generally the most presentable member, and so he found himself manning empty desks when the secretary had caught alight on the way to work. He herded kindergarteners away from burning playgrounds. He laid cinderblock foundations when other arms got tired. He'd leave with a pocket full of coins— flammable bills were out of fashion—and return to the pack with canned goods and biscuits.

The bottoms of the cans were stamped with expiration dates that were now as relevant as the *Late Night Show.* Sometimes the cans were dented, which Dutch had heard was supposed to be bad, but he'd yet to find out why. Often the labels were missing. Theoretically, one can was as good as another when survival was at stake, but Dutch found that hard to believe—especially when he realized he'd been given a can of fancy olives instead of pasta or corn.

Heating the food was never a problem.

Sometimes Dutch lay on his back on the asphalt and stared at the sun until it hurt to look. He thought about the ancient civilization that could have lived on that sun before it began to seethe and burn. He wondered if one day the fire that consumed Earth would warm some distant planet and change their seasons and grow their trees and heat their living rooms in the morning and light the side of his brother's smiling face.

Luis told Dutch that Dutch worried too much; that there was nothing about this smoking planet that was new. While spray-painting the curvaceous shadow beneath a pair of breasts on the side of the police department, Luis said that the ever-growing flames only made concrete the abstract reality of an individual's opportunities narrowing with the passage of time. Then Luis snapped his fingers at Dutch until he made Dutch aware that he wanted the can of cool teal. Luis had two years of a liberal arts education—the two years that instilled principles but not the two years that instilled when to shut up about them.

Dutch asked, "Would you still paint tits on walls if every wall already had them?"

. . .

THIS IS THE TRUE QUESTION AT THE HEART OF THIS STORY

I LIKE HOW YOU THINK I'M JOKING.

Some days Dutch wanted to be Anna-Sophia. She looked like something born out of a fire: thick, cinder-black hair; dark eyebrows that should've been too thick to be beautiful; smudgy brown makeup around hazel eyes. Her lips were red. Not the red of lipstick or the red of a Corvette but the red of metal heated to the point of surprise.

The most important thing about Anna-Sophia was that she didn't love the fire any less for it being unquenchable.

Some days in high school, the only thing that had gotten Dutch to the end of the day was the promise of striking a match. Sometimes he'd hear that scratch and it would give him a shiver of release, even if it was merely a piece of cardboard ripping or the sole of a shoe scuffed on ragged asphalt.

Now a match was a weapon, and a guilty one at that, and there was no release. But not for Anna-Sophia. Dutch watched her poised before the flames that burned eternally in the median of I-95, her lips parted, the reflection in her pupils darting like a nervous glance. As the firefighters—wielding concrete, not water—battled feverishly, her expression was one of deep satisfaction. The world was on fire, and she'd started it.

Anna-Sophia clutched Dutch's arm and laughed. Her eyes were misty with ecstasy. When she saw his somber expression, she released him.

"Ah, Dutch, you're such a control freak. It's not the same when you didn't start them, is it?"

Dutch said, "It's not that. It's just not the same when you have cake for every meal."

He could see she couldn't understand.

"I would like it to stop now," he said, simply.

He'd decided that a few weeks earlier. Months after everyone else had, but still, he'd gotten there eventually, well before the earth became another sun.

Anna-Sophia watched the firefighters pour concrete on brittle grass. They glanced fearfully up at the spitting sparks; all it took was one to catch ahold of their sleeve and they would be lost in a slow, impervious fire.

"I know everything there is to know about fire," she said. It sounded like a confession.

Dutch considered how, before all this, he might have wanted to hold her hand, or to kiss her, but now he only looked blandly at her fingers as he said, "Then put it out."

Anna-Sophia said, "You don't see, Dutch. It's not about the starting. It's about seeing it through to the end."

(She didn't say she couldn't.)

. . .

That night, the wind changed and sent a spark into Luis's paints. When the cans exploded it was like the whole planet sucked in its breath. The fire snaked across the asphalt they slept on and incinerated the mats beneath Luis and Alyssa. There was no evidence Joshua had ever been there.

Dutch was spared because he was on the roof, watching the stars through the rippling air. He heard the bark of the explosion, then Alyssa's abbreviated scream, and then silence.

He crashed downstairs. Anna-Sophia was crouched beside a glowing ember on the concrete floor, one side of her face dirty with soot. Her fingers were an inch away from the heat.

Dutch snatched her hand and tugged her to her feet. He was not gentle, but he was no rougher with her than she was with herself. He didn't ask if the others were still alive somewhere in the fire. It wasn't the sort of question that was relevant anymore.

He wanted to miss them, but he couldn't. The fires were burning him from the inside out.

"I know you think I'm not sorry about them," Anna-Sophia said, later.

Dutch was meditating on the difference between burning down a barn and burning down a person. He didn't look at Anna-Sophia; he was tired of looking at the flames.

(She had never said that she was sorry.)

· · ·

Dutch had once watched a television program about underwater volcanoes. Near volcanoes, where the ground fissured all the way to the center of the earth, the water was hot enough to boil but couldn't because of the weight of all the water lying on top of it. Life shouldn't have been able to thrive there, but it did.

Tube worms, looking like obscene lipstick tubes, clung to the rocks near the vents. The program had declared the tube worms masters of evolution and survival.

Dutch laid on his back and let the sun turn his closed eyelids bright red. Perhaps, in one hundred years, humans would have skin that didn't bubble in the heat. Perhaps, in one thousand years, they'd be able to survive on the beaches of ash that blew out of the flames. Perhaps, in twenty thousand years, humans would be able to walk through the fire. Evolution was a trust fund, but Dutch was poor now.

OR POSSIBLY THE
WORLD WILL BE
RULED BY FIRE
LIZARDS

Above Dutch's closed eyes, a familiar sound, unheard for hundreds of days, scratched into reality. Just the timbre of it, the impossibility of it, sent a rush through him.

He opened his eyes. He focused first on the heel of the hand inches from his nose, and then on the fingers above it, and then the struck match that the fingers held. A tiny, invincible flame glowed at the tip of it.

"Jesus Christ," Dutch said.

Anna-Sophia's hand didn't shake. "I know you liked it. I have another."

The fire slowly ate down the stalk of the match. He resented that she had been the one to strike it. It shouldn't have been struck at all, but if it had been, he wanted it to have been him. The memory of the sound tormented him.

"Let me up."

The flame pulled itself down the match toward Anna-Sophia's fingers. In the old days, instinct would've taken over: feel the heat of the nearing flame, shake the match, toss it in the sink. Watch it blacken and dim.

Unhurriedly, Anna-Sophia stood, dropping the match onto the concrete. The flame finished the cardboard and then, small and starving, it searched the surface of the concrete for sustenance. Dutch was surprised at how hard he had to struggle with the muscle memory of stamping it out. He couldn't stop staring at that new flame, irrelevant in a world of flames, and when he didn't move, Anna-Sophia grabbed his jaw and kissed him.

"Why would you do that?" Dutch asked. "There's enough in the world already."

Anna-Sophia pulled a book of matches from her pocket. They were stamped with the name of a hotel. All but one had been torn out.

"This one's for you," she said, pressing the matchbook into his palm. Her mouth was curved into something not quite like a smile. It was a face that saw into his soul, how badly he missed wanting.

Dutch ran his thumb along the match. If he was like Anna-Sophia, he could strike it and love the new fire for the hydra that it was. There was still release to be had.

Anna-Sophia smiled down at the tiny flame at her feet, captivated even by a fire the size of her thumb.

Dutch tore the match from the book. He'd torn too slowly; the tail end was ragged and spear-shaped. Now very much space between skin and match head.

Anna-Sophia looked up into his face.

He tugged the match between the striking surface and the cover, and there it was, the sound: the almost inaudible breath of the match head igniting. Then the rushing hiss of the pioneer flame bursting into the air.

Anna-Sophia's face was a cathedral lit by the sputtering match. Every want, every desire that Dutch had ever possessed—everything he had thought he'd lost—was in her expression. He'd never realized how what he'd taken to be adoration was really fear.

He could feel his heartbeat again, crashing chaotically in his ears. "Tell me you love it," she said.

Dutch lit her hair on fire.

(He didn't say that he didn't.)

When the match fell to the concrete by his feet, it went out.

I TOTALLY SHOULD
HAVE SAVED MY FLAMES
DOODLE FOR THIS PAGE.
CURSES!

I will help you:

290

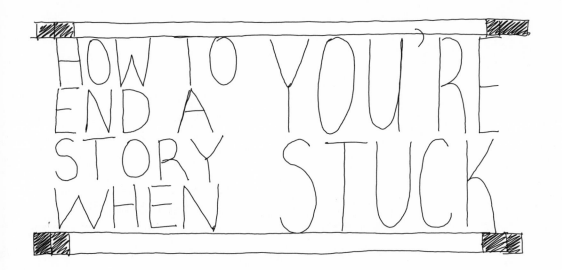

HOW TO END A STORY WHEN YOU'RE STUCK

→ KILL SOMEONE

→ KILL EVERYONE

→ BURN THINGS DOWN

→ MAKE THEM KISS

→ GET THE PIANO WIRE

→ START OVER

→ IT WAS ALL A DREAM

→ END MID-SENTE...

THE MERRY FATES WOULD LIKE TO THANK:

OUR AMAZING READERS

OUR CLEVER EDITOR

Our Wonderful Agents

The Merry Spouses... ...who love us.*

*put up with us.†
† usually.